Seasons of Friendship

Perveen Nadirshaw Tayabali

For my very dearest
Mamta, this comes
to you with lots of love –
Perveen xox

July 2023

Email: perveentayabali@gmail.com

ISBN-13: 9781726662123

Seasons of Friendship
A Novel

The characters are entirely fictional and bear no resemblance to any person living or dead.

List of Characters
and a
Glossary of Words
at the end of the novel.

for my beloved Chotu -
a walk down memory lane.

Prologue
Hirjee and Rustam
November 1943

'You put salt in Daulat's tea when I told you not to? Why don't you listen to anything I say?' asked Hirjee. 'You knew Daulat would gag!'

'*Haan,* I knew that, but Boka it was so funny,' Rustam grinned, though his bottom smarted from a recent spanking.

His eyes twinkled, picturing his nineteen-year-old sister at the breakfast table coyly batting her lashes at Homi, the young man sitting across her, then starting to gag, spill tea over the embroidered tablecloth, and rush off in mortified tears.

'Anyways,' muttered the nine-year-old, 'she deserved it. Why'd she tell Mumma to take away my mouth harmonica last evening? I wasn't troubling anyone, only practicing scales in the garden and she complained to Mumma saying I was doing peu-peu-peu like a cat, to irritate her and Homi. I know she did it jus' to get me into trouble.' He turned his wide brown eyes on Hirjee, 'You know, I heard her say to Mumma she's hoping Homi'll ask her to marry him. 'Yuck! How can Homi want to marry someone like her?'

'Don't know,' shrugged shy twelve-year-old Hirjee. Girls were a mystery to him, especially Daulat, who was very attractive.

'Girls! *Eugh!* I hate girls! I'm never going to marry!' proclaimed Rustam, scrunching his face and kicking at the sand with his grubby feet, while trying to strike sea creatures with bits of shell, creatures that scuttled away and burrowed in the sand.

Two boys sat in the mid-morning sun, on a broken stone wall, oblivious to the heat or the fresh sea breeze cooling their sweat-dampened faces. In the distance, the ocean glittered in the sunlight, and its incoming tide swirled onto the beach, leaving greyish-white foam to curl along the water's edge.

Rustam jumped down from the wall, grabbed the cowry shell Hirjee was studying, and ran off laughing.

Two boys raced down the beach on that sunny day, blissfully unaware of how close their seasons of friendship were destined to be.

One

Marina, Amy
May 1985

'Amy! Amy, wake up! Wake up!' Amy's sleep-filled brain heard the impassioned plea. She groggily opened her eyes and raised her hand to shield them from the light that had been turned on. Her mother stood by her bed in a dressing gown worn inside out, with un-brushed hair tucked carelessly behind her ears. A quick glance at the bedside clock showed her it was four-thirty in the morning and rain was thrumming outside her window. It was only the last week of May, but the monsoon had broken earlier than usual.

'Amy, get up,' her mother reiterated. 'Daddy's very ill. Go sit with him while I phone Dr. Guzder.'

The tiled floor felt cool under Amy's bare feet as she hurried into her parents' room. Their maid Rosy was already there, saying, 'Rustam*seth*, Marina*bai* is phoning Dr. Guzder, an' by God's grace, you will be becoming better. Don't worry *seth*, just sleep an' rest.'

Seeing her enter, Rosy gave her a worried look and padded silently from the room.

Amy's throat constricted at the sight of her father sweating profusely and clutching his left arm. Kneeling by his bed she took his cold hand in hers. Seeing her there, Rustam smiled reassuringly and said, 'Don't look like that my darling, I'm going to be fine.'

'Are you sick Dad?' her brother Jamsheed's voice queried from the doorway. He was thirteen, but looked much younger, standing in his striped pajamas, his eyes wide and fearful.

Marina's fingers trembled as she dialed Dr. Jehangir Guzder's number. Rustam was having a heart attack and she did not know what to do. The phone rang and after what seemed to her an eternity, the physician's sleepy voice said, 'Hello.'

Hearing Marina's description of Rustam's illness, the elderly doctor, wide awake by now, said with urgency in his voice, 'Phone Breach Candy Hospital and ask them to send an ambulance at once. Tell them it's an emergency! Try and keep Rustam calm, and I'll be with you as soon as I can. I will contact the Intensive Care Unit and arrange a bed.' He went on to say, 'Be brave, my dear. The Night Matron knows me and will do her best to accommodate my patient.' But for all his reassuring words, he sent a quick prayer to be successful in getting a bed for Rustam.

Replacing the phone, Marina dressed hurriedly. Her fingers felt numb, and she kept dropping things as she packed an overnight bag for Rustam, trying at the same time to calm her agitated husband who threatened to get out of bed and do the packing himself.

'Marina, have you packed my new pyjamas and my shaver? And what about my clean *sadras* and underwear…'

'Rustam darling, I've packed everything you might possibly need. If I've forgotten anything, Amy or I will bring it to the hospital for you. Please, darling, Jehangir said you must not upset yourself.'

She gave a sigh of relief when the paramedics arrived with the ambulance and her restless husband was put in their care. The rain had begun to ease, but the pounding sound of waves, beyond their garden wall, matched the frightened thudding in her chest.

Dr. Guzder arrived just as the paramedics were making Rustam comfortable on the ambulance bed and starting him on oxygen. The portly doctor clambered into the ambulance and, after looking at Rustam, told the driver to get to the hospital as fast as he could. He sat on the narrow seat beside Marina, as she held Rustam's icy hand between both of hers and Rustam clutched hers as if he never wanted to let go.

Amy drove Jamsheed in her parents' car to the hospital, keeping close behind the ambulance with its flashing blue lights and sirens wailing down the silent streets. The roads were wet, dark, and empty, lit at intervals by fluorescent streetlights. The first heavy shower had scattered the gulmohor's flame-coloured petals and they floated in puddles on the tarmac, like droplets of life's precious blood crushed beneath the wheels of the speeding vehicles.

'Amy, what's going to happen?' Jamsheed asked. 'How can Daddy become so ill? He's never ill! He can't be ill! Amy, he's promised to take me to a cricket match on Saturday. He bought those tickets months ago!'

'Don't worry, Jamsheed. If Daddy can't take you, ask Rayomand; he enjoys cricket, or ask Hirjee uncle. I am sure one of them will accompany you.' She gave him a reassuring look, while trying bravely to quell her own fears.

The ambulance whirled into the main gates of the Breach Candy Hospital and halted by the curved entrance of the porch. Rustam was put on a stretcher and rushed to the Intensive Care Unit on the second floor, with Marina and Dr. Guzder hurrying behind him. Before going up in the lift, Marina handed her handbag to Amy and said, 'Pay the deposit at the reception, darling, and please call Hirjee uncle.'

Jamsheed stood near Amy as she gave the drowsy operator Hirjee's telephone number. At its first ring, she heard her father's friend say sleepily, 'Hello?'

'Uncle, this is Amy. I'm so sorry to wake you, but Daddy's had a heart attack and has been admitted to the Breach Candy Hospital. He has just been rushed to the I.C.U. by Dr. Guzder!'

There was a shocked unintelligible sound at the other end of the line, and then she heard him say, 'Amy darling, I'll be with you as soon as I can. I'm sure things will be all right.'

Amy and Jamsheed went up to the second floor and stood outside the closed doors of the Intensive Care Unit, awaiting Hirjee uncle's arrival, desperately needing his comforting presence.

She prayed silently for her father to get better and when she saw Hirjee uncle and his son Rayomand hurrying towards them, her frightened mind eased a little. They had raced up two flights of stairs, too impatient to wait for the elevator.

Seeing their scared faces, Hirjee put his arms around them both. After waiting outside the closed doors for a while, Hirjee suggested that Rayomand give Amy and Jamsheed tea that Philomena their housemaid had insisted they take with them to the hospital.

Rayomand led the siblings to where red plastic seats lined the walls of the curved lobby. After they were seated, he poured hot sweet tea from a thermos into plastic cups.

Amy drank hers gratefully, leaning her tired head against the back of her chair, comforted by Rayomand's calm presence. Time crawled, but she came fully awake the instant she saw Dr. Guzder emerge from the I.C.U. supporting her mother, who was crying uncontrollably. Amy ran and put her arms around Marina, Dr. Guzder's sombre words of condolence making no sense. Jamsheed following behind her, gripped his mother's hand and asked in a terrified voice, 'What's happened Mummy? Hirjee uncle, why is Mummy crying? Mum?'

'He's gone! Oh God, I can't bear this!' Marina whispered. 'Rustam's gone! My darling, darling Rustam!' For a moment, everything whirled before her eyes. Her legs gave way and she would have fallen but for Hirjee, who reached out to support her.

Amy thought she would choke on the bile rising in her throat as it dawned on her that her wonderful fun-loving Daddy was gone. She was oblivious to Rayomand's arms holding her and Jamsheed. She heard Jamsheed crying, making horrid gulping sounds, and found her own cheeks wet with tears. Her mind refused to accept that she would never hear her father's teasing voice, be held in his arms, or feel his hand mischievously muss up her carefully brushed hair. She saw her mother turn blindly from Hirjee to reach out for her and Jamsheed, and they clung to each other, weeping brokenly for the person who had left them so suddenly.

Standing beside Marina, Hirjee felt utterly helpless. This could not be happening. In a daze, he tried comforting Marina and her children, while aching inconsolably at the loss of his oldest and dearest friend. He clearly remembered the day, when aged five, his father had introduced two-year-old Rustam to him. A close bond had developed when Rustam had trustingly taken Hirjee's hand in his and become the brother that Hirjee, an only child, had longed for.

Once, on a holiday in Tithal, Rustam had nicknamed him 'Boka' for 'being a boring old bookworm', a name only Rustam had ever used. It had been said tauntingly because Hirjee had wanted to read Sherlock Holmes rather than play 'catch' on the beach.

'Don't call me that!' Hirjee remembered saying, and Rustam had persisted. 'Boka, Boka, Boka!' he had chanted gleefully. Angered at being teased, Hirjee had flung his book down and chased laughing Rustam onto the beach. He had caught hold of him and they had wrestled on the sand.

Rustam had been everything that Hirjee was not; exuberant and outgoing, he had embraced life as if it were made especially for him. His parents had spoilt him because he was ten years younger than his sister Daulat. Rustam had blithely fallen in and out of scrapes and on many an occasion,

Hirjee had covered for him. Hirjee's father, Adeshir, had not approved of Rustam's volatility and often thought that he was far too indulged by his parents.

When Rustam qualified as a Chartered Accountant, Adeshir employed Rustam in his family firm, Dhanjibhoy & Dhanjibhoy Accountancy, only to please Hirjee. For years, Adeshir had worried that Rustam would do something unacceptable and cause problems for them at work. However, with the passage of time, he had admitted that Rustam brought cheer to their days with his easy banter and had increased their client base with his endearing charm. And on the day that Rustam had married Marina, Adeshir had finally given his seal of approval. He had admired Rustam for choosing a lovely girl from a good and well-established Parsi family.

Hirjee's darkest days had been made bearable by Rustam, especially after his wife Jeroo died.

As boys, they had fought like brothers, and as quickly forgotten the source of their ire.

They had shared laughter, and on occasion, tears.

As grown men, their friendship had deepened and become richer, knowing they would always look out for the other.

So much of his life had been entwined with Rustam's.

It was unbearable now that his brother was gone.

Two
Hirjee, Marina
May 1985

Doongarwadi, housing the Towers of Silence, is an enclosed haven situated in the midst of teeming Bombay. It is an oasis, hidden from view, on a low hill, sheltered by a small forest of tall flowering trees and shrubs. It houses different species of birds, especially peacocks.

They strut about with tails sweeping the ground or fanning out in a shimmering display of blues, purples and greens, dancing gracefully to impress their drab, brown females.

At Marina's request, Hirjee saw to the funeral arrangements and phoned Pune to inform Marina's parents, Tehmina and Shavaksha, of the devastating news. He sent obituary notices to the newspapers and requested family priests to perform the funeral rites. He organised a *bungli* at the Doongarwadi for the family's four-day sojourn during the funeral and subsequent prayers. He hired the second largest housing, as the largest was occupied by another bereaved family. The whitewashed brick building had a large central hall for prayers, a side room to wash and re-dress the deceased person, a kitchenette, a bathroom, two bedrooms, and a large, covered veranda.

During the funeral prayers, he sat between Amy and Jamsheed, shading his tired eyes. He looked at his friend lying on cold marble slabs and wiped the tears he could not keep from coursing down his face.

Sala, how could you die and leave us, when you had everything to live for? What brought on this attack? Were you worried about something? Why did you not share your problem with me? All you had to do was tell me. What will I do without you?

Marina sat beside her weeping parents, dressed in a white sari, her head covered by her sari *pullo*. She said and did all the things expected of her but was somehow removed from it all. It was as though she were watching a strange and unreal event happen to someone other than herself. But a sharp searing pain shot through her as she glanced down at her bare left wrist. The glass bangles she had worn since the day of her wedding had just been removed and smashed, a symbol of her widowhood.

She gazed in pain at the top end of the funeral hall where her husband's washed and dressed body lay on low marble slabs, covered by a white sheet. An oil lamp burned on the tiled floor beside him, and his much-loved face was serene, as if he had just gone to sleep. She remembered him saying each night, before they slept, 'Good night sweetheart, God bless you.' Today it was she who was brokenly whispering the words, 'Sleep well darling and God bless you, but how will I exist without you?'

Marina rubbed her burning eyes and wondered over and over, how this could possibly have happened. *Why had he, an apparently healthy man, suffered such a massive attack? Was it some deep worry? Something he had not shared with her. Was it genetic? Her head pounded in pain. She wondered if she would ever know. It isn't fair, she railed silently. I just want him back. Oh God! I want him back!*

The funeral hall, with its white painted walls, was filled with Rustam's family, friends, and work colleagues. The priests in their white flowing robes, who twenty-three years ago had officiated at his wedding, stood at three paces from the body, each holding one end of a cloth tape or *paiwand*, during the prayers. A square piece of cloth, the *paddan*, tied at the back of their head with cloth ties, covered their mouths and noses.

They began the ceremony by reciting the ancient Avestan prayers to Ahura Mazda, to bless the newly released soul. They prayed aloud, creating vibrations strong enough for the soul to break its ties with the land of the living and encourage its first steps onward. Finally, before the ceremony ended, a pie dog was brought into the hall on a leash and made to stand before the body, an ancient custom to verify that there was truly no breath in the still form.

After the prayers were over, the mourning family and friends filed silently past Rustam's body, which was placed in a metal bier. The bier was then lifted by four pallbearers and carried out of the hall to the Tower of Silence, to be disposed of in the way of the ancient Persians.

The priests walked somberly behind the pallbearers, and they in turn were followed in silence by Parsi men wearing round black cloth caps, *phetas,* or shiny black, turban-shaped *paghris* on their heads. Each sober pair held a handkerchief between them.

Since women were not permitted to accompany the cortège, Marina stayed behind with the ladies, watching the solemn procession leave the funeral hall, from the *bungli's* veranda.

Later that evening, after more prayers were recited for the departed soul, Hirjee sat on a wood-slatted bench on the veranda with Amy, Jamsheed, and Rayomand. Voices floated out to them from the kitchenette where Marina's mother Tehmina, helped by Rustam's cousins and aunts, was preparing the evening meal.

Out on the veranda, a soft breeze blew, bringing with it the smell of wet earth. A lone evening star shone from a gap in the cloud-laden sky and the last plaintive cry of peacocks was heard, as the birds settled in for the night.

Looking affectionately at Rustam's children, and wanting to lighten their sorrow, Hirjee began reminiscing about a time when Rustam was five years old.

'One Sunday afternoon,' he began, 'around four o'clock, your father came to tea with your grandparents and Daulat. As soon as he arrived, the two of us were packed off to play on the veranda adjoining the parquet-floored sitting room. The grown-ups, meanwhile, chatted in the living room, waiting for our bearer Parmal Singh to serve them tea and lemon cakes.

Lilavati, Rustam's fat ayah, squatted on her haunches near us chewing tobacco, unconcerned, as long as we played quietly, did not push and shove each other or dirty Rustom-*baba*'s clothes.

We were playing with my train set, when Rustam suddenly asked, 'Want to see something?' I said yes. He glanced at Lilavati to see if she was watching and deciding that she wasn't, he boasted, 'I have something you haven't seen in your whole life, but you must swear on your *kusti* you won't tell anyone.' As I had just had my *navjote*, I told him it was wrong to swear on the sacred thread around my waist. I told him if he told me not to tell anyone, I wouldn't.

'You promise?' he asked, and I naturally said yes, certain I would have seen it before. A five-year-old couldn't possibly have something an eight-year-old hadn't seen, right? Rustam put one pudgy hand into the inner pocket of his cotton jacket and gingerly pulled out a white mouse. I remember staring at the pink-eyed creature and being repelled by it. When he cheerfully asked if I wanted to hold it, I wanted to say no, no I don't! But being older, I swallowed my disgust and bravely held out my hand.

After all these years, I can still remember the mouse scurrying from Rustam's hand onto mine. As soon as the tiny claws touched my palm, the shock was too much for me and I immediately shook it off.

The white bundle of fur took off like a rocket, straight into the living room and into the path of Parmal Singh. Seeing the mouse race towards him, he hastily raised one foot to avoid stepping on it, unbalanced, and fell heavily to the floor. The large silver tea tray he was carrying, slid from his hands, smashing my mother's prized Minton-ware. There was milk and sugar scattered everywhere. It was fortunate he wasn't carrying the large silver teapot, which was full of scalding tea.

I can still see it all so clearly. Daulat was the first to notice us standing in the doorway, staring at the havoc we had caused, guilt written all over our faces.'

Hirjee paused, lost in time. Shutting his eyes, he clearly saw himself and Rustam as those frightened boys. A sudden tug at his sleeve brought him back to the present.

'Don't go to sleep, Hirjee uncle! Then what happened? What happened to you and Daddy?'

Observing Jamsheed's eager face, Hirjee thought, irrelevantly, that his eyes reminded him of Marina. Smiling at him, he continued, 'My father, Adeshir, was generally a mild-mannered man, but seeing Parmal Singh on the floor in tears at having broken Memsahib's foreign crockery - and my mother sobbing that her best china was reduced to a memory - he glared at us and asked in a thundering voice, 'Who is responsible for bringing a dirty *oonder* into this house?'

Your Daddy promptly said, in a quavering voice, that it was his fault, because the mouse belonged to him. But I said no that the blame was mine; the mouse had run into the living room because of me. I was immediately marched off to my room and as punishment, was deprived of my favourite lemon tea cakes. Rustam was considered too little to be scolded, but he accompanied me to my room to share my punishment. I remember him clambering onto my bed with his short plump legs and sitting by my side, holding my hand till it was time for him to go home.'

By the time Hirjee finished his tale it had become dark and the rain that had held off for most of the day had begun to fall in earnest, shrouding the electric lamps in the Doongarwadi compound, in a veil of silvery grey.

Amy leant her head against his arm and, holding his right hand between her own slim ones, thought him to be the kindest man in the whole world. A question occurred and looking at him she asked, 'What happened to the mouse, Hirjee uncle?'

His dark brows knitted in thought and after a brief pause, he said, 'You know Amy, I have absolutely no idea. But the dent where the tray fell still remains, and no amount of floor polishing has removed it.'

Three
Amy
May 1985

The days spent at the Doongarwadi were strange ones for Amy. Her mother seemed removed from everything; it was as if some part of her had followed her husband to the great beyond. She shed no more tears and Amy could not understand her mother's rigid control.

On the first day after the funeral prayers, their grandpapa Shavaksha said to her and Jamsheed, while wiping away their tears, 'Don't cry, my darlings. Shedding tears is not good for your father's soul. They say when you cry, the pull of your earthly love holds the soul back from its new journey to God.'

But it was hard because tears flowed so easily. She felt teary even when she shared a giggle with her granny Tehmina, reminiscing about Daddy teasing Tehmina about her inquisitive ways. 'Mamma,' she clearly heard her father's amused voice say, 'Do you have to know everything? Do you have to know about everyone, even if you don't know them?'

What surprised her in this place of sadness, was that Rayomand's presence gave her a feeling of peace. The sharp pain of her father's passing was just that little bit more bearable. Amy wondered why it should be so. She knew it was not just Rayomand's handsome face, but something she could not put into words. He looked a lot like Hirjee uncle, having inherited his height, marked brows and dark wavy hair, but he also had Jeroo aunty's aquiline nose and her wide mouth with its ever-ready smile.

However, being nine years younger than him, she was aware that he looked upon her as a child to be affectionately humoured. He was also engaged and soon to be married to a beautiful woman. In the past few years, they had met infrequently at family gatherings, but barely spoken to each other. She had been too shy, and he, though fond of her, had little time for a gauche teenager.

Two days after the funeral, with the rain having let up, Amy entered the rustic garden of the Doongarwadi's Fire Temple and sat on an old wooden bench. Watery sunlight, filtering through the leaves of surrounding trees, threw dappled shade on the stony ground; pomegranate and bougainvillea shrubs and straggly rose plants grew in earthenware pots, while all around her the warm morning air was alive with unfamiliar bird song. A soothing aroma of sandalwood smoke emanated from the Fire Temple, and she heard the sonorous voice of a *mobed*, lifted in prayer. She sat deep in thought, her hands lying loosely in her lap. She was so still, that a sparrow hopped boldly up to her, pecking at the ground with its hard beak, only periodically turning its head to look in her direction. She ruminated on her boyfriend Kayum, who had attended the funeral with her three girlfriends. He wanted more than just friendship and right now, she did not want to be romantically involved with anyone. Her friend Meena could not understand Amy's lack of interest. At twenty, she was already engaged to a man chosen by her parents and a few weeks ago, had said to Amy, 'How can you be like this, keeping Kayum hanging around? You've got to decide one way or another. If you don't, you'll be sorry when he ditches you and becomes somebody else's boyfriend.'

Amy remembered saying she really did not care if he did.

Personally, she did not think he was right for her and reminded Meena, that Daddy said he would send her abroad for further studies. But now with Daddy gone, Amy wondered if it still would be possible. Then her unruly thoughts came back to Rayomand and the day, seven years earlier, when he had rescued her, dangling from a *safed jamun* tree.

The year was 1976 and Amy and her parents were in Tithal, spending one of their many Divali vacations with the Dhanjibhoys. It was the year prior to Rayomand leaving for England, to train as an accountant. He too was in Tithal with his parents and his school friend Asif.

During the day, the two young men played cricket on the beach with little Jamsheed, and sometimes went swimming with him clinging like a limpet to Rayomand's neck. Amy, on the other hand, was a shy eleven-year-old, happiest reading her storybooks. Occasionally, Rayomand would tweak her pigtails just to tease her.

One morning after breakfast, Amy and her mother were in the garden. Marina sat with her sewing under the dappled shade of a mango tree while Amy sat cross-legged on the ground, chewing on a blade of grass.

'Mummy, tell me about Ram and Sita.'

'You want to hear the same story, again?'

'Yes Mummy, please?' Amy cajoled.

'Alright.'

Laying her work aside, Marina vividly related the adventures of Prince Rama and his brother Laxmana of Ayodhya. She described in detail, how Rama rescued his beautiful Sita from the clutches of the ten-headed ogre Ravana, who had abducted her; and how valiantly he and his brother Laxmana succeeded in killing the ogre, then aided by an army of monkeys, set fire to Ravana's kingdom. When the people of Ayodhya learned that their tall and handsome prince had rescued his beloved princess-wife, they decorated their homes with oil lamps and set off thousands of firecrackers. She ended the Ramayana by saying, '...And that is why Diwali is still celebrated today.'

Lying on the stubby grass with her eyes half closed, Amy was sorry when her mother's voice fell silent. She stared dreamily at the blue and white sky through a crazed pattern of green mango leaves, and in the secret recesses of her eleven-year-old mind, wished that someone handsome and brave like Prince Rama would one day love her with a similar kind of devotion.

For Amy, visiting Tithal during the Diwali vacations was a high point in her otherwise humdrum life, centred around school, homework, and the infrequent visits to her grandparents in Pune.

Amy loved wandering through the rambling old house built in the early nineteen-thirties by Rayomand's grandfather Adeshir. She enjoyed the welcoming feel of its highly polished furniture, brass lamps and potholders that shone when sunlight touched them. There were strange but comforting aromas wafting through the house on the salty breeze: of beeswax polish, fresh lilies and marigolds strung across doorways, of freshly baked crusty bread and the strong scent of leather-bound books in the fascinating library.

As soon as Hirjee uncle had inherited the property, the first thing he did was to convert the kerosene oil lamps to modern electricity. Bathrooms were overhauled and fitted with modern basins and running water. The old-fashioned wooden 'thrones' that needed to be cleaned by the jamadar, were replaced by toilets with proper flush tanks.

But Amy's favourite place was behind the kitchen, in the large fruit orchard with mango, chickoo, sitaphal and safed jamun trees, interspersed with tall coconut and targola palms. She would sit there for hours, under a shady tree and read her books.

To her perennial disgust, Rosy would insist she wear a floral-painted straw hat with pink ribbons, to protect her from the sun. Her one-year-old dachshund Mitzy, kept her company, flopping down beside her, panting in the heat, after chasing the mali's loudly squawking chickens.

One afternoon as she sat reading, she heard Rosy screech, 'Jamsheedbaba come down now, or I am shouting to Mummy!'

Amy looked up from her book and saw Jamsheed high up in a safed jamun tree trying to grab a branch bearing a fruit just beyond his reach. She jumped up from her stool, dropping her 'Little Women' on the ground and hurried to Rosy's side, calling, 'Jamshi, come down and I'll try and get it for you.'

Jamsheed promptly climbed down and pointed to a large fruit he wanted.

Worried that Amy might actually do something dangerous like climb the tree, Rosy turned to her saying sternly, 'Baby don't you dares do anything so foolish. Both of you be good now, an' waiting till I bringing mali Sitaram. He will be getting the fruit for you.' Rosy hurried away to fetch the gardener.

Seeing Jamsheed look expectantly at her, Amy thought rebelliously, if Jamsheed can climb this tree, it can't be too hard. She decided to disregard Rosy and give it a try.

Removing the offending hat, she began to climb. Just as she was about to break off a large fruit, she heard Jamsheed's high-pitched voice say, 'No, Amy no. Not that one, I want the other one.'

The other one was just out of reach. Gritting her teeth and trying hard not to look down, she climbed even higher, to get the one Jamsheed wanted. She caught hold of the fruit and gave it a tug.

Her foot suddenly slid from its perch, a branch, bare of leaves, slipped between the back straps of her denim overalls, pinning her to the tree. She found herself dangling in mid-air, desperately clutching the branch with its elusive fruit suspended directly above her. Below her, Jamsheed clapped his hands and jumped up and down, saying, 'Amy, Amy! You look so funny! You look like a monkey in the tree!'

Returning with the gardener, Rosy saw Amy and wailed, 'Oh Marymai! What I do now? I tells you not to climbing the tree an' you climbing it! Oh you bad, bad girl!'

Sitaram stared blankly up at Amy and asked in Marathi, 'Rosy, what is she doing there?'

Terrified by the sight of Amy hanging so precariously, Rosy turned angrily on the bemused man.

'Doing up there? How does it matter what she's doing there. You go now and fetch a ladder, an axe or anything to cut Amybaby free.' Her angry, imperious commands in Marathi sent Sitaram scurrying to fetch the necessary items.

Rayomand and Asif strolled into the orchard to ask Sitaram to break open some green coconuts. Hearing Rosy loudly berate someone, they headed in the direction of her strident voice.

They found Rosy and an excited Jamsheed staring up into a safed jamun tree. Looking up they saw Amy impaled on a branch and heard an agitated Rosy tell them that she had sent Sitaram to fetch a ladder and a machete. Ignoring Rosy and not waiting for Sitaram, Rayomand climbed up and smiled reassuringly into Amy's frightened face. Holding a protruding branch with both hands, he placed his right foot in the fork of the tree and rested his left foot on a branch just beneath Amy's dangling feet.

'Keep holding tight, Amy. I can't release you without the branch being cut, so rest your feet on my thigh and take some weight off your arms.'

With Rayomand by her side, some of her fear abated and she relaxed, grateful for the foothold beneath her.

Sitaram arrived, puffing in his haste, with a ladder and a machete. He leaned the ladder against the tree, climbed up and standing on the topmost rung began to hack at the branch. As it was being cut, Rayomand wrapped an arm around Amy to turn her towards him, in order to help her down.

With Amy freed from her restraining branch, her full weight fell on Rayomand; his foot slipped from the fork of the tree and they both fell onto the sandy ground.

He lay still, his breath knocked out of him, gazing into Amy's distraught face. Her look was so comical, and he was so relieved that neither of them had been injured, that he burst out laughing.

For a few seconds, she lay paralysed on top of him, then she scrambled up and instead of thanking him, kicked him in the leg and ran blindly into the house. Jeroo aunty, watching this piece of theatre from the veranda, held Amy close and soothed her wounded sensibilities.

For years after the incident, Amy had stubbornly insisted that she hated Rayomand. But now, sitting alone on the wooden bench, she acknowledged that she didn't hate him; she thought him very attractive.

On the fourth day at dawn, after the *chahram* prayers were recited, Marina and the Cooper family headed home in Hirjee's car. As they drove out of the tall Doongarwadi gates and down Kemps Corner, she was amazed to see everything still the same; people on the street going about their normal lives, unaware and uncaring that Rustam was gone and her life shattered.

Arriving home, the chowkidar by the gate hurried up to Hirjee's parked car and opening the door, offered her his condolences. When she unwillingly entered her apartment, their cook Anthony, the houseboy Raju, and Rosy were waiting solemnly to greet her. Rosy hugged her and Amy, and after politely greeting the rest, put a consoling arm around Jamsheed. A subdued Mitzy stood by the door, her tail drooping between her legs.

Marina accepted their commiserations and, scooping Mitzy into her arms, walked onto the veranda taking comfort from the dog's warm body. In the morning light, the sea beyond their garden wall was a dull, metallic grey. Her brown eyes disinterestedly followed the flight of a squawking seagull, dislodged from its rocky perch by a sudden wave.

How would she survive the rest of her life without Rustam's vibrant personality beside her? Who would make her laugh or exasperate her with his occasional intemperate behaviour? Everywhere she looked, she saw Rustam's presence. She now understood why some Indian wives of old, chose to follow their husbands in death and commit sati. It was just too painful to carry on living without a loved one.

Marina grieved for her parents who were shocked by their beloved son-in-law Rustam's sudden death. She was grateful to them for staying with her, to support her through the first month and attend special prayers for Rustam, at the Banaji Fire Temple.

These prayers were recited on the tenth and thirtieth day after his funeral in a large, carpeted hall, by four officiating priests, sitting cross-legged on a white sheet. They sat facing a silver *aferganyu* and periodically, while praying aloud, sprinkled frankincense on burning sandalwood sticks. On a wall behind them hung a large oil painting of Prophet Zoroaster holding a staff in his left hand and his right forefinger pointing heavenward, proclaiming the monotheistic belief in God. Sitting in the dimly lit hall, Marina felt a measure of peace; enveloped by the aromatic scent of sandalwood and frankincense. She listened to the intonation of the Avestan prayers, mesmerized by the flickering flames.

Her parents, both in their seventies, sat on either side of her. Her gentle father Shavaksha, once an owner of a thriving stone pulverising business in Pune, held her hand in his. Her mother Tehmina, an old-fashioned lady, sniffed occasionally and wiped her eyes.

Four

Hirjee, Marina
June 1985

Hirjee found the first weeks unbearable. Although he and Rayomand divided Rustam's large workload, he was aware that a new accountant was needed. But he could not bear the thought of someone else in Rustam's chair.

A pall of sadness had settled in the office. The staff reminisced about his impudent ways and Rustam's cheery morning greetings, calling out loudly to their elderly and now almost deaf chowkidar, '*Salaam*, Ram Singh,' and to his Gujerati secretary, 'Well Harish*bhai,* how's the world treating you?' And Harish returning with a grin, 'I'm fine boss. You are okay?' Then a quick look into Hirjee's room saying, 'Morning Boka,' and thence to Rayomand, often preceded with a quick thump on the back, 'Well *baba*, how's your sexy girlfriend?'

A month later, Hirjee finally decided to sort through Rustam's personal files and papers and hand them to Marina. He entered the musty unused office and throwing open the shuttered windows, let in fresh air. From a break in the clouds, the mid-day sun spilled into the room, creating a bright patch of light on the floral-tiled floor, illumining dust motes floating freely in the air. He glanced at the silver-framed photograph standing on the desk, of Marina taken in Mahableshwar, just before Amy was born. Her bright young face gazed expectantly into a future of happiness and contentment. Now, two decades later, she was suffering, and he was helpless to ease her loss.

Settling himself in Rustam's chair, he opened the file containing a list of all Rustam's investments. He knew there might be some dud shares as Rustam had, on occasion, taken small losses; but still, he was sure it would be an excellent portfolio. He was not prepared for the horror and anger that gripped him when he reviewed the investments. Hirjee realised that Rustam had disregarded advice given by him some months earlier. He stared transfixed at the evidence that clearly explained Rustam's heart attack. There was a sick feeling in his gut as he stared blindly out of the open window. A pigeon cooed irritatingly on the stone ledge of an adjacent office building, but his eyes looked inward to another day, upon another scene.

Three months earlier, Rustam had walked into his office and introduced him to Anand Nathani, a short bespectacled man with a very earnest baby face that successfully hid a shrewd and calculating business brain.

Hirjee remembered Anand's soft and persuasive voice saying, 'I am about to float a gold mining company on the Bombay Stock Exchange. Banks and large institutions are showing a lot of interest, because rich seams of gold have been discovered in one of the mines.' He had paused, smiled at Rustam, and continued, 'My colleagues and I are certain that the same will be found in the others once digging commences.' Then looking back at Hirjee he had said, 'As Rustam is my school friend and you are his good friend, I have come to offer both of you shares in the company, at an appreciable discount at issue.'

Hirjee recalled his instant dislike and irrational urge to ask Anand to leave his room, but because he was Rustam's friend, Hirjee had kept silent. Instead, he had asked Anand a great many searching questions which the man had answered credibly. Later, after Anand had left, Hirjee had tried dissuading Rustam from investing in a dicey gold mining venture. But Rustam had stubbornly seen it as a wonderful way to make a tidy profit.

'Rustam, we don't know where these gold mines are in Rajasthan's huge desert, or if these veins of gold actually exist.

I don't like buying into a new company without being able to verify Anand's claims. Let's wait till the company floats, then think of investing in it.'

'Wait? How can we wait? How can we miss out on such an opportunity?' Rustam had queried, annoyed by Hirjee's despondent view. 'But you can do what you want!' he had snapped. Then, with excitement building in his voice, 'Anand is an old school friend and I trust him. For goodness' sake, we were in the Boy Scouts together. Is it surprising he wants to share his good fortune with me? Look at the amazing opportunity he's offering us. I would be chump not to take advantage to increase my capital. I will soon be needing a lot more money than I have, to send Amy to America for further studies and then, have enough saved to send Jamsheed as well.'

With Rustam adamant about investing, Hirjee had grudgingly invested a modest ten thousand rupees and advised Rustam to do the same. But now he saw that his gullible friend had rejected his advice; had liquidated more than two-thirds of his bluechip stocks and bought into a company whose shares were not worth the paper they were printed on.

Just two days before Rustam's death, Anand's gold mining company had made headline news. The front pages of all leading Indian newspapers screamed, 'Gold? What Gold? A Scam to end all Scams!'

One intrepid journalist investigated the gold mines, by venturing into the inhospitable desert region. He found that although the mines existed, very little work was in progress and absolutely no gold had been discovered. He had uncovered an elaborate fraud. The police were called to investigate, but it was too late. There was no trace of the money invested by shareholders and the main perpetrators of the hoax had fled the country.

When he was calmer, he rang Marina and after chatting for a while, he said, 'I'd like to visit you one evening to discuss some details of Rustam's accounts. When is it convenient?'

Intrigued by his unusual request to want to discuss financial matters at home, Marina replied, 'Come this evening Hirjee, I'll be glad to have your company. I'm on my own as the kids are busy and Mamma and Papa have returned to Pune.'

Hirjee could barely concentrate all day as he brooded over how best to break the shattering news to Marina.

That evening, after work, as Hirjee hurried to his car in the rain, Ram Singh rushed up to him with an umbrella. Sliding into the driver's seat, Hirjee smiled his thanks and slipped some money into the elderly man's shirt pocket.

Hirjee's journey through pelting rain from Hutatma Chowk to Marina's home at Nepean Sea Road was at a snail's pace, the rush-hour traffic made worse by the monsoon. It was frustrating to drive slowly behind cars, buses and taxis attempting to get ahead by changing lanes. The buses and taxis were the worst offenders, inching forward, heedless of being sworn at by car drivers giving way to prevent their vehicles being damaged.

Coconut palms swayed precariously in the wind, their fronds blowing at right angles to the trees along the familiar Marine Drive coastline. Stormy winds forced huge waves to fly onto the main road, over the sea wall and concrete tetrapods, pouring onto windscreens of the slow-moving traffic, blinding drivers with cascades of grey water.

Hirjee negotiated Hughes Road and turned left at Kemps Corner on autopilot, his mind trying desperately to find words to soften the blow Marina was about to receive. 'Damn you Rustam for being such an idiot!' he said, aloud. There was little he could do to save Marina from worrying about the future. The money she would receive from his firm would not be enough to compensate for what Rustam had lost.

On arrival, he stood outside Marina's apartment with his dripping umbrella forming a puddle on the tiled floor. He stared ruefully at his damp trousers, wet from the slanting force of the rain, and rang the doorbell. Raju opened the door and greeted him with a toothy grin.

Mitzy raced up, barking madly, wagging her tail and fawning as if she had not seen him in years. Hirjee lifted her up, tickled her under her aging chin and had his face licked in response.

Marina, elegant as always, welcomed him with an affectionate hug and linking her arm in his, walked with him into the lamp-lit living room. Her eyes expressed concern while chiding him. 'Really, Hirjee! You should've cancelled coming here. We could quite easily have met on another day.'

She led him to a comfortable sofa and sat by his side, with Mitzy curled up on her lap. They chatted about the recent activities of a prominent political party in Bombay.

'Seems like another senseless political strike might be brewing, so make sure you stock up on essential foods Marina,' said Hirjee. 'Especially the *ukhra* rice Rosy loves to eat. Also see that Anthony has a spare gas cylinder in the kitchen. If you have problems getting a second one, let me know. If this wretched strike goes ahead, it will disrupt the movement of all trucks coming into Bombay.' He paused. 'Why don't these local politicians realise that strikes make life more expensive and difficult for the common man?'

They fell silent, as Raju put a cut-glass whisky tumbler and a jug of water on a side table for Hirjee and handed Marina a glass of freshly made *nimbu pani.* He also placed a plateful of steaming hot samosas on a coffee table before them.

The apartment was quiet, with Tehmina and Shavaksha having returned to Pune, Rosy at church, Amy dining at

Meena's, and Jamsheed studying maths in his room with his tutor.

Marina studied Hirjee and thought how neat he looked in his starched shirt and sober tie, so unlike Rustam, who generally wore his loosened around his neck, or not at all if he could help it. Hirjee's salt-and-pepper hair grew away from his forehead and thick eyebrows dominated a strong face.

At his continued silence, she gave him a questioning look. Something in his face worried her.

'What is it, Hirjee? What's wrong?' she asked.

At her questioning words, he lifted the wretched file out of his briefcase and handed it to her.

Brushing Mitzy off her lap, Marina took the proffered file and studied it. As she went through the list of investments, she saw that nearly every good share had 'sold' marked in red against it and the proceeds put into a gold mining company. She stared at the company's name in horror. It was a name everyone had read about in the papers. How could Rustam have sold their shares without discussing it with her? How could he have gambled so much of their savings in a new and dubious company?

Turning to Hirjee she asked, 'Did you know about this venture, Hirjee? And did you think it was safe to invest in it?'

Unwilling to look at her, he stared glumly at the Qum carpet on the floor and said, 'Yes I did, and no, I did not think it a safe investment.'

'Then why didn't you stop him?' Marina cried, a panic-stricken edge to her voice. Pushing the file aside, she stood up as if she could not bear sitting passively any longer.

Hirjee leaned forward, wishing he could do something, hating the feeling of utter helplessness as she paced distractedly in front of him. He kept his hands tightly clasped on his lap, keeping rigid control on the overpowering urge to comfort her. He loved Marina and had done, for as long as he could remember. He wanted to take her in his arms and tell her he would take care of everything, give her everything, but he couldn't. She did not want him. She loved Rustam. Had always loved Rustam and felt only affection for Hirjee as a trusted friend.

Marina stopped her pacing to ask, 'How could Rustam do this? How could he invest our savings in something as dicey as this?' She paused, as realization dawned on her. 'Of course! He would have known I would object. That's why he did not mention it! Why didn't you stop him Hirjee, why didn't you?' Tears of fear, anger and frustration poured down her face.

'Oh God!' she said, 'Now I know why he had such a massive attack! What shall I do Hirjee, what shall I do? How will I manage with most of our savings gone?'

Suddenly, in the face of her distress, his control slipped, and his impassioned plea was out: 'Marry me, Marina. Let me look after you!'

She stopped her frantic pacing and stared at him; then to his shocked surprise, began to laugh.

'How ironic,' the bitter hurt she felt made her say, 'I was married to one fool for over twenty years and now another wants to marry me!'

Her words were a dousing of icy water over Hirjee, bringing him back to his senses and reality. Fool! He berated himself, he truly was the fool she called him to say something so idiotic. He would have given anything, anything at all, to be able to recall his words.

Seeing the stricken expression in his eyes, Marina was immediately contrite. Stretching out her hands she took both of his cold ones in hers, her eyes wet with tears. 'I'm so sorry. So very sorry, Hirjee, I should never have said that. I thank you for everything but forgive me if I ask you to leave me alone just now. I have to be by myself to think.'

Marina went into her bedroom after he left and shut her door; her mind reeling from the news. She registered the sound of rain as it came down in torrents. She walked automatically to the half-closed windows to check that her newly hung drapes were dry. She stared out through the half-glazed veranda doors, at the slanting rain pounding on the veranda floor, thinking Rosy will be drenched when she gets home from church, her small umbrella no protection against this torrential downpour.

Marina paced her room wondering tiredly, how she would manage on the capital left after estate duty and taxes were paid.

How would she look after her home and take care of Amy and Jamsheed's education? She tried envisaging a life devoid of the comforts she and the children took for granted.

She felt mentally and physically drained.

She lay on her bed, staring blankly at the ceiling, wondering what she was going to do. Her parents would help, but she did not want to burden them at their age. Maybe she was overreacting. Maybe it would all work out. She could sell her apartment and buy a smaller, cheaper one in Pune, somewhere close to her parents in the cantonment area. Perhaps set up a flower shop on the Main Street, like the one she worked for, specialising in creating arrangements for nouveau riche clients. The business belonged to her friend Gitu and the two of them had worked together since its inception, five years ago.

Her mind kept shooting off in all directions. Exhausted, she turned over on her side into a foetal ball and covered her face with her hands, tears seeping from her tightly clenched eyes. They began to flow harder and before long, she was crying as uncontrollably, as she had the morning Rustam died holding on to her hand, for the pain of missing Rustam, for her children, for herself and Hirjee.

She recollected the evening Rustam had laughingly called Hirjee her Don Quixote and she his Dulcinea, after they watched 'Man of La Mancha.' His teasing had troubled her then, because she had never done anything to bring about Hirjee's devotion. She had been glad Rustam was not the jealous type. He knew how deeply she loved him.

Five
Hirjee, Jeroo

Hirjee clearly remembered the sweltering day in October 1944, when fifteen-year-old Jeroo entered his life and turned it upside down.

Jeroo was an orphan. She was the daughter of his mother's best friend and had come to live with them after her parents were killed in a road accident. Hirjee had been unimpressed by the plain, fair girl, with thin long plaits. Though saddened by her grief, he was thirteen and young enough to resent her invasion in his life. One day, while kicking a football around in his walled garden, he grumbled to Rustam, 'Why couldn't a boy have come to live with us? I would've loved an older brother. We could've played cricket, football, tennis, had so much fun! But a weepy girl, Rustam! What use is a girl? She doesn't play any games. When she comes home from school, she just follows Mumma around the house and the two of them keep gouss-goussing.'

He continued morosely, 'Mumma only loves Jeroo and has no time for me. I asked Mumma a question yesterday and she said, hmm, what is it? and continued talking to Jeroo.'

'Haan, Boka, I know. My Mumma also has no time for me. Every day she goes shopping with silly old Daulat, buying her saris and more saris, and so much jewell'ry for her wedding. If I say I want something, they both say Rustam stop troubling us and go out and play. I'll be so happy Boka, when my stoopid sister marries that stoopid Homi and goes to live with him.'

Years passed, but Hirjee never came to terms with sharing his parents' attention, especially his mother's, with a stranger he wished had never come. But in time, Jeroo's gentle and affectionate ways had him tolerating her as an unobtrusive older sister.

Jeroo was nineteen when she fell in love with Hirjee, a good-looking seventeen-year-old, knowing there was no hope of him ever returning it.

Two years later, when Hirjee's mother died, Jeroo, in her early twenties, quietly and efficiently took over the smooth running of their home.

Hirjee was deeply distressed by his mother's death and immersed himself in his studies. On attaining a First in his Bachelor of Commerce Degree, his father sent him to England to acquire his Chartered Accountancy qualifications. After successfully completing his degree, Ernst and Young with whom he had articled, offered him an excellent position in their firm. Much to his regret, he was forced to turn them down, because his father wanted him to join their family firm.

One evening, Hirjee's father called him into the study. After Hirjee was seated, he said, 'Son, just before Mumma died, she declared that her dearest wish was for you to marry Jeroo. You remember how much Mumma loved and worried about Jeroo's future because the poor child has no one besides us to look after her. She is our responsibility, and we must see her future is secure. You are twenty-four and I feel Jeroo is the ideal wife for you.'

Hirjee leapt off his chair, his sudden action toppling it over. He gazed at his father in stunned dismay.

'Pappa,' he exclaimed, 'You cannot honestly believe I can marry Jeroo; how can I, when I think of her as a sister? Besides, I don't even love her! You don't have to worry about Jeroo. I promise I will always look after her and see she never wants for anything, but marry her, I cannot. I just cannot! You must not ask that.'

Displeased, his father stared at him from under bushy eyebrows. 'Hirjee in matters such as these, a son has to bow to the greater wisdom of his father. Love-shmove is all nonsensical talk. It will come after you are married. Jeroo will make you an exemplary wife. I know she is very fond of you, just as you are of her, so what's all this fuss about? It's not as if she doesn't want to marry you. I have asked her, and she is very willing.' Suddenly, another disagreeable thought crossed his mind. 'You are not in love with another girl, are you? Someone I do not know of?'

'No, of course not! But that doesn't mean I can marry Jeroo!' Hirjee cried, and his father let out a small sigh of relief.

Hirjee rushed from his father's study to Rustam's home and found him cramming for his final B. Com. Examination.

Rustam was delighted to see him, but seeing Hirjee's morose face, asked, 'What's wrong, yaar? You look terrible! Don't tell me someone's run off with your non-existent girlfriend.'

Disregarding Rustam's poor attempt at humour, Hirjee swept a pile of jumbled clothes onto the floor and sat on the unmade bed. He ran his fingers through his hair and clutched it in frustration.

'What's wrong, yaar? Tell me!' Rustam demanded. 'You haven't had news that your C.A. degree is invalid, or anything like that?'

'Don't be an idiot. How could I possibly be told that my degree is not valid? Honestly Rustam, you say the stupidest things.'

'No need to be insulting yaar. Go away if you've come here to insult me. I've studying to do.'

'No, no sala, I am sorry. But Rustam, Pappa says I've to fulfill Mumma's dying wish by marrying Jeroo. Jeroo! How

can he expect me to marry her? He says Jeroo is willing. But Jeroo would never disagree with him.'

Rustam's jaw dropped in surprise, appalled by what Adeshir expected of his son.

'He can't force you to marry Jeroo. We're in the twentieth century, not in some bygone era, where sons and daughters had to marry according to parents' wishes. Be firm. Just say no!' He fell silent, then stated, 'I know why your father wants you to marry Jeroo.'

'Why?'

'Because he doesn't want his untroubled existence disturbed or have Jeroo's considerable fortune leave the family with her marrying someone else.'

'How dare you, Rustam!' Hirjee raged, leaping from the bed, his hands rolled into fists. 'Take it back at once! How dare you insult my father?'

'Wait!' Rustam cried shielding his head with both arms, to avoid the imminent punch. 'Sorry yaar! I didn't mean anything bad. Just saying, you must stand up to your father. You cannot marry Jeroo! Speak to Jeroo and ask her if she's being forced into saying yes.'

'I did,' was the grimly muttered reply. 'She says if I am agreeable, then she'll be happy to marry me. It's up to me to decide. Oh God, what shall I do?

In the end, Hirjee was no match for his father's uncompromising personality and after a short spell of resistance, acquiesced, and within the year, he married Jeroo. Over the years, he often wondered why Jeroo had wanted to marry him, a man two years younger and one who had never pretended to be in love with her. He respected and admired her for her many good qualities, but never shared his innermost thoughts or feelings with her.

Jeroo never reproached him or gave any indication that she missed his inability to return the absolute love she had for him. She seemed content with the knowledge that he was happy to be her friend. At twenty-six, she had been prepared to have him under any circumstances. On their wedding day, she had promised herself that she would make him the best wife in the world and hoped someday, that he would return her love.

Her sheltered existence had not prepared her for the reality of marriage and for the nights she would weep silently into her pillow after her husband dropped off to sleep.

It was only after Rayomand's birth that she found a measure of contentment. Her baby son filled her life by greedily demanding love.

When Rayomand began school, she poured her energies into charitable works, many of which were unknown to Hirjee.

After more than twenty years, Jeroo fell ill with a virulent form of leukaemia and the best doctors in Bombay could not save her. Hirjee sent her medical details to the Johns Hopkins Medical Institute in America but received a disappointing reply. They said if Jeroo were willing to be admitted to their hospital, they would consider using a new trial drug, but gave her less than a fifty percent chance of recovery. She refused their offer. Rayomand, studying in England, rushed home to spend the last few weeks with her and stayed by his father's side until after the funeral.

Hirjee was stunned by Jeroo's sudden illness and after her death, realized, how much he missed her love, good advice, and companionship. Things he had always taken for granted. There was a void in his life like a huge open crater and for many months he felt both lost and rudderless, in his own home.

Letters of condolence poured in from friends and people all over the world citing incidents of Jeroo's generosity and help. How little he had appreciated the extent of her charitable works or the kindnesses she had shared with people from all walks of life.

When their postman Suresh heard that Jeroo had died, he sat on the bench outside their apartment door and bawled like a baby. 'What are we going to do Hirjeeseth? What shall we do without our Jeroobai? Who will look after us now? Who will help us and our families?'

Philomena had been inconsolable. It had irritated Hirjee to see their middle-aged Catholic maid dressed in unrelieved black for the whole of the first year. He wondered why she mourned Jeroo's loss as though her most beloved sister had died. He understood later when Philomena explained how Jeroo had helped her. It seemed that as soon as Jeroo had discovered that Philomena had been sending all her pay to Goa for the upkeep of her sickly younger sister, she had set up a trust fund and arranged for Philomena's sister to be cared for in a home run by nuns. Her kind actions had freed Philomena from worry and distressing responsibility.

The days and months after Jeroo's death were unbearable and Hirjee was full of bitter self-loathing and grief. It was Rustam and Marina's constant warmth and friendship that had helped him cope with the pain. His life became less lonely and bearable once Rayomand returned home from England and began working for the firm.

Six
Rayomand, Anjali
June 1985

Rayomand drove home down empty streets, whistling softly under his breath. It was four in the morning, with the night sky thundery, threatening imminent rain. He hoped idly that the deluge would hold off till he was safely indoors.

He parked his car and was surprised to see light streaming from his father's study window, illuminating the concrete path and the shadowy croton hedges. His mood was mellow having spent the early part of the evening with friends at the Willingdon Club and later dining with Anjali in her apartment. The dinner was a complete blur, but the scent and taste of her was very much in his mind. He turned the key in the lock, opened the front door and silently let himself in. He headed to his father's study and was surprised to see him asleep at his desk, his head resting on his folded arms. Rayomand laid a hand on his father's shoulder, saying, 'Dad?'

Hirjee opened his eyes and squinted at the light in his room.

'You should go to bed. Need anything, before I turn in?'

'No son, nothing. But thanks anyway.'

Rayomand strolled into his room, unaware of the thoughts troubling his father. He brushed his teeth and climbed into his pajamas. He lay on his bed wishing Anjali was with him. His beautiful Anjali! She drove him crazy with wanting her. He wondered when she would agree to fix the day they could marry.

He had introduced Anjali to his father at a dinner some months ago. The two of them had chatted for a while, after which his father had moved away and spent the greater part of the evening, laughing and talking to Asif and Ashok's wives, Fatima and Anu.

Later that same evening, he remembered asking, 'Dad, did you like Anjali? Isn't she gorgeous?' He recalled his father's unsmiling look and words.

'Yes son, she is. But your mother would not have approved of her.'

'Not approved of Anjali?' he had retorted angrily. 'Why? What do you mean by saying Mum would not have liked her? You mean you don't like her. How can you say such a thing when you know nothing about her? Are you snobbish because she's an actress?'

'No,' his father had replied. 'It's just a gut feeling I have. She's too different from you and your conventional background. But of course,' he added, softening his words, 'I might be wrong about her.'

'You are wrong!' Rayomand had reiterated. 'I know she is the one I've been waiting for. Give her time Dad and you'll see just how wonderful she is.'

His father had never again repeated those worried sentiments about her, but his disapproval continued to rankle. Rayomand could not help wondering why Ashok and Anu did not care for her, though they never said anything to him. Or why Asif and Fatima kept Anjali at a polite distance. Anjali too had noticed his friends' thinly disguised aloofness and said with a shrug, 'It's understandable Rayomand. I'm so used to such reactions. I can't help my looks and no woman likes to be in another woman's shadow.' Enchanted by her, he did not care if the whole world disapproved. He loved her and was determined to marry her.

Lying on his bed, his head pillowed on his arms, he thought back to the time he first met Anjali at a wedding two years ago, in January 1983…

Ashok and Anu's wedding was celebrated at the National Sports Club of India. The venue was specially chosen to accommodate over two thousand guests. A tracery of lights adorned the trees and shrubs, and red carpets covered the scrubby and patchy brown lawn. Invitees sat at tables decorated with marigolds, with lighted candles in gilt containers vying in opulence with the gold and diamond bedecked ladies.

Rayomand was on the dais, chatting to garland-bedecked Ashok and Anu, who were seated on gilt chairs. Hearing Mr. Dharamsi Desai's happy booming voice, he turned and saw Ashok's father lead a man and a woman up to them. The man coming up the flower-decorated steps, had large diamond buttons in his silk kurta and behind him was a slim woman in a heavy brocade sari. When she floated into view, Rayomand found himself drowning in a pair of shining blue-green eyes. Her beauty rendered him speechless. He had never, in all his life, seen anyone like her. The almond-shaped eyes with their impossibly long lashes looked past him and he noticed just a hint of a smile on her perfectly shaped lips. Stunned by her beauty, he knew that she was the one he had been waiting for all his life.

Anjali noted the impact she made on the tall handsome man beside Dharamsi Desai's son. She knew she was considered one of the most beautiful women in India and if her male friends were to be believed, the most dazzling. She was attending the wedding with the South Indian film producer, Kumara Mangalam, with whom she had been living these past eight months.

His film, in which she starred as the heroine, was now complete and it was time for her to move on. She wondered, glancing in Rayomand's direction, if he belonged to the film industry too.

Some weeks later, Ashok's father, the owner of distribution rights to Kumara Mangalam's film, held a gala dinner at the Taj Mahal Hotel to celebrate its opening in cinemas all over Maharashtra.

Ashok invited Rayomand and four other school friends to the premier, and later to dine at the Taj. At dinner, Rayomand was seated beside Anjali, and he found her a fascinating conversationalist, with a wide range of interests.

She, at her naturally charming best, basked in his obvious admiration. It was a pleasant change to be with people who did not belong to the film industry, to be with men and women whose friendships went back to school days. When Rayomand led her onto the floor, she found it pleasurable to be with a man taller than her and one who moved with natural rhythm. It was good not to have sweaty hands caress her midriff or surreptitiously touch her breasts, or for her to pretend that their touch was pleasing. She relaxed in the easy convivial atmosphere and enjoyed herself.

Utterly bewitched by her, Rayomand began pursuing her with steely determination. He sent baskets of flowers and boxes of handmade chocolates each morning, with an invitation to dinner.

One Sunday morning, after another of his gifts arrived, Anjali's English mother Anna, in a voice made husky by years of smoking, said, 'Why don't you meet him? You've said he's handsome and wealthy, and it's abundantly clear he's obsessed with you. It's time you settled down. Get him to marry you and you'll be well placed in Bombay society.' She glanced at Anjali over a steaming cup of tea and saw her daughter's look of annoyance.

'Mum,' Anjali muttered irritably, buttering her toast, 'I'm not ready to give up my career. You know what happens to actresses when they marry, their work dries up! Producers stop giving them unmarried heroine's roles.' She continued, with an edge to her voice, 'Even the most beautiful actresses have to settle for roles as wives, or sisters-in-law. I don't need a man to look after me or to tell me how to live my life.'

Anna wisely refrained from saying more. Instead, she gazed at the ring on her finger, a deep blue sapphire set in a surround of diamonds, and thought of her dear Hans, a retired German captain of an oil tanker. He had proposed to her a few years ago and given her the ring and when she had declined, he had asked her to keep it as a memento of his love.

One day, when there was nothing special planned for her evening, Anjali suddenly decided to accept Rayomand's invitation. He could not believe his luck. His middle-aged Goan secretary, Mrs. Pereira, who took the call, was almost incoherent with excitement.

'Sir, sir, Miss Anjali Rani is on the phone. Wow sir, I didn't know you knew her, she w-wants to speak to speak to you. Oh, my goodness, sir,' she said, fanning her flushed face with both hands. 'I can't believe I have actually spoken to her! T-take the call sir, take the call, she's waiting!'

He was every bit as excited and enormously elated that she had finally accepted his invitation. He found it hard to sit still or concentrate on his work. When Rustam strolled into his office to leave a file on his desk, he teased, 'Something wrong baba, ants in your pants?' Rayomand was annoyed, until he saw the humour and grinned at the appropriateness of the comment.

That evening, after fetching Anjali from her apartment, he drove her to a restaurant of her choice, dining under the stars on delicious tandoori food, fascinated once more by her beauty and her free spirit.

For Anjali, it was a novel experience to be with someone who made her laugh. She was drawn to him and when they kissed good night, she was surprised to find herself returning his kiss. When he invited her out again, she readily agreed, and a few weeks later, allowed him to stay the night, responding unrestrainedly to his eager lovemaking.

It was soon clear that Rayomand was utterly besotted by her and Anjali knew just how to keep him taut with excitement. She let him kiss her or caress her fulsome breasts, at the most unexpected moments, then retreated, leaving him frustrated and constantly craving more. She was a stimulating companion, an innovative lover and someone who delighted in driving him to a fever pitch of jealousy.

Her clothes were superbly tailored, but provocative. She wore designer *kurtas* made from silk and *chikan*-work cotton, with demure chiffon scarves draped carelessly over her shimmering black hair. Her silk and georgette saris were stunning; her *pullo* wrapped enticingly around her shoulders, and her sari blouses worn knotted just beneath her breasts.

She revelled in the feel of power she wove over men, having determined a long time ago, never to allow a man access to the inner sanctum of her heart. All her affection was centred on her mother, the one person in the world whose love she knew was as unswerving as it was unconditional.

Seven
Anjali
February 1985

Anjali fumed as the word 'cut' was shouted for the umpteenth time. Chunky gold earrings weighed on her lobes, making her head ache, and she longed to remove the noisy silver anklets and colourful glass bangles that jangled on her nerves. She sat upright in her chair dressed as a feisty Kohli fisherwoman in a green and black-checked, nine-yard cotton sari, the front pleats pulled between her legs and tucked into the waistband at the back. The makeup man dabbed moisture off her face, expertly retouched her lips, the kohl around her eyes and the red dot in the centre of her forehead. Her personal dresser fussed with her hair making sure that the artificial hibiscus tucked in her bun was secure, while another minion kept a fan trained on her to keep her cool.

Outwardly, her face was serene and unruffled with none of her inner irritation visible. She had learned the art of forcibly switching off from the noise and bustle by reciting lines in her head. She did this now as the irate director debated with the choreographer whether to decrease the number of dancers.

'Anju*beti,* wake up!' a hoarse voice whispered in her ear and her eyes flew open. Her face registered displeasure seeing Pratap Khanna, her stocky, rotund agent of ten years, standing beside her.

'Anju*beti*, something frightful has happened.'

Anjali was suddenly afraid.

'Pratap is it my mother, has something happened to her?'

'Your mother? No, no she's fine,' he replied, thinking worriedly, if only it were as simple as that. 'It's something else, something much more serious.'

'Serious? What is it? What's happened? Tell me!'

'No *beta,* I cannot, not here, with all these curious ears listening to our conversation. Meet me outside as soon as the shoot is over. I'll be waiting for you.'

Two hours later, Anjali entered the private air-conditioned lounge of a nearby hotel and sat with Pratap on a red leather sofa. She studied an improbable arrangement of plastic palms 'growing' in the centre of the room, while Pratap ordered two glasses of chilled mango juice. Through closed windows, the muffled roar of early evening traffic and the urgent ringing of cycle bells, as cyclists wove their way down the crowded streets, could be clearly heard.

She waited impatiently till the elderly Maharashtrian waiter, unimpressed by '*filumwalla*-types,' ambled back with their order and placed the drinks before them. The glasses dripped moisture, leaving wet stains on the glass tabletop.

'Well?' she asked, once they were alone.

Pratap grimaced, drawing out a large envelope from his leather case. From it he pulled out some photographs and handed them to her.

Anjali stared in horror. If these photographs were published, she would be ruined. She was in them with her friend Hirok Gupta, the Steel Industrialist, a short powerfully built man, with the keen intelligence of an erudite Bengali gentleman.

Anjali had been introduced to the now forty-year-old widower, eight years ago, at the Premier of her hit film, Dil ki Dhadkan. It was the film that had first proclaimed her thespian skills as a heroine and not as a supporting actress; a film in which her name was emblazoned on all the posters and hoardings around the city.

Intrigued that she had read and enjoyed the works of the Bengali writer and poet, Rabindranath Tagore, the industrialist was even more astonished to discover she could recite verses from Tagore's 'Gitanjali', in Bengali. At the end of the evening, fascinated by her, he had invited her, along with the director and some of her co-actors to spend a week with him on his tea estate in Darjeeling.

Hirok's guesthouse in Darjeeling resembled a Swiss chalet and looking out of her lavish bedroom window, Anjali had a superb view of the hillside and the mountains beyond. The air was clean and crisp and each day she saw new and exotic hill birds instead of the common pigeons, crows and pariah kites found in the cities. Great eagles glided effortlessly on air currents. On the mountain slopes, covered in terraced rows of fresh green tea bushes, hill women in their colourful costumes picked tea leaves, tossing them into wicker baskets suspended by straps from their forehead.

That week, her first to the Northeastern part of India, proved to be an unusual experience for Anjali. Hirok was a generous host and his staff ensured that his guests' every need was met.

One morning just before dawn, Anjali accompanied Hirok to his favourite scenic site. There, spread before her, were the spectacular snow-clad peaks of the Himalayas gradually emerging with the first light of the sun. Anjali stood enthralled in the pre-dawn hush, broken occasionally by the call of a song thrush. As she silently watched colours of pink and gold wash across the sky, Hirok recited Vedic verses in Sanskrit, in praise of the wonder unfolding before them.

'Hail, ruddy Ushas, borne upon thy shining car,
thou comest like a lovely maiden by her mother decked
Through years and years, thou hast lived on and yet thou'rt ever young.
Thou art the breath of life of all that breathes and lives.

Awaking day by day myriads of prostrate sleepers, as from death,
causing birds to flutter from their nests and rousing men to ply with busy feet
their daily duties and appointed tasks, toiling for wealth, or pleasure, or renown.'

The lyricism of the stanzas and the breathtaking grandeur of the Himalayas deeply moved her, touching some hidden core, and she was grateful to Hirok for sharing these precious moments with her. It was a new experience to be with him and enjoy his intellectual companionship. Her hungry mind was drawn to his and she could sit for hours listening to him. For the first time in her life, she was with a man she genuinely respected.

At the end of the week, not wanting to part from her, he asked her to accompany him to Zurich, where he was chairing an industrialist's conference.

She was hesitant, but both her film agent and producer encouraged her saying, 'Arrae Anjali devi, you must accept this offer. Gupta-ji is very rich and influential, and we must try and get him to invest in your new film.' She accepted his invitation, delighted to make this unexpected trip to Switzerland. On the day of their departure, she arrived at the Sahar Airport with Hirok in his limousine and waited in the V.I.P. lounge before boarding Air India's Boeing 747. She gloried in the unaccustomed luxury of First Class, with crew fussing over them, wanting to gratify their every need. She knew it was Hirok they wished to please, but she did not care, and as she basked in his reflected glory, she promised herself that one day soon, they would do the same because of her.

In Zurich, their luxurious hotel overlooked picturesque mountains, luminous in the summer sun. During the day, with Hirok busy at the conference, she was free to wander and shop to her heart's content. It was wonderful to know that she could walk into any shop and be able to afford anything she wanted. She often wished her mother could have been with her. Someday soon, she told herself, the two of them would share a holiday, just like this one.

Anjali came to know Hirok as a tender and poetic lover. He, in turn, gloried in her exquisite beauty and showered her with expensive presents. They both knew this holiday was just an interlude in their busy lives and would soon be over, with each returning to their separate worlds.

One morning, halfway through their trip, Hirok asked Anjali, 'How would you like a numbered bank account here in Switzerland?'

Resting languidly on lace-edged pillows, she turned her shining eyes on him and gave a dazzling smile. 'A numbered account? You can do that? Can you really open an account for me? Hirok, Hirok, I would love one. It'll be the best thing anyone has ever done for me. How terrific to be able to save some of my earnings abroad.'

Hirok smiled, and continued, 'Okay. I'll have it all set up for you before we leave. But remember, you must be careful not to speak of it to anyone. It is a totally illegal transaction and punishable by law. If anyone ever finds out, you'll find yourself in serious trouble.'

Thrilled by his generous suggestion, she beckoned him excitedly to her bed and flinging off her silk-embroidered kaftan, threw her arms around his neck and gave him a long seductive kiss; her hands hurriedly pushed the brocade dressing gown off his strong brown shoulders and eagerly pulled him on top of her, murmuring low enticing words.

They lay on the bed in a wild tangle of sheets, the morning sun streaming onto their heated bodies through the long paned windows, as Anjali leisurely commenced to thank Hirok in all the wanton little ways he most enjoyed.

Her easy friendship with Hirok had deepened these past eight years. He was her trusted friend and the one she turned to in times of trouble.

He knew about her involvement with other men and was not bothered, because he too enjoyed the companionship of other women. As neither pretended to be in love with the other, their relationship worked very well. Hirok had funded some of her most successful films and made sure that a part of her earnings went like clockwork into her Swiss account.

'Well?' Pratap's fractious voice penetrated her reverie. He had been speaking, but she had not heard a word, as she continued to stare at the photographs of her in Hirok's bed. Hirok's head on her bare breasts, his face obscured, but hers clearly visible with her rich black hair fanned out on the pillows. She looked at Pratap in distress. 'How could these have been taken? Hirok always assured me that the staff at his Calcutta guest house are his most trusted.'

Pratap looked at her through horn-rimmed glasses and muttered, 'The photographer who took these photos wants twenty-five lakhs for them.'

'Twenty-five lakhs? Twenty-five lakhs! Is he crazy? I won't pay him so much money. I can't pay that kind of sum!'

Pratap went on, 'He says the 'hush money' will have to be sent to an account in Mauritius. He says that he will hand over all the photographs and the negatives only after the money is deposited. He warns us though, that if we inform the police, these pictures will immediately be printed in every Indian film magazine.'

'Pratap!' Anjali wailed, 'Suppose he only pretends to hand over the photographs and negatives, and continues to blackmail me?'

'Yes, that's true, but what to do? That possibility will always be there. We will notify Gupta-*ji*. He'll know how to recover the photos and frighten the man as well.'

Anjali never knew how much money changed hands, or how Hirok managed it, but within days, Pratap delivered the photographs and all the negatives to her.

'Here Anju*beti*,' he stated, with relief in his voice, handing her the incriminating package. 'Here! Take the lot and destroy them. But Anju*beti*, I must tell you there is a deal struck with the photographer.'

'A deal? What do you mean by a deal? How can a deal be made with a blackmailer?'

'Easily. To soften his loss, Hirok says we are to let the man take photos of you and give him some kind of inside scoop, that only he will be allowed to publish.'

'No! I won't,' she exclaimed angrily. 'How can Hirok expect me to do such a thing?'

Pratap thought for a bit. Then his eyes brightened, and he struck his forehead with the palm of his hand.

'Hai! That's it! Anju*beta*, I know just what we must do. You know how curious the film magazines have been, wondering if you have met the man of your dreams. *Arrae beti*, listen to this brilliant idea! We will arrange a 'special' photo shoot for the photographer and let him take as many pictures as he likes and have him announce your engagement to Rayomand.' He then went on with rising excitement, 'Anjali to marry her Prince! I can see it all so clearly. You dressed as a Kashmiri princess with Rayomand by your side, wearing a black silk Nehru jacket. I know the man will be delighted. Such an amazing scoop will earn him a lot of money.'

'What? You want me to become engaged to Rayomand?'

'Yes, of course! Why are you so shocked?' he asked, annoyed by her uncharacteristic reticence. 'He is your boyfriend, no, and you have been with him for over a year, and he's crazy about you.'

'I know, but somehow it doesn't seem right; what if it affects my popularity?'

'That's a chance we must take. Anyway,' he added philosophically, 'You don't have to marry him if you don't want to. All you must do is get engaged.'

One evening, Anjali was invited to a wedding at the Government House, as an honoured guest of the Governor. After being photographed with him and his granddaughter and groom, and having met and charmed all the right people, she turned to Rayomand and whispered, 'I'm tired of this, let's leave.'

Bored out of his mind, he heard her words with delight and clasping her hand, wove his way out of the crush, politely pushing past her many admirers. Once in the privacy of his car, he drove down the winding Walkeshwar Road to the Taj Intercontinental Hotel at Apollo Bundar.

He parked under the porch and handed his keys to a waiting hotel driver. They walked into the foyer, with Anjali keeping her head lowered to avoid recognition, her face partially obscured by her long loosely draped scarf covering her head. They took the lift to the 'Rendez-Vous' restaurant and as they entered, the head steward, recognising Anjali, obsequiously led them to a secluded table overlooking the bay.

After studying the impressive menu, they ordered lobster thermidor with all the trimmings and later, over coffee, Rayomand asked for the hundredth time, 'Anji baby, when will you put me out of my misery and marry me?' He watched her study him through her lashes and braced himself for his usual rejection. But when she gave him a dazzling smile, saying, 'Ray, I've made up my mind and yes, I will marry you.' he thought he had misheard her.

'Did you just say you'll marry me?' he asked incredulously, and when she nodded, he gave a low shout of joy. He reached impulsively to take her in his arms, but Anjali immediately shushed him, saying, 'There's no need to advertise it to everyone in the room! I'm happy to be engaged

Ray, but you'll have to be patient with me until the ten films I'm in are complete. My agent, Pratap Khanna, will know how to break the news to the public without it affecting my popularity. He will want us to pose for some studio shots, to publish them in papers and film magazines.'

Her words doused his enthusiasm and he felt strangely let down being told he must wait. But although bemused by her sudden wish to be engaged, he was delighted by her acquiescence and agreed to everything she said, including a photographic session.

Eight
Hirjee
March 1985
[Three months before Rustam's passing]

It was a warm Sunday evening and after a tiring game of golf, Hirjee entered the hushed air-conditioned library of the Willingdon Sports Club. He thought in amusement of the hot-shot lawyer who, unhappy at losing a close-fought game, had challenged him to another round the following Sunday.

After choosing a book from the crime fiction bookshelf, he walked to a chair by one of the many plate-glass windows and before sitting down, paused to admire the neat green lawn and the golf course beyond. Finding a magazine lying open on the armchair, he bent to remove it and his hand stopped in mid-air. He stared in shock at a full-page photograph of Rayomand and Anjali seated side by side on a sofa, with Rayomand's arm resting proprietarily on her shoulder and her flawless face gazing directly into the lens of the camera. She was leaning against Rayomand, with the silky material of her sari having slipped and her voluptuous cleavage partially on view. The caption to the photograph blazed, 'Stop Press! Anjali to marry her Prince!'

No! It can't be! This is dreadful. This cannot possibly be true. Hirjee felt deeply wounded that Rayomand had not said anything to him. He sat down and tried to make sense of what he had just read. Then he stood up, needing to find Rustam. Knowing him, he would be in the card room, playing bridge. Taking the lift to the ground floor, Hirjee walked to the card room and through the closed glass doors saw Rustam engrossed in watching a hand being dealt.

At the sound of the door opening, Rustam looked up, surprised to see Hirjee beckoning him to come out. He excused himself and followed Hirjee on to the lawn. He could see his friend was uncharacteristically agitated.

The two of them walked in silence, past the thick green hedge and rows of red and yellow cannas separating the lawn from the golf course. The setting sun threw long shadows as rooks, crows and pariah kites flew leisurely to roost in the dark copse of trees and the first chorus of cicadas rose in the air. They walked on, oblivious to the other club members who were seated on the lawn, enjoying their drinks and snacks placed on square wooden tables.

Hirjee stopped, and turning, said, 'Rayomand is marrying Anjali!'

'I know, Boka.'

'You know and you never mentioned it to me? How long have you known it?'

'Since yesterday, when Amy came across an article in a film magazine and showed it to us. When I approached Rayomand this morning and congratulated him, he told me not to say anything until he had spoken to you.'

'What shall I do, Rustam? How can my foolish son think of marrying her? I have seen them together and I know she doesn't love him. Why must he choose Anjali when there are so many other lovely girls?'

Like my Amy, Rustam thought, and knew the same lay unspoken in Hirjee's mind.

'How can he let me find out like this?' Hirjee continued angrily.

'Calm down, Boka. There must be a good reason why Rayomand hasn't spoken as yet. Give him a chance to tell you. Whatever you do, do not get angry or say anything you will later regret. You must not spoil your relationship with him. Remember he is a grown man and free to make his choices.'

Rustam's sensible words lessened some of Hirjee's agitation, but he knew he must tread carefully with Rayomand, who was very protective of Anjali.

On returning to his apartment, he was met by Philomena, who informed him that Rayomand was home and would be dining with him. He longed to march into the living room where Rayomand sat reading and shout at him in frustration. He had the most incredible urge to shake him - something he had never done - not even when Rayomand was a boy. But he took heed of Rustam's council and kept a firm check on his temper.

Both men were subdued at dinner; their usual camaraderie visibly missing, as each nursed his thoughts.

Rayomand silently debated how best to broach the subject to his father, knowing it would be unpalatable. He had waited all week for the perfect moment to speak, but while he procrastinated, the story had appeared in print.

After the dinner dishes were removed and a bowl of fruit placed before them, Rayomand finally spoke of his engagement. He was astonished at the calm way his father accepted the news, but the involuntary muscle twitching in his father's jaw was a sure sign that he was upset.

Finally, Hirjee spoke. 'I know you have chosen your life's partner and I wish you well. But I ask you, please, to take your time before you make this commitment final.' Getting up from his chair, Hirjee went into his study and closed the door.

Rayomand sat on, feeling a strange sense of disquiet. A part of his mind was bemused by Anjali's sudden wish to be formally engaged. She had told him, often enough, that marriage was not for her and until now, had skirted the issue or made a joke of his wanting to marry her.

A week later, on a Sunday morning after church, Philomena was taken aback when Rosy asked her in Konkani, 'Philo, why haven't you told me that Rayomand*baba* is marrying that actress, Anjali? Why have you been so secretive? If Amy*baby* were getting married, I would have rushed over and shared the news with you. You would have been the first to know!'

Philomena stared at Rosy, unwilling to believe her words. 'You are wrong, Rosy,' she replied firmly. 'I don't know where you have heard such nonsense, because I know my Rayomand would never do something like that. *Chhee, chhee*! How can you say that he is marrying someone so unsuitable? No, no! Can you imagine what Jeroo*bai* would say? You are definitely mistaken! Rayomand hasn't said anything to me, so it can't be true, and you shouldn't spread false rumours.'

Justifiably annoyed, Rosy snapped back, 'I tell you it is true! Just last evening Amy*baby* showed me the photograph of the two of them in a film magazine, and it was clearly printed that they are to be married.'

Philomena's eyes began to brim with tears and kind-hearted Rosy was immediately contrite. Putting an arm around her friend's shoulder, she said, 'Philo, Philo, don't be upset, it's already done. You know you can't do anything. Whatever God ordains, will happen.'

'No, no Rosy, my Rayomand can't marry that woman. I won't let him marry her! I'll tell him he can't marry her. I'll say Jeroo*bai* would never permit it.'

And Rosy, looking sadly at Philomena, said, 'Philo take my advice and don't make too much fuss. We all know she has been his girlfriend for more than a year and you must realize that you can't change anything. You must accept that Rayomand will be marrying the actress. Philo, they are already officially engaged!'

Philomena arrived home deeply distressed and snapped at the elderly cook Hari Prasad, for speaking to her. She busied herself in the kitchen, making tea, mumbling under her breath, and then marched with the tray into Rayomand's bedroom. She glared at Rayomand as he sat in bed reading the 'Sunday

Times of India'. In a querulous voice, she asked, '*Arrae* Rayomand*baba*, is it true what Rosy is saying, that you are engaged? Engaged to marry that low-class actress woman?'

Rayomand was taken aback at her outburst. He had been unaware till now of her dislike for Anjali, who never bothered to waste her charm on home help. 'Don't be so rude Philomena,' he scowled, taking the tray from her. 'Of course, I'm marrying Anjali. You know I love her.'

'Ohh!' Philomena cried, beating her thin chest with the palms of her hands. 'Ohh, my poor Jeroo*bai*, what must she be feeling in heaven that I have not looked after you properly, for you to even think of marrying that woman!'

Rayomand was amused at the strange picture Philomena presented, of not having 'looked after him properly.'

'Rayomand*baba*,' Philomena threatened, 'If you marry that low-class woman and bring her here to live, then even though I promised my saintly Jeroo*bai* to always look after you and Hirjee*seth*, I will leave and go home to Goa!'

'Do as you damn well, please!' Rayomand retorted in anger.

Hearing his incensed words, Philomena's exacerbated nerves snapped, and she burst into tears. Unable to watch her weep, Rayomand got out of bed and bending over, put his arm around her thin shaking shoulders to give her an affectionate hug.

'Don't cry, you silly old thing,' he said gently. 'You know Dad and I cannot do without our Philomena.' At his cajoling words, she sniffed and wiped her eyes with the back of one work-worn hand. *Thank you, Jesu,* she sent up a prayer, *at least Rayomandbaba still loves me.*

Some days later, while playing snooker with Ashok at the Bombay Gymkhana Club, Rayomand heard him say, 'I hear that you're marrying, Anjali?'

'Yes. I'm sorry *yaar*, for not informing you and Anu personally. But I asked Anjali just a few days ago and she finally said yes.'

'But you can't marry her Ray, she's not marriage material! I blame myself for introducing you. Anu is livid with me and thinks I have done you a big disservice. She doesn't like Anjali at all.' At his school friend's outburst, Rayomand turned on him in anger, 'What's wrong with everyone?' he raged. 'Till now, all anyone said was wow Rayomand, you're so lucky. Now when I say I'm engaged to her, not one person is happy.' He stormed past Ashok, slammed the snooker cue back in its place and left the billiards room.

A few days later, Ashok invited him for a drink at the Bombay Gym, and sitting across from him at the bar, he apologised.

'Sorry about the other evening Ray, I was totally out of line saying the things I did. Man, if you love Anjali and she loves you, then Anu and I wish you both every happiness.'

Taking his friend's outstretched hand, Rayomand accepted the apology, but Ashok and Anu's disapproval continued to rankle.

Nine
Rayomand and Amy
Late July 1985

One evening, four months after their much-publicised engagement, Rayomand's mood was grim on the tennis courts of the Bombay Gym. Anjali had cancelled their evening for the third time in ten days. Earlier in the day, there had been a call from her secretary to say that madam was unable to keep their appointment, because she was going to be busy all evening discussing a new film. The secretary also informed him that Miss Rani was leaving for Delhi the following day and would call him on her return, two weeks later.

Rayomand had coped with her last-minute change of plans before their engagement, because after each occasion, she had made it up to him in exhilarating ways that kept him yearning for more. But now her casual attitude both frustrated and annoyed him. He tried stifling the anger growing in him. He had known from the start that his involvement would entail having to share her with the public and accept as part of her profession, having to travel to different parts of India.

He showered in the men's changing room after a punishing set of tennis and headed home. It struck him while driving, that it was quite a while since he and his father had been out together.

Rayomand turned his key in the lock and entered the apartment to find his father about to go out, dressed casually and looking extremely fit for a man in his early fifties. Although he and his father were both six feet tall, his father's broad physique made him appear shorter.

'Got a hot date, Dad?' he quipped, and Hirjee, surprised to see him home so early looked quizzically at him and asked, 'Are you free this evening? Would you like to join me and the

Cooper family for dinner? It's Amy's twentieth birthday and when I rang this morning to wish her and found she had nothing planned, I invited them to dine with me. Marina was hesitant, but I know Rustam would want them to enjoy themselves.'

Rayomand's immediate response was, 'I would love to Dad, tell me where you are taking them, and I'll meet you there as soon as I can.'

Delighted by his answer, Hirjee asked him to be at the Nanking Restaurant by eight.

Rayomand entered the Chinese restaurant a little after eight and looking around the room saw the Cooper family seated around their favourite table on the mezzanine floor. He went up the spiral staircase to join them and when he kissed Amy, to wish her a happy birthday, he was surprised to see her blush. It suddenly struck him that she had grown into an attractive young woman. Where was the little girl he used to tease? There was something coquettish in the way she swung her thick shoulder-length hair and looked at him through her lashes. The last time he had met Amy was at her father's funeral in May, two months earlier. She had looked pale and drawn then, but today she glowed with the freshness of youth. His gaze wandered around the table, and he was happy to see Marina relaxed and laughing at something his father had just said. She had become thinner and there were new lines of pain etched around her eyes.

Jamsheed excitedly claimed Rayomand's attention by asking, 'Did you hear the cricket commentary today? What did you think of Sunil Gavaskar's batting? I wish I could have watched it live!'

Looking into Jamsheed's wide-eyed face, Rayomand pleaded guilty to not having time to listen to the match on the radio. He said, 'Jamsa, unlike a scrubby schoolboy I know, some people do have to work and keep their noses to the grindstone. But if you want to enlighten me, I am all ears.'

That was encouragement enough to set Jamsheed off on his favourite pastime. He told Rayomand all about the players, the number of runs taken, the sixes that were hit and made comparisons with the thrilling match played earlier in Sharjah, when the Indian team brilliantly won the Rothman's Trophy! He burbled on, almost without taking a breath, till his mother asked him to give others a chance to talk.

Their table was covered with all their favourite dishes. Hirjee ordered fried tiger prawns, duck cooked in a special sauce, sweet and sour chicken, fried rice, spring rolls and American chop-suey topped with a fried egg. For dessert, they had vanilla ice cream and lychees steeped in sugar syrup.

Sitting across Marina, Hirjee was happy to hear her laugh. This was the first time in weeks that he had seen her so relaxed. He watched her gently tease Rayomand about his childhood penchant for eating sweets.

'I remember you stuffing your mouth till your cheeks bulged. I am surprised,' she laughed, 'That you have any teeth left. I know Rosy was the culprit who spoilt you.'

Hirjee looked at Amy sitting on his right, gazing at Rayomand with shining eyes and wondered how his son could miss seeing the jewel in front of him. He wished for the hundredth time that Rayomand was marrying Amy instead of Anjali. He knew his wilful son was heading towards a future of unhappiness if he persisted in marrying the actress.

After dinner and as it was still early, Rayomand suggested he treat them to coffee at the Sea Lounge, to round off the birthday.

Jamsheed thought it a wonderful idea.

'Yes, yes!' he cried, at this unexpected treat and was annoyed when his mother said, 'No darling, I'm sorry, you know you have school tomorrow, so we have to get back home.' Looking at Rayomand, she added, 'You can take Amy for coffee if you like and bring her home later, while we go home with Hirjee.' Turning to Hirjee, she added with her lovely smile, 'That is if you don't mind?'

Rayomand drove Amy to the Taj Mahal Hotel and parked the car in front of the imposing stone-faced building. Turning to her he asked, 'Feel like a stroll before we go up to the Sea Lounge?'

Surprised by his question as she stepped out of the car, she replied shyly, 'Yes, if you like.' Being with him on her own was something she had only ever fantasized about. But now, she could not think of one thing to say. He will be bored with me, she thought to herself, and wished that she possessed the gift of clever repartees like her school friend Zia, or even Pinku, whom nothing ever fazed.

The night was warm and clear, with a light breeze blowing off the sea. Dark clouds hung low on the horizon with the promise of more heavy rain to come. These past two days had been hot and humid, a break from the continuous torrential downpour and winds that had buffeted the city. At ten-thirty on this warm night, there were almost as many people strolling along the promenade of the Gateway of India, as there were at five in the evening. Hawkers enjoyed a brisk trade selling roasted chickpeas and peanuts, fresh coconuts, and ropes of sweet, scented jasmine. Some toy sellers strolled by, carrying heavy rectangular boards attached to long wooden poles. On the board's flat surface, toys in plastic and paper hung from cords stretched horizontally across. There were brightly coloured whistles in the shape of singing birds, kaleidoscopes made from cylindrical rolls of cardboard and small pink and yellow plastic hens that laid round white eggs when the body was pushed down on a flat surface. The hawkers sold all sorts of boxed games and gas balloons for children, who scampered around while their parents ambled slowly or sat on the broad parapet by the sea, unconcerned about the lateness of the hour.

Tongue-tied, Amy walked beside Rayomand terribly aware of his tall presence. She wished her mother had not suggested that the two of them go off on their own. She felt stupid and shy with him, something she never was with boys her age.

She had been relaxed at dinner, laughing at stories Hirjee uncle and Rayomand related for their amusement. She had even innocently flirted with him, utterly unaware that he had found the experience unexpectedly charming.

They paused by the side of a crippled beggar, and she watched Rayomand put money into his battered tin cup. The man gave them a toothless grin and invoked Allah's blessings.

They walked on.

Glancing at Amy, Rayomand instinctively felt her shy discomfort. He did not want her to be uneasy with him and being as fond of her as he was, found he wanted to be her friend. He impulsively reached for her hand and in trying to put her at ease, spoke of a time when he had been saved from drowning by Rustam.

'Dad saved you? Really?' Amy asked, forgetting her shyness. 'When did this happen? How come I don't remember the incident?'

'Because you weren't born then.'

'Well,' she declared impatiently, her eyes bright with curiosity. 'What happened? Tell me!'

He smiled at her eagerness and said he would tell her over coffee in the Sea Lounge.

They entered through the double doors of the 'old-world' part of the Taj Mahal Hotel, built in 1903 by the Parsi industrialist, Mr. J. N. Tata. They went up the grand carpeted stairway to the Sea Lounge and sat by one of the windows overlooking Apollo Bandar. The stretch of sea before them was dark, broken by silvery lines of rippling foam, and in the distance, they could see pinpoints of light, steamers far out on the horizon, moving slowly, to destinations unknown.

'Are you sure you want to hear about the incident,' Rayomand asked. 'I don't want to bore you.'

'You won't!' was her impatient reply.

'Okay,' Rayomand said. 'I was around six or seven years old, and your parents were newlyweds. They had accompanied Dad, Mum and me to Mahableshwar, and stayed with us at the Race View Hotel.

'I remember being a spoilt little pest and wonder now how Rustam put up with me, or how Marina tolerated my constant intrusion. I was like a persistent puppy trailing him wherever he went. The only time he was free of me was when Mum insisted I lay down for a couple of hours in the afternoon and later, forcibly put me to bed by seven-thirty in the evening. But I don't need to tell you this, because you know how good-natured your dad was, and looking back, he deserved a medal for being so patient.'

Rayomand gave her a mischievous look before saying, 'Perhaps he was just using me. Maybe, he was practising for when he would need lots of patience for a daughter who was yet to be born.'

'Wretch,' Amy giggled. 'I never troubled Daddy. I loved him too much. So, what happened?'

'Rustam was my hero. To me, he could do just about anything. Come to think of it, he must have taken a lot of ribbing, for we made a strange pair, a tall young man with a six-year-old constantly in tow, trying to walk and talk like him.

One morning, I decided I wanted to go fishing on Yenna Lake. Dad and Mum tried dissuading me, saying there were no fish to be found in the lake, but I was adamant. I insisted I had seen them the previous evening, jumping in and out of the water as we walked along the promenade.

I remember your dad saying very seriously, that I had only seen frogs and imagined them to be big fish. If I tried fishing there, I would end up catching a large brown frog, which would be *masala* fried and served up as my dinner! It sounded horrid, but I was not going to be put off from my fishing expedition.'

He paused as the waiter brought their two cups of frothing cappuccinos with chocolate wafer biscuits and placed them on the table before them. After taking his first sip, he continued. 'The next day, after my forced afternoon nap, Rustam drove me and my friend Sunil, the gardener's son, down to the lake. We carried homemade fishing rods with safety pins as hooks and worms that Sunil had dug up from the hotel's kitchen garden.

I confess, Amy, I was secretly worried that I might catch a frog because I more than half believed Rustam when he said that if I caught one, I would have to eat it. But I put the horrible thought from my head, determined I was going to catch a big fish and show them all.'

'That was terrible of Daddy,' Amy said, feeling sorry for the six-year-old.

'Yes, I know,' Rayomand replied. 'Well, the three of us got to the lake and after Rustam hired a brightly painted rowing boat, we clambered into it. It was a sunny afternoon, the calm surface of the lake rippling each time a cold breeze skittered over it. Taking the oars, Rustam rowed out to the middle of the lake and pulling in the oars, asked us to put worms on the hooks and catch our frogs.'

'That sounds horrid! Didn't you know frogs don't eat worms?'

'Nope,' Rayomand grinned. 'Not then. But I do remember feeling squeamish forcing a wriggling worm onto a safety pin and made poor Sunil do it. Rustam sat back watching us, thoroughly enjoying our conversation about the best way to catch fish.

I remember waiting, for what seemed like ages when, peering into the water from the side of the boat, I saw a really big fish swim past our wriggling bait. Sunil, I shouted, Sunil *dekho, dekho,* a fish! And in trying to show him just where I'd seen it, I leant over just a bit too much and the next thing, I was swallowing huge quantities of dirty, freezing, water of the Yenna Lake.

I learnt, much later, that your dad seeing me fall head-first into the lake, reacted instinctively. He pulled in the oars, yanked off his heavy jacket and sweater, and dived into the icy lake. People on the pier rushed into motorboats and came out to help us. Men pulled Rustam and me out of the water. My wet clothing was immediately discarded, and I was wrapped warmly in Rustam's sweater and dry jacket, while he was lent a shawl to wrap around him. Then someone drove poor Sunil, freezing Rustam and me, back to the hotel.

It was a long time before I wanted to go near the lake and a longer time before Mummy trusted Rustam to take me out on his own.'

'Did you fall ill?' Amy asked.

'Nope, I was fine, not even the hint of a sniffle - but your father was confined to bed with flu. Poor Marina, her holiday was completely ruined having to nurse Rustam for the rest of the trip!'

They came home after midnight and standing on the landing outside Amy's apartment, spoke in low voices. 'Thank you so much,' Amy said looking up at Rayomand. 'I've had a wonderful evening. I woke this morning feeling miserable, missing Daddy terribly, then Hirjee uncle rang and insisted on taking us out, saying Daddy would definitely want us to celebrate my birthday.'

Looking into her wide brown eyes, Rayomand smiled and lightly brushed her cheek with the back of his fingers. He waited while Amy inserted her key in the latch and before she could turn it, the door opened. Rosy glowered at Rayomand, while Mitzy ran in circles around them, wagging her tail.

'*Baba*,' Rosy grumped, 'Is this, the time, so late, late, bringing Amy*baby* home?'

In answer to her question, Rayomand laughed, put his arms around her plump shoulders and gave her a hug. Her irate ways never bothered him. They were old friends. Just this evening he had been reminded by Marina how Rosy had spoilt him as a child, sneaking forbidden sweets from a jar kept in the pantry. He then turned to Amy and said softly, 'Happy birthday, Amy,' and thank you too, for a really good time.'

Ten

Hirjee

July 1985

Hirjee entered his study after dropping Marina and Jamsheed at their apartment. He switched on the desk lamp and gazed around his favourite room. Most of the décor belonged to the era of his father and grandfather.

Two 18th-century Chinese porcelain vases, each on highly polished tables, stood on either side of one large window. The drapes, at the white-painted metal-grilled window, were drawn back to let in the night breezes. His gaze moved to the 'the grand-mother clock,' so named by Rayomand when he was little because though quite large, it stood on a carved table and not on the floor.

Along one wall, were glass-faced cabinets made of walnut wood, with leather-bound books collected by his father and grandfather. He had added to the collection, and now, looking at them, thought he ought to be ridding the shelves of some of the unwanted ones. He would speak to Rayomand about it.

Another glass-fronted cabinet held his precious collection of netsuke. He had had an electrician install lights on the shelves, to illuminate them. Each piece had been carefully selected and bought, over many years, from the Chor Bazaar. They were now doubly precious as they had been acquired with Rustam when they had gone antique hunting on Sunday afternoons.

The only 'new' object in the room was his fifteen-year-old leather chair, which had replaced his old, scarred leather one. He had done it after Jeroo had said, looking at it in distaste, 'Really Hirjee, how can you continue to sit in a chair with broken springs? You must let it go! You'll injure yourself someday. You must agree it's seen its day and now belongs in a *jari-puranawalla's* shop!' He had ruefully agreed and the two of them had ordered this beautifully handcrafted leather chair.

He remembered when in this very room, his father had asked him to marry Jeroo, and he had reacted with disgust and anger. Sitting back in the chair, he placed his long legs on a footstool and brought his wandering thoughts back to the present. He was so relieved that, at dinner, Marina had behaved towards him in her normal friendly manner. They had met today for the first time since that disastrous evening when he had broken the news of Rustam's failed investment and foolishly asked her to marry him.

Why did he love Marina? For years he had been tormented by the same question. Why his best friend's wife? Marina, who had never encouraged him, nor given the slightest hint she cared for him in any way other than as a friend

He recalled the morning Rustam had told him he had found the girl he was going to marry. He remembered it as clearly as the day he first set eyes on Marina, because that instance, was seared in his heart; both incidents were fresh in his memory as if they had occurred yesterday…

It was a Sunday morning in May 1961, Hirjee and Rustam lounged under a shady gulmohor tree after a swim in the Willingdon Club pool. It was a warm day, the air filled with the sound of children playing and splashing in the water and the cawing of ubiquitous crows. Rustam lay on his deckchair deep in thought and finding him uncharacteristically silent, Hirjee asked, 'A paisa for your thoughts? I've been watching you sala and not once have you turned your wolfish eyes on girls going past in swimsuits. Are you okay?'

Rustam grinned, 'Only a paisa? You wound me! My thoughts are worth much more than that!'

Hirjee, laughed, 'Sala, you've never had a thought in your head quite so expensive.'

In mock anger, Rustam gave him a shove nearly toppling him off the rickety deckchair onto the coarse grass, and after Hirjee laughingly righted himself, he was surprised to hear Rustam say, 'I'm getting married.'

'What? Getting married? When? When did you decide to marry? How come you've never mentioned this to me?' He was about to call out the news to Jeroo, who was teaching young Rayomand to swim in the shallows, when Rustam grabbed his arm and shook him, almost throwing Hirjee off his deckchair again.

'Shut up!' he hissed. 'Did I say you could spread the news to all and sundry?'

'Sorry yaar, I didn't mean to upset you; but you drop a bombshell and expect me not to be surprised? Who is this amazing girl, who has stolen Casanova's heart?'

Rustam lay back on his deckchair, arms folded behind his head, and gazed dreamily up at the canopy of gulmohor trees, ablaze with bloom.

'Her name is Marina, Marina Vehvaina and she lives in Pune.'

'Not Shavaksha Vehvaina's daughter?'

'You know the family?'

'No, but I remember being sent to do some auditing for Mr. Vehvaina's company when Pappa was alive. Shavaksha's daughter can only be around twelve or thirteen at the most.'

'Twelve or thirteen? Don't be so ridiculous. She's not twelve or thirteen. She's the most glorious twenty-year-old you could ever imagine and I'm going to marry her.'

'Really? So, when's the wedding?'

'Don't know,' was the sheepish reply. 'I haven't asked her yet. It's all very strange,' Rustam carried on. 'I've just realised, lying here, that she's the one I've been searching for all my life.'

Hirjee was busy in the months prior to Rustam's marriage, having taken over much of Rustam's workload, so that Rustam could get on with his courtship. Marina's parents wanted their only daughter's wedding to be performed in Pune and Rustam's father, who was recently widowed, readily agreed.

Hirjee and Jeroo met Marina for the first time at a formal engagement ceremony, held four days before the wedding, in the Vehvaina's spacious home. Marina's father was at the front door welcoming guests and seeing Hirjee, he called out, 'Welcome, welcome Hirjee! Do come in.'

On being introduced to Jeroo, Shavaksha said, 'Welcome my dear, so pleased to meet you. It's so good of you both to come and grace this occasion.' Taking Jeroo's arm affectionately in his, he ushered them into the crowded living room. The room was redolent with the heavy scent of lilies and roses and scented garlands that were strung across every door lintel.

As they walked into the living room, a worrying thought flashed across Hirjee's mind. He hoped Rustam knew what he was doing - marrying someone seven years younger than him.

Rustam was in the centre of the room dressed in a knee-length white cotton coat and trousers, with a black pheta on his head, and his fiancée Marina was beside him in a pale pink sequined sari, her head covered by the sari's pullo.

The couple stood side by side on a low wooden stool decorated with chalk design, placed within a circular pattern of chalk, on the tiled floor. On a table by the stool was a large silver tray with three silver containers, one had a paste made of kumkum powder and the other two had pieces of rock sugar and rosewater. The tray also contained fresh betel leaves, some raw rice, a coconut, areca nuts, flower garlands, a sari, monetary gifts for the bride and groom, and jewellery for the bride. On another table, there was a lighted oil lamp and a garlanded picture of the Prophet Zoroaster.

On seeing Marina for the first time, Hirjee's breath caught in his throat. There was a buzzing in his ears and his brain screamed - it's not fair! It should have been him standing where Rustam so proudly stood. In the unexpected ways of life, he knew he was looking at the person he had yearned for, someone who could never ever be his; the girl who was going to be his best friend's wife.

He heard Jeroo's concerned voice ask, 'Are you all right, Hirjee? You don't look very well. Should we just wish the happy couple and leave?' Suddenly, he was brought back to the present. He made his wife a non-committal reply and, painfully schooling his features and thoughts, smiled and joked his way through the most appalling day of his life.

Rustam never discerned the depth of his love for Marina. But Jeroo, bless her kind soul, had known from the start, that the love she so desperately wanted, was given unasked, to his best friend's wife.

Now, sitting in his dimly lit study, Hirjee thought guiltily of the pain he had unintentionally caused Jeroo. In his own way, he acknowledged, he had loved her; how could one not love someone so generous and selfless? But in all their married years, Jeroo had been unable to ignite the fire that Marina, so unconsciously had lit.

Eleven
Amy
Late July 1985

Amy, Meena, Pinku, and Zia, having guiltily skipped class, sat in the open-air Naaz Restaurant overlooking Chowpatty Beach. They had come here in Pinku's car, to celebrate Amy's birthday, albeit a day late.

The scent of wet earth and white stargazer lilies was heavy in the air after the recent downpour. Colourful crotons and gnarled woody-stemmed bougainvillea grew in the garden, and gulmohor and piltoforum trees looked lush and green with the rain having washed off the grime and dust.

Seated at a table, Amy looked affectionately at her three friends, Meena, Zia, and Pinku. Their friendship had begun in kindergarten, at the age of four. Amy often teased Zia about her antics on their first day. Amy, who had kissed her mother goodbye without making a fuss, though inwardly terrified, had been shocked to see Zia wailing and clinging to her poor flustered mother's skirts.

Meena sat opposite her, very demure in a lemon-printed sari, with her long thick plait draped over one shoulder. Zia, her hair stylishly cropped, sat near Meena in well-fitting jeans and a short-sleeved top. Pinku dressed in a loose *kurta* and *churidars*, faced Zia, her curly mop of hair in need of a good brushing, and Amy, sharing the banquette with Pinku, wore a new cream printed shirt tucked into her favourite blue jeans.

Meena, always the shy one, had for the first years at school tagged behind forceful Zia and Pinku, but secretly considered Amy 'her bestest friend'. The ever-exuberant Pinku's real name was Lakshmi, named after the goddess of wealth, and of the four friends, she had the duskiest colouring, her pet name a misnomer. Her father adored her and sincerely believed that his business had flourished after her birth, and now because of her, he was a *crorepati* several times over.

On this bright but sultry morning, they sipped ice-cold Coca-Cola, oblivious to the strong aromas wafting from plates of hot samosas, potato spinach *bhajjias*, and spicy coriander chutney before them. Unable to wait any longer, Zia asked, 'Is it true Amy, what Meena says? You actually had a date with the divine Rayomand yesterday?'

'How come nobody mentioned it to me,' complained Pinku. 'Why am I always the last to know anything special that happens to anyone?'

'Because you never know how to keep your mouth shut!' Zia interjected.

'Girls,' Amy cut in, 'It wasn't a date!'

'Did you go out with him, or didn't you? If you went out alone with him, then it was a date,' Pinku declared.

'It wasn't like that,' Amy said, trying to squash their enthusiasm. 'Hirjee uncle invited Mum, Jamsheed, and me to the Nanking for a Chinese meal and Rayomand decided to join us. That's all.'

'That's all?' Zia asked in disappointment. 'What about your coffee at the Sea Lounge?'

Amy looked reproachfully at Meena, who looked sheepish. 'Sorry,' Meena apologised. 'I know you said not to speak of it till you told the girls, but you know Zia, she somehow squeezed it out of me!'

'So?' Pinku cried. 'What happened? Tell us. Tell us slowly, describing everything in minute detail.'

Amy laughed. 'It was magical!' The girls let out a collective sigh as Amy spoke of her first time alone with the man of her dreams.

'Fool!' Pinku said forcefully when Amy finished narrating her story. 'Amy, I'm sorry, but the man is a fool!'

'Why would you say that?' Amy exclaimed; annoyed Pinku should call Rayomand a fool.

'Because he is,' Pinku reiterated. 'He is a bloody idiot, running after that cheap actress woman who has slept with more men than we ever will, in twenty lifetimes.'

'Speak for yourself,' Zia interjected.

'Zia, you don't mean that!' Meena retorted; her sensibilities offended.

'Of course, I do. Life's too short not to live it fully. You just stick to your goody-goody Suresh. Marry him and have fifty children. I'm going to enjoy myself and have lots of lovers.'

'*Hai, hai!*' Meena cried, utterly shocked. 'How can you say that? What would your parents say if they should hear you? If you're not careful Zia, they'll lock you up in your room and marry you off to the first suitable man who comes along.'

Zia pointedly ignored her, saying, 'Girls, we have to plan how to make Rayomand fall for our Amy and ditch the bloody actress.'

'Zia,' Meena reprimanded, 'Don't use bad language.'

Zia continued as if Meena had not spoken. 'We have to collect all kinds of gossipy stuff written in the papers and post it to Rayomand. Make him open his eyes. Just recently, I read a small item in a magazine that some photographer took hidden photos of her having sex with a man, but it was all hushed up.'

'Yes, yes,' Pinku added. 'That's a wonderful idea, I agree with Zia. It's our duty as your friends to save this stupid man who can't see dross for gold!'

It amused and touched Amy that her friends were prepared to go on a mission to save Rayomand. 'Girls, you know you can't do that!' she said. 'It's a free country and Rayomand can choose whom-so-ever he wishes to marry. Can you blame him for wanting to marry someone as beautiful as her? God, I would give anything, anything at all, to have even a quarter of her good looks!'

'Why would you want to look like that painted doll?' Pinku asked, wrinkling her nose in distaste. 'You know you're beautiful and that any number of boys want to go out with you, but you're so fussy. Walking with your nose turned up at everybody. Take care,' she added, 'That you're not left on the shelf!'

'Amy on the shelf?' Zia scoffed, 'You just watch. She'll be married before any of us.'

'Definitely before you,' Pinku teased. 'You've just said you don't want to marry but have lots of lovers!'

They carried on this interesting conversation till Meena reminded them that they had been out of class for over two hours and should really be heading back.

Later that afternoon when Amy returned home, Rosy was waiting impatiently for her at the door. 'Amy*baby,* go to Mummy's room she's waiting for you.'

Noting her grim face, Amy asked, 'What's happened, Rosy? Did something happen to Mamma and Grandpapa? Are they ill?'

'*Nai,*' Rosy muttered. 'Just go in no, Mummy is waiting.'

Amy felt the first stirrings of unease. Something had to be very wrong for Rosy to tell her to hear it from Mummy when Rosy knew everything that happened in the home.

She entered her mother's bedroom and found Jamsheed sprawled on her father's bed, reading a comic. Her mother was sitting on her bed, her head leaning against the headboard, knees pulled up and her hands resting on them.

Seeing her enter, Marina smiled and held out her arms to give Amy a hug. Taking off her sandals, Amy sat cross-legged beside her on the bed.

'What's happened, Mum? Why is Rosy so secretive about everything?'

Marina wondered how she was going to find the right words to finally break the shattering news Hirjee had given her. She knew Amy would take everything bravely, and in her stride, but Jamsheed was going to be very upset. Taking a deep breath, she plunged in.

'Amy and Jamsheed, I have unsettling news to share with you. Do you remember the evening, some weeks ago, when Hirjee uncle came to visit, and I developed a raging migraine? Well, that was the day he told me that Daddy had lost most of our life's savings by investing, without my knowledge, in a gold mining company. You both know the one I mean. It's been in the newspapers continuously these past weeks. The one that has swindled so many innocent people; this so-called school friend of Dad's defrauded him and as you know, hundreds of others as well!'

'You mean we are poor now?' Jamsheed asked, in an awed voice.

'Not very poor,' Marina said. 'Not like the people you see sleeping on the streets. But yes, with Daddy gone and no proper income coming into our home, you can say we are not very well off. What is left of our savings will not be enough to run this apartment or keep Raju and Anthony.' She fell silent, then carried on speaking almost to herself, 'I will have to make some monetary provision for our Anthony. He is too old now to find another job.'

'Will Rosy go too?' Jamsheed asked, for although he and Rosy had daily battles about just about everything, he could not imagine life without her.

'No. Thank God. She insists on staying with us. I don't know what I'd do without her.'

'Mum,' Amy asked, 'Do you want me to stop studying? I could earn you know. Be a receptionist or something, and with what you make from the florist shop we might make ends meet.'

Marina looked affectionately at her daughter, so caring and unselfish. It was just like her to make such a suggestion.

'Shall I stop school too?' Jamsheed queried, happy at the thought of no more studies. To be free of studying Math, Hindi and Marathi! 'I'm quite tall for my age and people think I am sixteen years old, instead of thirteen.'

Marina smiled and shook her head. 'No, you will still have to go to school.'

'So, what shall we do?' he asked.

'Well, I was thinking that once the monsoon is over, around Divali time, we must put our apartment up for sale and move in with Mamma and Grandpapa till we find a place of our own, preferably near them, if it is at all possible. You'll like that, won't you?'

'Yes,' he said, 'But what about my school? How will I come to Bombay every day?'

'No son, you won't,' Marina countered. 'I'm afraid I cannot afford to send you to the Cathedral School anymore. You'll have to go to another one in Pune.'

'Another school? Ma, no! You can't do this to me. I can't leave my school and go to another one. Please, please don't make me leave it!' he cried.

'I'm so sorry, I wish I didn't have to, but we just cannot afford to live as we are, in such an expensive city.'

'Can't Hirjee uncle help us? He could easily look after us, he is so rich!'

'Jamsheed, how can you say something so foolish?' Amy cried, appalled by his words. 'You know we could never take money from Hirjee uncle.'

'Why not?' he said, belligerently. 'Or' he turned to his mother, 'I can live with Rayomand and Hirjee uncle. I'm sure if I ask Hirjee uncle he'll let me stay with them and pay for my schooling. Please Mum can I, huh Mum, please can I ask him?'

Marina wished she did not have to make her pleading son unhappy, but what he asked was impossible. Hirjee would be more than happy to look after Jamsheed and would think himself privileged to do so. But she could not bear the thought of taking charity from him.

'Stop being more of an idiot than you already are,' Amy scolded Jamsheed. 'You're thirteen and much too old to behave like a baby. You're not making things easier for Mummy with your foolish requests. You know perfectly well you cannot ask Uncle to pay for your schooling, or for you to live with him and Rayomand.'

'You're such an old grandmother!' Jamsheed raged. 'Rayomand won't be living with Uncle much longer, so I'll be doing Uncle a big favour by keeping him company!'

Marina bit her lip to keep from smiling at her son's logic. 'Sorry Jamsheed darling,' she said gently. 'What you propose is not going to happen. You will have to come to Pune with me and be the man I need in our new home, now that Daddy's not here to look after us.'

Jamsheed stared at his mother, blinking back tears, and nodded. He got off the bed clutching his Batman comic and went into his room, shutting the door behind him.

'Mum,' Amy asked, putting an arm around Marina's shoulders. 'Shall I warn the principal that I'll be leaving soon and not sitting my final exams?'

'No, darling. When our apartment is sold, you must stay at the college hostel, complete your degree, then come to Pune after your exams.'

Twelve
Rayomand
July 1985

Anjali found everything going wrong during a filming session in Delhi. Her co-actor continued to fluff his lines and after thirty-five takes, was still unable to get them right. The make-up assistant spilled Anjali's expensive, liquid face foundation, narrowly missing her elaborate costume, and to add to all that, an attractive actress called Mona - whose role in the film she had reduced by dropping a quiet word in the director's ear, said with false sympathy, '*Arrae* Anjali *devi.* I was too shocked. Too, too shocked, you know, to hear that your boyfriend, no sorry, sorry, he is your fiancé, was seen outside the Taj Mahal Hotel in Bombay, walking hand in hand - that too late at night, with a ver-ry beautiful girl.'

'Yes Mona-*ji* I know,' Anjali lied, smiling sweetly at her. 'I knew he was taking his little sister out that evening. You are quite right, she is a very pretty girl, and you know Mona-*ji*, I love her very much. I am so lucky to have such a lovely sister-in-law.'

The woman's face fell, much to Anjali's delight, but inwardly she was livid with Rayomand. How dare he go out with other women when she was away? She ignored the fact that she never took her engagement seriously and spent time alone with men she thought might be useful to her career.

Back in her hotel suite, she paced up and down in her room, Mona's spiteful words ringing in her ears. Pratap, who was with her, said, '*Beti*, I advise you not to give credence to that nasty woman's gossip. You know perfectly well Rayomand is not someone who fools around with other women.'

'And how would I know that?' Anjali countered. 'Can I look into his mind? Can I know what he gets up to when I am away? No, something must've happened. He must have gone out with someone!'

'Anju, Rayomand is a good man. Don't judge him by your own yardstick.'

Her eyes narrowed and she glared at Pratap knowing what he said was true but needing an outlet for her frustration and anger. It was useless to pick a fight with him; he was too pragmatic. It was like speaking to a blank wall.

After prowling some more, she decided to phone Rayomand and ask if what she had heard was true. Her traveling clock said it was four in the afternoon, so he would still be at work. She remembered his request not to call his office and that made her even angrier. How dare he tell her not to call him at work? Who did he bloody well think he was? Lifting the receiver, she asked the hotel operator to call Rayomand's office, completely forgetting his warning that the staff sometimes listened in to their conversation on the general office line.

The phone buzzed on Rayomand's desk, and he heard Mrs. Pereira's animated voice on the intercom saying, 'Miss Anjali Rani wants to speak to you.' As he was busy with an important client, he asked his secretary to inform Miss Rani that he would return her call shortly.

The phone buzzed a second time and a subdued Mrs. Pereira said, 'Sir, I think Miss Rani is very agitated and insists on speaking to you.'

Annoyed at being forced to take the call, he gave a curt 'Hello,' and that was the last straw that snapped Anjali's fragile control. She screamed down the phone at him.

'What d'you mean by telling your secretary you're too busy to answer the phone? Who d'you think you are, treating me this way? How dare you, you who are engaged to me, be seen around Bombay with other women? How dare you,' she repeated at a higher pitch, 'Embarrass me by going out with women while I'm away working in Delhi?' She suddenly burst into loud sobs. 'I hate you. I hate you!' she stormed. 'You're just like all men; unfaithful, bloody bastards!' Then she slammed down the receiver.

Transfixed, Rayomand stared at the handset in disbelief; no one had ever spoken to him in this way, and he was shocked to the core. It was doubly appalling that Mrs. Pereira could have heard some of the conversations.

He somehow got through the afternoon and was still furious when he left work at six o'clock. Driving to the Bombay Gymkhana Club, his mind was in turmoil with the knowledge that his relationship with Anjali had been based solely on worshipping her beauty, her quick and intelligent repartees, and her incredible prowess in bed. He knew almost nothing of her life because he did not read gossip columns in magazines or mix with the film crowd.

He was livid that she had not let him explain the innocent nature of the outing, and felt she insulted not only him with her crass words but Amy too.

Arriving at the Bombay Gym, he played a hard game of tennis, swam twenty lengths, and did everything he could to force the anger out of him. Later, when he joined friends at the bar for dinner and drinks, he picked at his food and drank more than normal.

When he rose to leave, Asif, who was with him at the bar, offered to drive him home but Rayomand refused the offer.

'I'm fine *yaar*,' Rayomand slurred. 'It'sh ridiculoush to think, I'm too drunk to drive. I never drink too much. I'm abs..' he suddenly hiccupped '… 'solutely fine, couldn't be finer!'

Unimpressed, Asif accompanied Rayomand to his car and waited while Rayomand tried inserting the key into a frustratingly swaying lock. Finally leaning his head against the doorframe, Rayomand turned to him saying sheepishly,

'You're right *yaar*, I can't find that damned lock, it keepsh jumping from side to side.'

Asif drove him home, with the car hood down. The cool night air helped to clear most of the alcoholic fumes; Rayomand rested wearily, with his eyes shut, till they reached his place. Asif got out of the car to see him to the door but having largely recovered, Rayomand declined. 'I can manage. I'm not so woozy anymore, but thanks for seeing me home. I appreciate it.'

'Tchh,' Asif replied, 'That's what friends are for.'

Hirjee sat alone in his study, unable to concentrate on the book open in front of him, going over his conversation with Marina earlier that evening. While chatting, she had casually mentioned her plans to sell her apartment and move with Amy and Jamsheed to Pune. He told himself he was being extremely irrational, to be upset. Pune was not far. He would still see her, speak to her regularly on the phone, and look after her interests.

He rested his head on the back of his chair and thought of the changes wrought with Rustam's passing. If only Rayomand had been marrying Amy, instead of Anjali. He had recently learnt from friends in Calcutta, for whom it was common knowledge, that whenever Anjali visited the city, she stayed with the industrialist Hirok Gupta. Sadly, Rayomand had decided that she was the one for him and despite knowing Hirjee's aversion to his choice, still planned on marrying her.

He had avoided attending the elaborate engagement dinner in March, hosted by Anjali's film agent Pratap Khanna, saying that he had to be in Coimbatore that day and Rayomand had not insisted he attend. Marina and Rustam had gone and told him it was a grand affair.

Seeing a light in the study, Rayomand looked in and glimpsed his father at his desk. It was worrying how often he found

Hirjee working late into the night. He knew his father missed Rustam, but wondered if there was something more that was worrying him. He pushed open the door and at the sound, Hirjee lifted up his head and asked, 'Well, had a good evening?'

'Yes thanks, but why are you up so late? Can't you sleep? Care to share what's troubling you?'

Hirjee looked at Rayomand. At over six feet, his son seemed to fill the study. 'Care for some hot coffee?' he asked Rayomand, indicating a thermos on the desk that Philomena had filled, before going to bed.

Lowering himself into a leather chair, Rayomand reached for the coffee his father had poured into the thermos' cap. 'Well, I'm listening. Tell me what's bothering you.'

Holding his own cup with both hands, Hirjee spoke almost to himself, 'What possessed Rustam to throw his money away on such a disastrous investment? Why did I not realise, knowing him as well as I did, that he would be tempted? I should have known. He was a trusting idiot. I know I advised him against investing, but obviously, I did not do it forcefully enough to prevent this debacle. I blame myself. I looked upon him as a younger brother. I should have been able to save him from this! And now my best friend's gone, leaving his family in such a difficult situation, and I am unable to help them because Marina will never accept financial help from me!'

His father's agonised words made Rayomand aware of something he had always somehow known - that much as his father loved and missed Rustam, it was his love for Marina that was tearing him apart.

Hirjee continued, 'Marina called this evening to say she has decided to sell her apartment in October and move to Pune. She says she'll stay with her parents till she finds a flat somewhere near them. Jamsheed will have to leave the Cathedral school and move to Pune.'

'Poor Jamsheed,' Rayomand murmured. 'Even though he fools around at school, he loves it. What about Amy? Will she give up her studies here? And will she be able to join another college in Pune, in her final year?'

'Jamsheed will go with Marina when her apartment is sold, but Amy will stay behind till she completes her B.A. exams. When Marina leaves for Pune, Amy will move into the Sophia College hostel.'

The two men sat in silence. Then Hirjee said, rubbing his eyes, 'Amy is such a lovely girl, Rayomand, how I wish you were engaged to her.' He was sorry the instant the words left his mouth and was stunned by Rayomand's violent response.

'Shame on you Dad, what's wrong with you? How can you even suggest such a thing? You know I love Anjali and just because you can't marry Marina and set her world to rights, you think that my marrying Amy will solve your problem, and theirs! You have never made the slightest attempt to know Anjali,' he said, raising his voice. 'She is beautiful and an extremely brave and hardworking woman, who has struggled in a difficult profession to get to the top!'

Shoving his heavy chair back with a loud screech, he slammed the cap of the thermos on the desk, spilling its remains on the polished surface.

'You'll have to think of something else to help the Cooper family, because I'm sorry, I cannot oblige!' He pushed past Philomena who was standing in the doorway, gaping at them both, woken by the sound of his raised voice.

Hirjee heard Rayomand's door slam shut and turned to Philomena, who was busy wiping the spilled coffee from the desk and told her to go back to bed. It was almost dawn by now and the crows had begun their morning chorus.

He barely slept for two hours before he was wide awake, thinking of his son's angry reaction to his thoughtless remark. He knew it had been a stupid thing to say. For all he knew, being nine years younger, Amy might not want to marry Rayomand. He would have to apologise because he did not like distressing his son. Rayomand was right. Hirjee was aware that he had never attempted to know Anjali. If his son loved her, there had to be something special about Anjali and it was up to Hirjee to make a greater effort to know her.

He left the house before Rayomand was awake, drove to the Willingdon Club for a swim to clear his head, before heading to work.

Rayomand stared blankly at the papers spread before him on his desk. He had been over the same sets of figures for the past hour, but the numbers on the account sheets looked like squiggles. His agile mind could usually discern at a glance whether the neat sets tallied or not.

He hated discord. Especially with his father with whom, he got on rather well. It never bothered him that he lived in the family home, sharing it with Hirjee. In fact, in a city like Bombay, with space at a premium, he would have been hard-pushed to find a place he could afford to buy.

Years ago, his father had said when he was ready to marry, he could have the top floor that was being used as a guesthouse. He considered himself fortunate to have such a large and comfortable home to live in. He was ashamed to have lost his temper last night. The two of them rarely clashed, because his father was gentle-natured and loathed confrontations. Rayomand could not ever remember being scolded by his father. It was his mother who, on occasion, had rebuked him for some misdemeanor pointed out by Philomena.

What had made him react so violently? It had to be Anjali's phone call and the alcohol he had consumed. He knew his father loved Amy and wished she could be his daughter-in-law, the next best thing to having Marina as his wife.

What a strange family they would be if his father married Marina and he, not that that could ever happen, married Amy. Amy was a pretty girl, but much too young for him. What was his father thinking to even mention such a thing!

He knew he owed his father an apology. Earlier that morning, before he left for work, Philomena had barely wished him, but her disapproving glances had spoken volumes. Anwar Singh, their bearer, had served him breakfast without his usual smile, and by then, Rayomand would not have been surprised if their old cook Hari Prasad had marched out of the kitchen, and reprimanded him!

Unable to work, Rayomand went and tapped on his father's door, 'May I come in?'

'Of course,' Hirjee replied, with a smile.

'I'm sorry, Dad. I apologise for last night. I should never have spoken the way I did.'

Hirjee walked around his desk and hugged his son. 'It is I who needs to apologise. I should never have said what I did. You were right to say I've not attempted to know Anjali. I haven't! She must be very special if you love her so much and I promise to make every effort to get to know her better.

Thirteen
July 1985
Anjali

Pratap Khanna watched Anjali's histrionic performance as she screamed down the phone, the sexy sound of her voice lost in the harsh tones of anger, tears streaming down her cheeks in a mixture of frustration and fury.

He rose from his cushioned chair after she slammed down the receiver and, sauntering over to the cabinet, poured a large whiskey soda for himself and a gin and tonic for Anjali who was now sitting at her dressing table, dabbing hot tears from her face.

'How could he? How could he take another woman out, Pratap?' she asked, studying her flawless features in the triple mirrors. 'Am I losing my looks?'

Pratap looked impassively through his horn-rimmed glasses and asked, 'Why didn't you ask Rayomand if the story was true, before jumping down his throat and mauling the man?'

Anjali smiled at his laconic question. 'I did, didn't I? But Pratap,' she replied, petulantly, 'He's engaged to me! How dare he go out with anyone else! You know perfectly well,' she continued, 'If there's even the slightest bit of gossip worth spreading, then there must be a grain of truth somewhere.'

'Anjali,' Pratap warned, 'I would go easy with a man like Rayomand. Though he's crazy about you, he does not strike me as someone who'll allow a woman to push him around. If you go too far, he'll leave you.'

Anjali stared at him, wide-eyed. 'Did you say he would leave me? Pratap, no man ever leaves me. I leave them!' She raised one perfect eyebrow. 'Maybe it's time I left him.'

Swivelling around on her stool she said, 'He's begun to bore me, Pratap, with his very proper ways, his proper father and his very proper friends who look down their snooty noses at me, especially the women. The men would be only too happy to change places with him.' She giggled and continued, 'One night at a party, a so-called friend asked if I would spend the night with him and was very disappointed when I said no.'

Pratap let his eyes wander over the volatile and beautiful woman before him, surprised that he had never felt the slightest urge to sleep with her. He knew her too well. Now, after her passionate bout of weeping, where most women would have swollen eyes and reddened noses, Anjali's face looked wonderful. She was a strange mix of generosity and great warmth of spirit, but she could also be cold and calculating. She had a strong selfish streak and was very possessive. No, he was one of the few men not sexually attracted to her. Finishing his drink, he walked to the door, intending to return to his room and continue reading the new script in his hand.

'Do remember you have a dinner invitation to be at Cabinet Minister Jitenbhai Kapur's at eight-thirty. Let me know when you're ready because a limousine is booked to take you there.'

Pratap walked down the hotel's ornate corridor, with its white pilasters and gilt-framed floor-to-ceiling mirrors, thinking it was an honour for her to be invited to entertain visiting Russian Diplomats. He entered his room and sitting on a cushioned sofa by a plate-glass window, stared at the sprawling city of Delhi, the new film script forgotten in his lap. He missed Sushila, his mistress of nearly thirty years. She was more his wife than his mistress and lived in a small apartment in Andheri, a crowded suburb of Bombay. She was not beautiful or even highly talented, but she made him feel good. He loved her and had always been faithful to her.

His wife, Kaushalya, lived in Ludhiana with his parents and he had always made sure that they were monetarily comfortable. Thanks to Anjali's earnings, he had done very well for himself. His two daughters, who he rarely saw, were married into wealthy families and busy rearing their own children.

He brought his thoughts back to the present and to Anjali and felt a deep sadness. She was not the same Anjali he had met when she was eighteen, struggling to get ahead, urging him to fight for better film roles for her. She was now twenty-eight and at the pinnacle of her career. In another few years, it would be difficult for her to play the role of an innocent, young heroine.

Her mother was right. Anjali should seriously think of settling down. Rayomand might not be the ideal man for her, but he was wealthy and would give Anjali a status in society that an actress, with her reputation, could never otherwise achieve. It would be a miracle if she could find another man to love with the intensity, she had felt for Nirmal Singh, the property magnet she had met in Simla when she was twenty-three.

Pratap recalled that the studio had rented Nirmal Singh's palatial home in Simla and the entire cast and film crew had been accommodated there.

He had been present when Anjali had first met Nirmal Singh while being filmed in the rose garden. It had been as though a current had passed between them. An immediate reunion of two souls. A strange understanding that had gone deeper than anything they had ever known. The moment had a magical quality. A moment of sheer stillness, transcending reality.

Anjali had fallen in love with the whole-hearted dedication she gave to everything, and it had seemed then, that Nirmal had returned her love with the same untamed intensity.

The crew had stayed in Simla for three months, until all the main scenes for the film had been shot, and throughout, Nirmal had remained devotedly by Anjali's side.

Anjali had glowed. Happiness had transformed her. It had lent her an incredible radiance that the camera had faithfully captured.

However, when they left Simla, Pratap had been surprised when a subdued and dry-eyed Anjali returned to Bombay with the film crew. Up until then, he had been certain that Nirmal Singh would insist on her staying behind, by proposing marriage.

On the journey back to Bombay, Anjali had shared some of her heartbreak. Nirmal had proposed marriage but had said that before they could marry, he had to find a suitable husband for his younger sister. He had wanted Anjali to give up her career and to live with him before they married. Nirmal, the rich and spoilt darling of his family, had been supremely confident that Anjali would do as he asked. It had been impossible for him to think that she would do otherwise. He had thought that she loved him far too much to live without him.

Pratap had heard the searing pain in Anjali's husky voice. She had told him that when she had asked Nirmal if he had given a thought to what his family would think if he married a woman he had been living with, he had replied high-handedly that as he was the head of his house and because he paid for everything and everyone, his family had no say in the matter. This unseen despotic side of him had shocked her. She had lived too long in India not to be aware of the strict social mores found in close-knit Indian families and had felt that Nirmal was doing her a great disservice. If she lived openly with him before marriage, she would never be accepted by his close-knit aristocratic family. She had to leave. As much as she adored him, her fiery independent temperament would never tolerate his domineering rule.

Pratap thought about that magical summer with great regret. Soon after Anjali left Simla, Nirmal, shocked by her rejection of him, had barely waited a few weeks before he and his younger sister had married the son and daughter of a rich landowner from Lahore.

Anjali's friend, the industrialist Hirok Gupta, had been wonderful. Learning of her heartbreak, he had come from Calcutta to Bombay and whisked her away to Darjeeling, where she had spent a month in the peaceful Himalayan surroundings learning how to hide her heart. To hide it so deep, that never again would she let it be exposed to such intense pain; and on her return, she had shed no more tears. Her friendship with Hirok had strengthened and undergone a change in the quiet time away from Bombay and the film world. He was no longer just another inconsequential lover, but a good friend.

On her return from Darjeeling, offers of work poured in after the run-away success of her film shot in Simla. Producers and directors fought over who could sign her quickest.

But Anjali had changed. Steel had pierced her soul and that gift of loving innocence she had presented to her lover, was left behind forever in Nirmal Singh's rose garden.

Two days after her angry phone call to Rayomand, Anjali's emotions had calmed down and on quiet reflection, she knew her behaviour had been thoroughly unreasonable. In the past, whenever she was upset, Rayomand had sent presents and flowers and made constant phone calls to jolly her out of her petulant mood. Now, there was an ominous silence. At Pratap's insistence, she finally called Rayomand and used her considerable charm, to break down his polite barrier. She apologised in her best soothing manner and blamed her outburst on having a bad day. She said she had waited for him to call and say everything was all right and that he still loved her, but since he hadn't, she had phoned him instead. She said she couldn't bear to think her darling Rayomand was angry when she loved him so much.

Pratap, listening to the conversation, made a rueful face and mouthed not to overdo it. Anjali, enjoying her new role as the contrite lover, stuck her tongue out at him and carried on with soothing words of love, telling Rayomand he was the only person in the world she could rely on, who would always look out for her and be faithful. She listened to Rayomand's explanation of the innocent outing and was satisfied. Two weeks later, on her return, she invited him for dinner.

When Rayomand entered her chic living room lit with aromatic candles, she greeted him with a slow erotic kiss, her tongue curling languidly around his, as if she would suck in his very soul.

His breath caught in his throat and, holding her hungrily, he found he could not wait. He caught her to him, his senses reeling, passionately aroused as always.

Her low words whispered in his ear increased his desire to lay her on her satin sheets and make impatient love. His incredible Anjali. His beautiful Anjali. Only Anjali could fill his universe.

They helped each other undress, throwing off their clothes, and scattering them to lie where they fell. They lay on her bed in a tangle of arms and legs. Rayomand delighting in Anjali's smooth, scented skin. She drove him crazy. His mind was on fire. Then much too soon or so it seemed to him, she was frantically clutching him and moaning his name over and over.

As they lay spent in each other's arms, Anjali was delighted by Rayomand's total surrender. Pratap was wrong to think that she would ever lose him. He was too much in love to ever go away - unless of course, she thought naughtily, it was she who discarded him.

Later, they wandered arm in arm onto the veranda and while waiting for dinner to be served, stood looking out at the brightly lit Worli Bay. By now, the torrential rain had cleared, and stars glimmered through gaps in the cloudy night sky. Anjali's veranda was a lush garden, with bougainvillea spilling over the balcony rails in a rich cascade of colour. Lilies, ferns, and palms grew in specially created beds that were discreetly lit. The perfume of night flora hung heavy in the air.

Anjali and Rayomand reclined against satin cushions and gold tasseled bolsters, on a floor mattress covered in silk. On a low revolving table, decorated with lilies and roses, were silver and enamel trays filled with steaming *moghlai* dishes, each chosen especially for Rayomand's delectation. Over the years, Anjali had perfected the art of captivating her men and knew just how to keep them malleable in her gracefully manicured hands.

Fourteen
Marina
Aug. 1985

The months after Rustam's death were painfully hard for Marina. He was with her in her dreams every night. In the morning, her hand automatically reached for his, and each time, on feeling the empty bed, her tears flowed afresh.

Sitting listlessly on her veranda, partly shaded by the swaying fronds of a coconut tree, Marina held her head in her hands. When would the pain stop? When would she learn to accept that she had to carry on with life stretching like a long bleak road in front of her? There were times when she wanted to seek oblivion just to be with him. However, for a practicing Zoroastrian, she knew it was wrong to even think such thoughts. But on a day like today, it felt particularly unbearable. She had forced herself out of bed this morning, to sit on the veranda for her cup of tea, before getting ready for work. Her body hurt, her throat was on fire and her head throbbed with an intensity she had not suffered in a very long time.

Rosy brought the tea and after one look at her, bundled her back under her sheets, stroking her hair but scolding all the while. 'Don't you even thinks of getting out of bed. I will be phoning Gitu*bai* and telling her you are ill. Look at you. You have the fever and the bad cold! I telling you every day, eat Marina*bai* eat! But no! Enough Rosy enough, you say, I'm not hungry. See, see, what's happened? You not looking after yourself properly at-all at-all since *seth* died. Now, you just staying in bed and I bringing you a glass of salt water to gargle and hot lemon-brandy-honey mittcher to drink. It will be making you better.'

She hurried into the kitchen, muttering under her breath about intelligent women not taking care of themselves and ticked off poor Anthony for using all four gas rings on the cooker when she needed one to heat water.

Lying in bed, Marina heard Rosy's irate voice through the kitchen door. The normal everyday sounds seemed terribly magnified. She wished Rosy would speak softer because her voice was causing flashing lights in her head.

Later, when Amy came home from Sophia College, Rosy said, 'Oh thank the Lord, Amy*baby*, you're home. Come, come see, Marina*bai*, she's not at all well. She has the bad cold.'

Hurrying into her mother's room, Amy was shocked to see her mother's face flushed with fever. She had noticed Marina looking poorly these past few days, but her mother had assured her she was fine and not to worry. Amy had not been satisfied but thought it was due to money worries and the raw grief her mother was feeling at being parted from her husband. Amy laid the back of her hand on Marina's forehead.

'My goodness Mum, you are burning with fever!'

'No, no, I'm fine,' Marina said, trying to allay Amy's fears, her voice a little more than a croak.

'Fine? You are anything but fine!' Amy countered. 'I'll ask Dr. Guzder to come as soon as he can.' She recalled the last time Jamsheed had had a high fever and her mother had applied cold damp towels to bring his temperature under control. She immediately asked Rosy to get a basin of cold water and do the same, while she tried getting hold of Dr. Guzder.

Arriving two hours later, Jehangir Guzdar was shocked to see how ill Marina was and was worried she had pneumonia. He looked sternly at Amy. 'You should have phoned earlier to let me know your mother was ill. She now needs to be hospitalised.' Amy's eyes stung with the unjust rebuke, and it was Marina who answered. 'It's not Amy's fault. Honestly, I was fine until today. Jehangir, I know you can make me well with your prescriptions. I'll take whatever medication you prescribe, but I am not going into hospital.'

'Marina,' he said worriedly, 'For a sensible person, you are being very difficult. Amy and Rosy cannot look after you in this condition. If you don't get proper treatment, you will become more ill.'

'No Jehangir, no. I have full faith in you. I know you can cure me at home. Please, please don't put me into hospital,' she beseeched in a barely audible whisper. In the face of her distress, Jehangir gave in and prescribed heavy antibiotic tablets. He handed the first dose to Amy from his medicine bag and asked her to send Raju with the prescription to get more from the chemist. After Dr. Guzder left, Amy said, 'Why are you being so stubborn Mum when you know you need to be admitted? What's wrong? This is so unlike you.'

'Amy,' Marina whispered hoarsely, 'We cannot afford the hospital bills. As soon as I'm admitted, the bills will add up by the thousands of rupees. Don't worry darling, I'll be better soon. Jehangir is an old worry bug - seeing a serious illness in a bad bout of flu.'

Amy was unconvinced, but, like Dr. Guzder, she gave in and right through, the long night, she and Rosy stayed by Marina's side, sponging her heated body with cold washcloths to lower the fever.

The next morning, Dr. Guzder was back to check on Marina and was concerned to find her condition worse than before.

'Marina *dikra*, these antibiotic tablets are not working. You need to be in hospital on intravenous medication.' He tried his best to persuade her, but Marina refused to agree.

Amy was frantic with worry, not knowing what to do, whether to phone her grandparents and ask for their help and advice against her mother's wishes or to ring Hirjee uncle. She finally decided to speak first to Hirjee uncle and then to her grandparents. She did not want to frighten the elderly couple with her news, knowing her mother did not want to burden them with having to share costs.

She rang the office and Rayomand answered the phone.

'Amy? Hi!' he said cheerily. 'How nice to hear from you. How are all the family?'

'I'm so sorry to disturb you, Rayomand, but I distinctly asked Hirjee uncle's secretary to put me through to him.'

'No, no, it's always a pleasure to speak to you. Dad's away in New York. He's been gone some days now. Didn't he tell you or phone to say goodbye?'

Amy suddenly remembered Hirjee uncle's visit the night before he left, but with her mother being so unwell, she had completely forgotten.

'Yes, he did. I remember now. I'm so sorry to have bothered you,' Amy said, tears welling in her eyes, threatening to fall.

Something in Amy's voice troubled Rayomand. 'Is everything all right, Amy?'

'No,' she replied tearfully. 'Mummy is very ill, and I don't know what to do. She needs to go to hospital. Dr. Guzder is desperate to admit her, but she refuses because she says we can't afford the hospital charges.'

There was a short pause, then Rayomand said, 'Leave everything to me, Amy. I'll come over and we'll sort this out.'

After speaking with her, he rang his father and informed him of Marina's illness and her refusal to be admitted. He also related a conversation he had just had with Jehangir Guzder, who felt Marina needed immediate hospitalisation and to be placed in Dr. Jamshed Sunavala's care.

'What do you mean Marina won't go into hospital?' Hirjee exclaimed. 'She must go and go at once! Rayomand, see that she does. Assure her that the firm will look after her medical bills, and she must not worry about a thing.'

'Yes, I will.'

'Rayomand, I'm coming home.'

'No Dad, there's no need for you to do anything so rash. You continue your assignments and I'll keep you informed about Marina's progress. Don't worry,' he comforted, 'Marina will get well.'

Amy felt better after speaking to Rayomand. She was sorry Hirjee uncle was away but believed Rayomand would persuade Mum better than she could. Jamsheed, just home from school and standing beside her, gave Amy a quick hug. She was touched by his surprisingly caring gesture because he was not given to outward demonstrations, especially to her.

Rayomand arrived at the Coopers' apartment soon after Amy's phone call. He sat on Marina's bed and was shocked by how ill she looked. Taking her burning hand in his, he spoke gently. 'Don't worry about the hospital, Marina. The firm has always looked after your medical bills and just because Rustam is not around, that has not changed. I've rung Jehangir Guzder and he has organised an ambulance to come for you.'

The doorbell went as he spoke, and he heard Raju open it. Marina looked at Rayomand with gratitude and lightly squeezed his hand. Her mind was playing tricks on her because Rayomand seemed to float in and out of her view, but his words penetrated her consciousness and she felt more at ease.

Jehangir Guzder entered her bedroom with the paramedics, and in no time she was whisked away to the Breach Candy Hospital, tucked into bed, and started on strong doses of intravenous medication.

There was a strange sense of déjà vu for Amy. It seemed like yesterday that they were here for Dad. She was not aware of her cheeks being wet until Rayomand wiped them with his handkerchief.

Amy, Jamsheed, and Rayomand stood silently outside the door of her mother's private room because it was crowded with doctors and nurses.

Dr. Guzder had mentioned earlier to Rayomand that Marina's resistance was low, and he was extremely worried. Now, standing in the corridor outside Marina's room, after conferring with his colleague, he said to Rayomand and the frightened siblings, 'My friend, Dr. Sunavala, one of the finest doctors I know, has taken charge. Having seen the chest x-rays taken by Dr. Tayabali and read Dr. Palia's pathology reports, he confirms my diagnosis that Marina has pneumonia. But my dears,' he comforted, 'Under Dr. Sunavala's excellent care, your mother will get well.'

Amy was familiar with Dr. Sunavala's wife who had been her paediatrician and now Jamsheed's, and when she was introduced to Dr. Sunavala, she was comforted. She asked Dr. Guzder, if she ought to inform her grandparents and after giving her question some serious thought, he said, 'No, don't call them just yet. They're both elderly and the news will frighten them. Let's wait for a day or so.'

Jamsheed stood close to Amy, clutching her hand, terrified that his mother might die, and Rayomand sensing their fear, put a bracing arm around them both. 'Come now, Marina is going to be just fine. Dr. Sunavala and Dr. Guzder will put her back on her feet.' He tousled Jamsheed's curly hair and gave his shoulder a squeeze. 'Smile, big man,' he said and looking affectionately at Amy, kissed the top of her head.

Rosy brought them hot cocoa and sandwiches, and when evening visiting hours ended, the three of them had a hard time persuading her to go home. She was adamant she wanted to stay near Marina*bai*. It was Rayomand who found the right words to quieten her agitation.

'Rosy, Amy and Jamsheed need you at home to organise food, so that they can eat at regular intervals. If you don't do it, who will look after them? What you can do tonight is to light candles for Marina*bai* at St. Steven's Church and pray she gets better soon.'

Her mulish expression softened, and she replied, 'Yes *Baba*, you're right. I will come again tomorrow.'

Amy, Jamsheed and Rayomand spent the first night at the hospital, sitting on hard red plastic chairs. Around three in the morning, Jamsheed fell asleep, and Amy dozed, with her hand in Rayomand's.

Rayomand blamed himself that neither he nor his father had thought to let Marina know that their firm would continue to look after their medical bills. Sitting between the siblings, he silently recited the Avestan *Yatha Ahu Vairyo* and *Ashem Vohu* prayers, for Marina's quick recovery. It was an unusual experience for him to be responsible for two young persons who seemed to think, with him around, everything would be fine, because he said so!

This was the first time in his carefree twenty-nine years that he was responsible for another's wellbeing. When his mother had been ill, it had been his father who had been in charge and he, a helpless spectator. The few weeks he spent with his mother in hospital had left him feeling both vulnerable and helpless, because he had been unable to alleviate her pain or her illness. In these past years, if problems arose, his father took care of them, unless they were work-related. To have Amy and Jamsheed rely on him to deal with the doctors and look to him for reassurance, brought forth a latent, protective side to his character, that he hadn't known existed.

He sat in the dimly lit waiting room, on his uncomfortable chair, his long legs stretched out before him. Amy had drifted off to sleep, her head resting against his shoulder, her legs curled up on the seat. He studied her face as she slept trustingly and noted that it had lost its childhood fullness. Her long lashes fanned out on her unblemished cheeks; her face partly obscured by the fall of her silky hair.

He suddenly had the most ridiculous urge to hold her, to stroke her hair and taste her lips. He wondered what it would be like to really know Amy, to know what she thought and felt, and if she were in love with anyone? This day spent in Amy's company had been a new experience for him. He could not ever remember just sitting with a girl or holding her tenderly, wanting to make the world right for her.

It's because I've known her since birth, he rationalised, and smiled, recollecting the first time he saw her at the Saint Elizabeth's Nursing Home. He had gone there reluctantly with his parents because he was uninterested in seeing a newborn. He remembered being disappointed and badly let down by Rustam. How could he have produced a daughter instead of a son?

When Rustam had proudly shown him his red-faced, wrinkled, newborn daughter, he remembered how difficult it had been for him to conceal his distaste and not say, '*Eeyugh*!'

The evening of her birthday, when they had dined at the Nanking, he had enjoyed her quick appreciation of the ridiculous when he teased her, her infectious laughter, and the way her dark brown eyes mirrored her thoughts. It was a humbling experience now to see total trust in them.

He shook his head to clear it of these thoughts. He ought not to be thinking about another woman when he was engaged to Anjali. However, he just knew that one day Amy would make some man a wonderful wife.

He deliberated on the intense anger he had experienced some weeks earlier, at Anjali's loud and unrestrained behaviour over the phone. She had apologised and later made it up to him and he had accepted her apology, and yet, the doubts still niggled. He tried to bury the seeds of disillusionment lodged firmly in his mind, but a part of his brain told him that her contrition did not ring true. His idealistic view of Anjali, as 'goddess', had crumbled and he was battling the knowledge that Anjali was human like everyone else. He was being critical and small-minded. It had been big of her to apologize. It could not have been easy for a proud woman like her.

The next day, Rayomand insisted on taking Amy and Jamsheed home for a few hours to freshen up if they wanted to spend another night at the hospital. Rosie made sure that Amy and Jamsheed were fed before Rayomand returned to take them back to the hospital, promising to visit them later with some hot cocoa and sandwiches.

On the second night, while Jamsheed slept with his head resting against Rayomand's arm, he chatted softly with Amy about their various likes and dislikes; about books they had both read, what Amy should do after her degree and the job she should look for once she was settled in Pune. The one topic they both assiduously avoided was Anjali.

On the third morning, after Dr. Guzder informed them that Marina was on the mend, Rayomand cajoled Jamsheed back to school, saying, 'Mummy will worry when she learns you've been missing school, Jamsa. She's so much better, it's only a matter of time before she's home again. You don't want to trouble her, do you?' Jamsheed reluctantly agreed, delighted by the knowledge that Rayomand would be fetching him after school, and bringing him to the hospital, in his air-conditioned Maruti.

Amy was astonished at how easily Jamsheed, who was normally so argumentative with her, was handled by Rayomand. She also knew that she had coped with the first two critical nights because of him. It felt utterly natural to be with him and have him take charge.

Rayomand met Amy's friends during visiting hours when they burst in, in a noisy group and flocked around Amy, chattering cheerfully like sparrows. He was amused by the curious glances thrown his way and Zia's loud stage whisper in Amy's ear, 'Not 'the' Rayomand, Amy?' He saw Amy colour, turn away without replying, and answer Meena's many questions about her mother's illness.

Both Zia and Pinku chatted to him as if they had known him forever. Which, in fact, they felt they did, because they had often discussed his love affair with Anjali, in great detail. Amy was relieved when her indiscreet friends left, but Rayomand was happy that their visit had cheered her.

Later that same evening, he insisted on taking the two of them home.

Amy finally rang her grandparents and informed them of Marina's illness and her hospitalisation.

The very next morning, her grandparents were on the early train to Bombay and Amy went to the crowded Victoria Terminus station to fetch them. Her grandparents greeted her with hugs and kisses and once the *cooli* safely stowed their bags and personal gear into the boot of the car, her grandmother launched into a mixture of worried questions and reproaches. Both grandparents were justifiably upset that she had shouldered the worry of Marina's illness on her own, especially her grandmother.

'Mumma,' Amy said, hugging her, 'I was not entirely on my own. Rayomand was with us, and he took care of everything. It's thanks to him and Dr. Guzder that Mummy is better.'

Fifteen
August 1985
Marina

It took five days for Marina to feel strong enough to sit up in bed. The fever and antibiotics had left her feeling drained and the slightest effort made her heart thump fast and tears slide down her cheeks.

She gazed around the clean room with its pale blue walls. There were floral curtains on either side of the glass-panelled double doors, which opened onto a long open-air veranda, overlooking the grey-green waters of the Arabian Sea.

From her bed, she could see the dull afternoon sun emerge from lowering clouds. She followed bright flashes of white seagulls hovering in the monsoon air, before diving into the rough, white-crested waves. Her gaze shifted to admire the scented bouquets on the shelf in her room. Hirjee's basket was the largest. He was still in the States and Amy said he called every day to inquire after her. She was told that he had threatened to fly back when first informed, but stayed on after being reassured that she was in Dr. Sunavala's capable hands.

Her mother Tehmina had been with her all morning, relating how Rayomand, Amy and Jamsheed had kept vigil in the waiting room during the crucial seventy-two hours. She said she and Pappa were most upset with Amy for not calling them immediately and sharing the seriousness of the illness. Amy, she said, had called them only when Marina was out of danger.

Listening to her mother's account, Marina thought how like Amy not to worry them. Marina loved her mother, but her constant chatter tired her. She was secretly relieved when her private day nurse told Tehmina that Marina needed to rest, and walked her to the lifts, suggesting she visit later in the evening.

Marina's mind drifted to Hirjee and his constant love for her, and then to Rustam, with whom she had spent twenty-three happy years. Rustam had been a kind father and a loving husband, if at times a little wearing, especially when he wanted his own way. He would have been shocked had he known how greatly his occasional flashes of temper had upset her. They were never long-lived, and he had always apologised afterwards.

Over the years, she had given in to most of his wishes, sometimes at the expense of her own, and at times joked that she had three children including Rustam, and if one counted Mitzy, four. But there were occasions when she had dug her heels in. Especially when she disagreed with a particular action, as she would have done had he told her about the gold mining investment. He must have known that she would stop him making such an investment and because he had made up his mind, he did it without informing her.

Sitting up in bed, unable to read or concentrate on anything, Marina recalled her chance meeting with Rustam on a warm Saturday afternoon in late February, in the early sixties.

One Saturday afternoon, in Late February, twenty-year-old Marina was at the Pune Club having tea with her parents and their friends.

She was wearing her favourite knee-length floral skirt, a sleeveless Peter Pan collared blouse and red-heeled sandals, and walking quickly to the ladies' room. Her handbag was open as she checked for her comb, and walked straight into a young man, who reached out to steady her. Her red leather purse with all its contents had flown out of her hands to lie scattered on the tiled floor. On becoming aware of warm hands clutching her bare arms, she stepped back, covered in confusion at being so clumsy. He immediately released her.

Before she could apologise, he said, 'It's all, my fault. I should have seen where I was going. But this glorious vision walking towards me, blinded me with her radiance.'

Marina smiled at his nonsense and begged his pardon. She knelt hastily to collect her possessions and he did as well, helping her reclaim a lipstick that had rolled almost onto the lawn. He handed it to her with a grin, saying, 'To be honest, I'm delighted to have bumped into you!'

Making an incoherent reply and without waiting for introductions, she fled into the ladies' room. A little later, when she rejoined her parents, she saw this same young man sitting beside her mother, chatting as if he had known her all his life. Her father introduced him, saying, 'Marina, meet Rustam Cooper. It's an amazing coincidence! I've just learnt that his maternal uncle and I were best friends at a school here in Pune.'

Rustam, unable to believe his luck at having literally walked into the loveliest Parsi girl he had ever seen, wasted no time in getting to know her better. One look at her old-fashioned parents and he knew they would not permit her to go out anywhere with him alone.

He was in Pune that weekend, from Bombay, to watch a friend's horse run in the Pune Gymkhana Races. During tea, he impulsively invited the Vehvaina family to watch the race with him and his friends the next day.

The following afternoon, Rustam made sure he was seated beside Marina in the members' enclosure, and advised her to bet on 'Latino Filly,' the horse he had come to watch. His friend Dadi had told him it was a foregone conclusion that this filly would come first.

Marina bought a five-rupee ticket and eagerly waited for her horse to win.

The gun went off.

The filly flew out of the starter's stall and suddenly to everyone's horror, veered to the right, and into a horse racing beside her. Her surprised jockey flew off her back and narrowly missed being trampled. Dadi's filly raced like the wind without her rider, until she reached the finishing line and just as he predicted, came in first, only to be disqualified.

Lying in bed, she recalled the times Rustam had visited Pune.

At first, he came on alternate weekends and her mother was always delighted to see him. He would arrive laden with all sorts of wonderful things from Bombay, often bringing mithai from the Parsi Dairy Farm, mainly ones her mother loved. He loved Tehmina's cuisine and in exchange, fed her choice bits of exciting Bombay gossip.

On learning that her father had problems with his business accounts, he offered to clear them for him. Marina was highly amused by Rustam's clever tactics of winning her parents' approval. At first, their outings were 'en famille' and later, after he formally asked her parent's permission to marry her, he was permitted to take her out, as long as they stayed with a group of Marina's friends.

Tehmina wanted Marina to marry right away. She was impatient with her daughter for wanting to complete her B.A. Degree. She dropped dark hints about girls losing 'good' boys by making them wait, and not snapping them up immediately. But Marina told her not to be so old-fashioned.

At first, she and Rustam followed her parents' dictates and spent time in the company of friends, but soon they used to slip away after meeting with them. They parked in quiet bylanes and kissed hungrily. For Marina, newly awakened to these unknown passions, it was a scary but delightful experience. She was in love with her wonderful Rustam, and it was as hard for her to wait, as it was for him. But more than anything, she wanted to complete her college degree before she married.

One evening, after another frustrating session, Rustam begged her to marry him and not make him wait any longer. He said he was going crazy without her in Bombay, that he was totally unable to concentrate on anything, and his work was suffering. He told her she could complete her degree in Bombay after the wedding, and sitting beside him in the darkened car, looking into his pleading face, she gave in.

When her parents were told that she was ready to fix a wedding date, her mother's happiness was complete.

One day, whilst getting her trousseau organised, Marina said, wistfully, 'Ma, I wish I could have had just a few more months to finish my degree.'

Her mother stared at her in shock. 'How can you say such a thing? You're lucky he didn't find another girl, while you've been dithering. You're very fortunate that a boy from a good family, highly educated and earning well, wants to marry you. How can you let such ridiculous thoughts about a useless degree even cross your mind? Marina,' she stated sternly. 'No degree-bigree can possibly compare with marrying such a suitable boy.'

Marina's wandering mind came back to the present. She sighed as the nurse made her comfortable and she looked at Hirjee's bouquet. Hirjee, who had kept a promise he had made to her years ago, to do anything he possibly could for her. He had always been such a wonderful friend and yet, when she had met him for the first time, and subsequently for quite a while, she had been sure he disliked her intensely. She remembered meeting him at her engagement and the look on his face when their eyes had met. A look that had made her recoil in shock. She had turned away, wondering what she had done to upset him. His wife Jeroo had hugged her and wished her happiness, but Hirjee had barely managed to say the words. Rustam, as usual, had been oblivious to the drama unfolding before him. Marina had seen concern in Jeroo's eyes and thought it was because Hirjee appeared to dislike her.

Marina recalled Jeroo's many kindnesses to her. When she had first come to live in Bombay, Jeroo had helped her get used to living in the large cosmopolitan city. It was Jeroo who had ensured that Rosy's name and her own were added to Rustam's ration card. Impressing on her the importance of the small booklet; a document establishing one's right of residency in the city.

Jeroo had introduced her to the crowded Grant Road Market, where one bought everything from, fruits and vegetables, to pulses, grain, and fresh fish.

An amazing place, rich in pungent smells and raucous sounds, especially the fish market, which was housed in a large hall, its concrete floor wet with fishy seawater. Bright-eyed Kohli fisherwomen squatted on raised concrete platforms, dressed in colourful, tightly draped nine-yard saris, their baskets of freshly caught fish before them. They sold pomfrets, *ramus*, *bombil*, prawns, live crabs, lobsters, eels and chopped-up pieces of shark, calling out in their loud voices, '*Yaa bai ithe yaa! Yaa seth ithe yaa*!' enticing customers to their stalls. These straight-backed women, Jeroo warned, were volatile and not to be crossed because they could fight loudly like 'fish wives.' Many of them were incredibly rich. The chunky gold earrings they all wore were so heavy, that their ear lobes hung down an inch.

Jeroo had shown her the best places to shop for household items, taken her to Colaba Causeway, to the crowded Crawford Market, to Bhindi Bazaar and to the Parsi Dairy Farm shop, that sold sweets and supplied creamy buffalo milk to their home.

She had also introduced Marina to their friends, but Hirjee, though always polite, had remained coldly aloof. There were times when Marina had seen a fleeting expression in his eyes, which puzzled her. She had questioned Rustam if he knew why Hirjee disliked her, to which he had replied, 'Dislike you? He doesn't dislike you. On the contrary, he likes you very much. He always has good things to say about you.'

She had not believed him until March 1965, when she and Rustam had been holidaying with Jeroo, Hirjee and eight-year-old Rayomand in Mahableshwar, a hill station, 4,400 feet above sea level. The five of them had chosen to stay for a week at the Mahableshwar Club instead of at the Race View Hotel, because rooms at the Race View had been unavailable.

One morning on a chilly but sunny day, Marina sat on a bench in the club's garden with a warm shawl draped around her shoulders. It was peaceful there, with the quiet broken only by the clip-clopping sounds of horses going down a nearby lane and the quarrelsome chatter of the saat bhai, dun-coloured birds that moved in flocks of seven.

She was five months pregnant and feeling lethargic and opted to stay behind when Rustam and Jeroo accompanied Rayomand on his pony ride.

Well wrapped against the chilly air, a cushion placed behind her back to ease her discomfort, she sat reading her book under a tree. But soon, unable to concentrate, she put it down because the baby began to move inside her.

She was staring dreamily into space, when, hearing footsteps approach, she looked up to see Hirjee by her side.

'Are you okay?' he asked. 'Do you need anything?'

'No thank you,' she replied, surprised by his question because until now he had been polite, but aloof towards her.

When he turned to move away, she said, impulsively, 'Don't go. Stay. Keep me company.'

After he was seated beside her, she asked him a question that had been upper-most in her mind, one that had been troubling her for quite a while.

'Why do you dislike me so much Hirjee? What have I done to upset you? Are you afraid, even after knowing me for

three years, that I will come between you and Rustam's friendship? I won't!'

'Dislike you, Marina?' he exclaimed. 'No! I don't dislike you. I only wish that were so. Rustam is my best friend and I, fool that I am... I'm in love with his wife. If there's anyone I dislike, it's me, for not being strong enough to control my feelings. And I have tried,' he sighed. 'Believe me, I've tried.'

Shocked by this unexpected and astounding confession, Marina sat in frozen silence, not knowing what to say, or how to lessen his distress.

It was Hirjee who finally spoke, saying with a forced smile, 'Don't look sad, it's not your fault. I shouldn't have said what I just did. I'll be fine. But always remember, if you are ever in need of help, know you can always rely on me.'

Neither of them had ever referred to that morning and for some unknown reason, she had not shared the conversation with Rustam. It was somehow too personal.

After his startling outburst, Hirjee had been much more at ease with her.

It was as if a painful sore had been lanced and he had come to terms with his life and his marriage to Jeroo.

He had proved a wonderful friend to her and with the passage of time, she, just like Rustam, had come to rely on his advice and friendship.

Now, after all these years, when she most needed his support, he was beside her like an anchor in her sea of uncertainty. She smiled sadly at a recent memory when he had impulsively asked her to marry him and she had hurt him by calling him a fool; her dear, affectionate Hirjee.

But she loved Rustam, had always loved Rustam, her fun-loving, wonderful Rustam.

Sixteen
Rosy
August 1985

Mitzy lay curled up beside Rosy as she sorted through clothes needing to be ironed. The afternoon was dull and humid, and she had debated, after her lunch of boiled rice with mackerel in coconut curry, whether to rest or not, before deciding against it.

The apartment was quiet without Amy and Jamsheed in the house. Everyday sounds wafted in through the open windows, of cars and double-decker buses trundling down the road, unintelligible voices of people talking in the driveway and the constant cawing of crows. She swatted at an annoying fly and checked that the surface of her upright iron was hot by sprinkling water on it. As ever, Marina was uppermost on her mind. She ruminated on the injustices of life and her mind drifted to the day Marina was rushed into hospital. She recalled her anger, at not being allowed to stay, but Rayomand had been right; it was better for her to be here to look after Amy and Jamsheed and see that they were properly fed and go to church in the evening to light candles and pray to Mary*mai* and baby Jesus for Marina's recovery.

Poor Marina, Rustam*seth's* death had been terrible for her. 'Tchh, tchh, tchh!' she clicked her tongue. No one should love someone so much. I cannot bear her suffering. Our apartment is so empty without her! Why should she have to suffer when she is so kind and patient, even with that idiot Raju, who I would have kicked out of the house a long time ago! Why did Rustam*seth* have to die so young? Why must life be so unfair?

She had visited St. Stephen's Church every evening after visiting hours, at the hospital, walking carefully to avoid puddles on the pavement. The after-office hour traffic on

Bhulabhai Desai Road was terrible. Cars inching their way down the congested thoroughfare. The shopping street was crowded with affluent people and trendy teenagers going in and out of brightly lit stores or standing outside Snowman's Ice-cream Shop, oblivious to children begging for carelessly discarded change.

At 8.30 pm on the first evening, the church was empty, its prayer hall silent after evening Mass. She lit four milky-white candles and placed them on a metal table by the pulpit. The flickering flames, bright beacons in the dimly lit hall, stood upright on a bed of spilled wax. Kneeling on a worn cushion in an empty pew and bowing her scarf-covered head, she recited the Lord's Prayer in Konkani and sent prayers to Virgin Mary, Baby Jesus, Saint Stephen, and Saint Anthony, to ease Marina's difficulties.

Rosy's mind began to wander, and in her thoughts, she was back in Goa.

Rosy Pereira was born the seventh child in a family of eight. Her father Joseph Pereira was the prosperous headman of a village in Goa, on the outskirts of Panjim. Rosy grew up in a rambling, hundred-year-old house surrounded by acres of paddy fields. The house with its high ceilings and wooden rafters housed all manner of creatures, especially house lizards and sparrows that nested in spaces, where the rafters entered the wall. The floors inside the house had beautifully coloured tiles imported from Portugal, while the veranda and terrace were patterned in mosaic tiles. The house had been built by her great-grandfather, during the Portuguese rule in the late nineteenth century.

Her father's paddy fields were famous for the cultivation of aromatic ukhra rice, a favourite of the Goanese people. He also owned a small orchard with mango, cashew and guava trees. Within the walled compound of their home, huge jackfruits hung grotesquely on jackfruit trees and the slim trunks of the coconut and toddy palms were twisted and bent by the monsoon winds.

As a child, Rosy ran barefoot in the orchard, playing with her younger sister Marie and village children her age. During the mango season, her small, brown face and her sister's, were permanently smeared with yellow juice. Her mother Esperanza would berate them, in Konkani, 'Look at the two of you. Go! Go immediately and wash your yellow faces at the well. You'll be sorry when your skin has painful eruptions due to the dried sticky juice!' But they rarely listened to her scolds. What was the point of washing when their faces got messy again? There were times when they crept out at night into their neighbour's field and cut stalks of sugar cane, tore them open with their strong white teeth and chewed on the creamy coloured cane, sucking on the delicious, sweet juice. Those were her happy years.

At the age of seven, she was enrolled in a school run by nuns, belonging to the order of Saint Francis Xavier. She hated sitting in an enclosed classroom, scratching alphabets in chalk on a black slate, while sunshine streaming in through the windows beckoned her to come and play; the screeching sound of chalk on slate still rang in her ears. The nuns taught her how to read and write and do basic maths and speak in pidgin English.

When she was older, she helped in the paddy fields, transplanting young rice shoots into neat rows, wading through knee-high water, the hem of her skirt pulled above her knees and tucked into the waistband. Transplanting was backbreaking work, and it was equally hard harvesting the rice, bending over double to slice stalks with sharp sickles.

Her father was kind and good-natured, with one failing: his love of whiskey. He brewed it himself and shared it with his neighbours, on those nights, the air was filled with the pungent aroma of strong spirits. The neighbourhood men gathered on the steps of her father's house would drink, sometimes sing, and occasionally get rowdy and come to blows.

Her intoxicated father would become unmanageable and verbally and sometimes physically abuse her mother, for trying to get him to bed. Those were times when Rosy, sharing the bed with two of her sisters, would pretend to be asleep. Her father was always repentant the next day and silently bore Esperanza's scolding with patience. He would go to the market in his horse-drawn tonga and buy sweets for them all and occasionally, gold earrings or bangles for his long-suffering wife.

Rosy was twelve years old when her father decided to hand the management of the land to her oldest brother, who had his own flourishing cycle hire business. Her second eldest brother, who worked as a chef on a cargo ship, was not interested in looking after the family property.

For the next three years, Joseph lounged under shady trees, his beloved whiskey by his side. Esperanza tried to encourage him to look after the farm and their household, but alcohol was slowing his once sharp mind. One day, without warning, he slid into a coma due to cirrhosis of the liver and within a week, he was dead. No one thought to take him to a hospital and as a child, Rosy just assumed that however ill a man was, he was supposed to die in his own bed.

Her carefree life changed drastically after her father's death. Her four older sisters were already married and living away from home. Two of them lived in Goa, and the other two in Kohlapur and Hubli.

Her eldest brother Robert, his wife Liza, and their children, shared the family home, but her sister-in-law did not get on with Esperanza. The two women disagreed on everything and often had violent screaming bouts. After Joseph died leaving the property to Robert, Liza insisted her husband sell the family home and much of the surrounding farmland

and move to live in a modern house, which she refused to share with her mother-in-law.

Once the house was sold, Rosy, Marie and Esperanza were moved into a small two-bedroom flat in the middle of Panjim. Her mother hated living in the stifling city after a lifetime in the country and the money she received each month from her son was barely enough for the three of them to live on.

At the age of sixteen, after completing her school-leaving examinations, Rosy gladly accepted her aunty Celine's offer of work in Pune.

Rosy, a thin young girl with light brown eyes and pale brown skin, her eyes, a throw-back on some Portuguese ancestor, was employed by Tehmina Vehvaina. Her aunty Celine, Esperanza's unmarried sister, had been working as a cook for the Vehvaina family, for the past twenty years.

Celine's relationship with Tehminabai was tempestuous. There had been innumerable occasions when she had thrown up her hands in anger and threatened to leave. Each time, the crises had been averted, with the intervention of Shavakshaseth. But Celine was aware, that for all Tehminabai's irritating ways, she was a kind and generous mistress.

Rosy's new job was to look after ten-year-old Marina. At first, Rosy was very homesick, missing her mother and sister, but found a measure of comfort in caring for the gentle child. She soon settled into her new job and happily conversed with Marina in Pidgin English and learnt to speak to Tehminabai in broken Gujerati.

One afternoon, while walking Marina home from school, she spoke of her visit to the 'Basilica of Bom Jesus' in Panjim, a church dedicated to Saint Francis Xavier.

'This church, no Marina, it is ver-ry big. The blessed San Francis's body, it is in a coffin, all gold an' carved and

ver-ry lovely. Sometimes on special feast days, I'm thinking after nine, ten years, the Fathers opens the coffin an' many peoples go past it. San Francis's body after so many years no, is become very dark and small. You know Marina,' she said making a face, 'One day, when the casket was opened no, some crazy woman, what happened to her, no one knows, but when she seed San Francis's body, she suddenly bited off his big toe.'

'She bited off his big toe? Oh Rosy, yuck! How can you say that!' Marina cried aghast, sickened by the tale.

Rosy grinned, 'I don't reely knows. But I'm only telling you no, what they say. Maybe she had the sudden giddiness and her head falling on the foot, breaked the toe. Or she kissed it an' broked it. Who knows! But the toe, no, is now inside a round glass box, fix-ed in the middle of something like a hand-mirror.'

On Rosy's eighteenth birthday, she met Santana de Souza, a shipmate of her brother Christopher, for the first time. He was a tall man of twenty-eight, with a ready smile and winning ways. He dressed smartly, wore his hair slicked down and sported a thin moustache. The attraction was mutual. After that first meeting, he visited Pune each time his ship docked in Bombay and began asking her out.

Tehmina disliked him instantly. She told Rosy and Celine, that she smelt alcohol on his breath, and he was not to be trusted. She warned Rosy in Gujerati, 'You be careful, Rosy. He's not the sort of man you should be going out with.' Unfazed, Rosy replied politely but firmly in Gujerati, 'He's my brother's friend Bai, so it is all right to meet him.'

Frustrated, Tehmina tried enlisting Celine's help. 'Can't you see Santana is not a good man? Can't you smell cheap daru on his breath each time he visits Rosy? He thinks his foul-smelling hair pomade hides it, but I know. I know when someone has drunk that vile stuff! If you're not careful, your innocent niece who is stubbornly foolish, will get into trouble. Then what will we do hunh? As her aunty, it is your duty stop her.'

Celine, fully aware that Bai was justified in her assessment of Santana, shrugged her shoulders fatalistically and replied, 'What can I do Bai? Rosy won't listen to me. She's not a child or my daughter. You also know that we bring our own destiny. If this man is meant for Rosy, then neither you nor I will be able to stop her.' However, recognizing her mistress's concern, she tried warning Rosy.

'Leave me alone, Celine,' Rosy snapped back angrily in Konkani. 'You and Bai are making a big thing out of nothing. You know he's Christopher's friend and now he is mine. I like going out with him and he is very good to me; so, don't interfere and mind your own business!'

For the first time in her life, Rosy was attracted to a man and imagined herself deeply in love, like heroines in Hindi films. She was angry with Tehminabai and Celine for interfering. It was exciting to go out with him on her days off, in new dresses especially stitched by a tailor in the marketplace.

The first time Santana put his arms around her and kissed her, her legs felt weak, a warm fluttery feeling blossomed in her stomach, and she knew it had to be love.

Santana tried to get Rosy to sleep with him, but the strong puritanical teachings of the nuns at school, stopped her giving in.

Two years later, he finally asked her to marry him.

When Tehmina learnt of the engagement, she vigorously voiced her displeasure. But in the face of Rosy's determination, she gave in and generously paid for the church wedding. The Vehvaina family attended the four o'clock ceremony but left after the cake was cut and a toast drunk to the young couple. They did not stay for dinner in the church hall. That night, for the first time, Rosy became aware of how much alcohol her husband had consumed.

Santana rented a small flat in a crowded locality of Pune and insisted Rosy stop working for the Vehvaina family. He proudly informed her that he earned more than enough to support her and did not want her working in anyone's home, especially not in Tehminabai's house. He disliked Tehmina as much as she disliked him. He told Rosy, that as his wife, she had to stay home to look after him. In the throes of first love and caught up in the excitement of caring for her handsome husband, she readily agreed.

But once he re-joined his ship, she began to feel lonely, missing Marina and Celine's companionship as much as they missed her cheerful presence around the house. There had been occasions when she and her volatile aunt had quarreled, but they were family, and their quarrels had soon blown over. Now, living alone, she missed her daily gossip sessions with Celine and the hearty laughs they had shared. She began visiting the Vehvaina household and spending more and more time there, happy to help Celine in the kitchen or in organising Marina's school clothes, doing just about anything to occupy herself.

When she was pregnant and found the first few weeks difficult to manage, she gladly accepted Tehmina's invitation to live with them again.

Six months later, Santana arrived unannounced and was surprised to find the flat empty. He had been heavily drinking all day and was annoyed that Rosy was not at home, waiting for him. He knocked on their neighbour's door and was furious to learn that Rosy had been living with the Vehvainas, for some months. He stormed out of his flat and jumping into an auto-rickshaw, headed to their home.

That weekend, the Vehvaina family were visiting Bombay and Celine was on annual leave in Goa. Rosy was on her own in the house sewing baby clothes in the kitchen and listening to Hindi music on the radio, when Santana burst in through the unlatched back door.

'Your ungrateful bitch,' he yelled in Konkani. 'I give you a wonderful house to live in and you prefer to be a slave in somebody else's! Especially this one, when I told you never to do so!' He rushed to her and grabbing her arm, yanked her off her chair. His alcoholic breath made Rosy gag.

'Come! We are going home and if you ever set foot in this house again, I will break both your legs.' With his face contorted in anger, he began to pull Rosy out the door.

But Rosy was not about to take any man's bullying lightly. Her temper flared at his arrogant unreasonable behaviour and she snatched her arm away from his, and shouted in Konkani, 'Stop this! Stop this at once! Who do you think you are? Some great rajah-bajah or something? Bursting in and ordering me around. You, who have not sent me any money to live on for the past three months, how dare you think you can bully me. You foul-mouthed drunkard! You think I'm some poor frightened woman? I am not! Get out of here before I scream the place down and call the police.'

The alcohol he had consumed made him see red; her sharp reply snapped his fragile control and he forgot she was pregnant.

He grabbed her by the hair and slapped her hard for daring to defy him. Once he started to hit her, he could not stop punching and kicking her.

'Stop, Santana stop! Oh Jesu, stop!' she screamed, before falling on the floor and curling into a foetal ball, trying to protect her precious baby from the blows raining on her. But her drink-fuelled husband was beyond rational thought.

'Help, help, help!' she screamed in pain, each blow to her body like shards of glass cutting through her.

Hearing her loud and agonised cries for help, neighbours rushed in through the wide-open back door, horrified to see her on the floor doubled over, trying to protect her pregnant belly from his vicious beating and screaming in pain. It took more than two men to yank the berserk man away from her and to forcibly restrain him. Some hurried away to call the police and a doctor, pushing past gaping crowds standing in the doorway.

Rosy was taken to the emergency department of the Pune Hospital and that night, she nearly died; the vicious beating resulted in her losing her baby. Santana was placed in police custody and jailed for three years.

As soon as Rosy was better, Tehmina and Shavaksha insisted she come home to live with them. Between Tehmina and Celine, they nursed her back to health and when she was better, she began working for them again, but the happy bubbly Rosy was no more.

For months after the incident, fifteen-year-old Marina would get out of bed each time she heard Rosy sobbing and sit by her cot to comfort her. She was shocked and frightened that anyone could hurt her favourite Rosy so badly.

Whilst in jail, Santana developed fever with severe breathlessness and the jail authorities admitted him to the Pune Hospital. There, his illness deteriorated and within a few weeks, he succumbed to sub-acute bacterial endocarditis. Within three short years of being married, Rosy was a widow and vowed never to marry again.

Seventeen

Amy

August 1985

Whilst continuing to iron, Rosy watched a cleaner in a building opposite theirs shake a small carpet and bang it hard against the outer wall of the veranda, sending clouds of dust into the air. Silly woman, she grumbled, how're we supposed to keep our homes clean if people do such stupid things?

Her wandering thoughts returned to Marina and Marina's first encounter with Rustam. She remembered an excited Marina returning from the Pune Club and pulling her into her bedroom, whispering that she had met the most handsome and the most wonderful man in the whole world.

She recalled Rustam's courtship, of his weekend visits laden with flowers and sweets for the family, and the generous tips he gave her and Celine. However, after her bitter experience, she was very wary of men and the idea of marriage. She warned Marina to be extremely careful before agreeing to marry him. 'Men,' she opined, 'But not our dear Shavaksha*seth*, is not to be trusted.' But she agreed with Marina that Rustam seemed alright and as far as she could tell, did not drink cheap liquor.

On Marina's wedding day, Tehmina gave her and Celine, new silk saris, gold earrings and four gold bangles each.

A few days before the wedding, Marina hesitatingly asked her if she would come and work for her in Bombay, and on hearing her emphatic, 'Yes, yes, Marina*baby*! I am definitely coming!' Marina had joyously flung her arms around her.

Rosy finished ironing and was folding away the ironing board when the doorbell rang and Mitzy ran out barking excitedly. It was Tehmina, returned from visiting Marina.

'Rosy,' she announced in Gujerati, her hands laden with flowers and sweets, 'I'm so happy! Marina is coming home tomorrow. Tell cook Anthony to make fried pomfret, yellow *daal* and rice, and *rava* for lunch and see that everything is in readiness for her.'

The next morning, Tehmina bustled about in a fever of excitement, ensuring Raju cleaned the house thoroughly and hung floral garlands. After breakfast, she lit an oil lamp, placed fresh garlands around a framed picture of prophet Zoroaster and one of smiling Rustam, then, covering her head with a cotton scarf, recited prayers of thanks to *Sarosh Yazad* for making her daughter well.

Jamsheed refused to go to school the next day, knowing his mother was coming home. He informed Tehmina and Amy that he would be going, 'With Hirjee uncle to fetch Mummy from the hospital.'

Hirjee arrived by ten a.m. as excited as all of them, to be fetching Marina home. Jamsheed and Shavaksha accompanied him to the hospital and while they waited in his parked Mercedes, he hurried up to her hospital room and found her dressed and eager to leave. It distressed him to see how weak she was and how glad to have the support of his arm.

As they made their way back to his parked car, he noticed Shavaksha surreptitiously dash tears from his eyes. Jamsheed rushed to hug his mother and, after making sure she was comfortably seated, gently closed the door.

The long days in hospital with nothing to do but rest, had brought Marina a strange kind of calm. Her raging torrent of grief was now a dull ache. She knew Rustam would always be with her, but a sense of acceptance pervaded her body. She was fully aware she had to carry on with her day-to-day living and try and make her home as happy as possible. Her children had suffered, and they looked to her to give their home its sense of security. She shelved the thought of selling the apartment for now, finding it too difficult to cope with, telling herself she would deal with the problem when she was stronger, trusting in Hirjee to guide and steer her in the right direction.

With Marina home from the hospital, and her visiting parents back in Pune, Amy's daily life settled once more into its humdrum routine. But some things had changed. She was aware of strange new longings and was surprised by the intensity with which she missed Rayomand.

The time spent with him at the hospital had a bittersweetness to it. She missed him acutely and wished she had not felt duty-bound to inform her grandparents quite so soon. If only she could have had a few more days in his unexpected company.

Things had changed with their arrival and Rayomand had resumed work. He had continued to visit Marina at the hospital, but the time spent with all of them had been shorter, with no opportunity for Amy to be alone with him.

During those early days and nights, Amy had been sure Rayomand had also felt a sense of closeness between them. She had seen tenderness in his eyes and her heart had thrown away caution. What was she going to do? Why did she crave the one person who could only bring her heartache? She chided herself. How could she possibly think he could care for her, especially when he was marrying the amazingly sophisticated Anjali. Wake up, Amy! Stop this futile dreaming. Rayomand is not for you. There will be someone else; someone special, just waiting for you.

When she was much younger, she remembered asking her grandmother, 'Mamma when do you think I'll marry?' and Tehmina had replied, 'Marry? Amy dear, that's in God's hands. The right man, whoever he is, will come knocking on your door, carrying a lighted lamp.'

Amy remembered teasing her by saying, 'But Mamma, what happens if the lamp goes out before he finds my door?' And Tehmina had stared disapprovingly at her over her reading glasses, unamused.

One evening, Amy's three friends came to the apartment to pay her mother a visit. They sat beside Marina's bed, chatting politely to her, before repairing to Amy's bedroom.

Sprawling on Amy's bed, they debated the exciting topic of 'Amy and Rayomand,' oblivious to Amy exclaiming, 'For goodness' sake, there is no Amy and Rayomand!'

Zia could not understand Amy's refusal to further her cause and was unwilling to drop the subject. Not one to give up easily, especially an idea as important as this one, she continued with her trend of thought, 'You cannot just sit around and do nothing, Amy. You have to win Rayomand away from that witch!'

'Don't be silly, Zia! He's nine years older and if he thinks of me at all, it's pityingly. He is sorry for our family. He most definitely does not see me as a grown woman. How can he? I've looked frightful each time we've met, all red-nosed and teary; be real for once. Can you actually see him, with his hands clutched desperately to his heart, saying, oh Amy, I can't live without you, Amy I'll die without you!'

'Yes, I can!' was Zia's staunch reply. 'You're far more beautiful than that witch.'

'Honestly, Zia! Don't keep calling her that. We don't know her. She may be an amazing person.'

'Hmm, she is,' Pinku agreed. 'We know she's fantastic in bed. Look at the number of men she's had.'

'Pinku!' Meena exclaimed. 'You shouldn't say such things.'

'Meena,' Pinku declared mischievously, 'You'd better get used to these sorts of things, for Suresh will say and do a lot more of those sorts of things when you marry.'

Colour flooded Meena's cheeks, and she looked away.

Eighteen

Sept 1985

On a warm Sunday morning in early September, Hirjee and Rayomand sat on their balcony, consuming a leisurely breakfast of Hari Prasad's spicy omelette with hot chapattis and strong Assam tea. A pedestal fan whirred noisily, circulating humid air. It was 8.30 in the morning and promising to be another hot day. The monsoon was almost over, and heat had begun. By October, Bombay would be sweltering.

Hirjee laid down the Times of India newspaper he was reading and said, 'Some American clients of mine are visiting Bombay, Rayomand, and I plan to invite them with some other friends, to dine on Thursday. Are you free?'

At Rayomand's nod of affirmation, he continued, 'Do invite Anjali and any other friends. I know it is short notice, but the Americans are only visiting for four days.'

'Did you say *invite Anjali*? I thought you couldn't stand her. Are you sure you want me to?'

'Quite sure, I want to get to know her better. I realize I've been remiss in my attitude.'

Rayomand smiled, acknowledging the special effort being made. 'Thanks, Dad. I will. I know once you get to know her, the two of you will get on famously. But don't blame me if your foreign men friends and all your male guests have eyes only for her.' Although he joked about Anjali's ability to have men fawn over her, and hated her blatant encouragement of them, he was much too proud to let her know. He only hoped that once they were married and she, secure in his love, would not crave such adulation.

Later that same morning, when he met her at the Breach Candy pool, he extended his father's invitation. Anjali, aware of Hirjee's dislike of her, debated whether to attend or not.

But, ever the consummate actress, she smiled and gracefully accepted.

Hirjee had spoken of the planned dinner to the Cooper family, while visiting with them the previous evening.

'I'm hosting a dinner on Thursday for some American clients I recently met in New York. They fly in on Tuesday morning and will be staying at the Taj. They'll only be here for four or five days, then off touring Delhi, Agra and Jaipur, before returning home. Please say that you and Amy will come?'

Taken aback at his invitation, Marina instinctively refused. 'No, Hirjee. I cannot. It's been only four months since Rustam's death, and I can't face so many people.' Turning to Amy sitting by her side, she said, 'But Amy, you can go. You'll like that won't you darling?'

Amy was prevented from answering because Hirjee immediately declared, 'Of course you can, Marina. I want you both to come. You'll know everyone there apart from the Americans.' He leaned forward, saying, 'You must start going out. You cannot bury yourself at home. You think Rustam would want you to do that? I tell you he wouldn't!'

Marina was about to insist she was not ready to attend dinners, when she saw looks of acute disappointment on both Amy and Hirjee's faces. Stifling negative impulses, she smiled at her two, favourite people, and said, 'Thank you. Amy and I accept. We would love to come.'

A smile lit his face and taking her hand, he gave it a friendly squeeze, aware of the huge effort she was making. Twirling the whisky and ice in his glass he spoke of his plan to ask Rayomand to invite Anjali.

'I don't know how, but I must overcome the unreasonable dislike I feel. I hope by meeting her more often, the two of us will become better acquainted. I must accept the fact that she's going to be my daughter-in-law.'

Amy's heart had sunk when her mother voiced doubts about accepting the invitation. She knew she could not go without her mother. Rayomand would most probably be there with Anjali and without her mother's support, she could not face them. And yet, she longed to see Rayomand again.

Fortunately, when her mother said yes after her initial hesitation, Amy wanted to skip for joy. She had not seen nor spoken to Rayomand for almost a month. She knew Anjali was back, for how could one not know of her whereabouts, when she was prominently portrayed in film magazines and newspaper columns.

She wondered what it would feel like to be in the company of the famous actress while seeing Rayomand again?

She must train herself to feel nothing. She must be sensible and accept that they would be married soon.

She was impatient to share the thrilling news with her friends in person and not on the phone.

It was late afternoon by the time she met up with them after class, in the college garden. The four of them lay their study books on the dusty grass under a gulmohor tree and sat on the books, brushing aside Meena's worry about sudden bird droppings. On hearing that Amy was going to a dinner party with Rayomand and their hated Anjali, they became as excited as her. They immediately began to discuss the pros and cons of the invitation, oblivious to everything around them; to the bittersweet scent of crushed grass, the smell of gasoline fumes, or the aroma of spices emanating from nearby apartments.

'Amy,' Zia stated. 'You must look your best, your very, very best so when Rayomand sees the two of you in the same room, he'll definitely prefer you to that twenty-eight-year-old witch!'

Amy laughed at Zia's immoveable faith in her ability to make Rayomand see her, with Anjali in the same room.

'That man needs thick glasses,' Pinku grumbled. 'Not being able to see which one of you is truly beautiful,'

'Amy,' Zia added. 'You have to fight for your man.'

'Zia,' Amy sighed, 'How can you be so stupidly stubborn? He's not mine. And never will be. He loves Anjali!'

'Amy,' Zia said, seriously, 'We all know where a man's brain lodges when involved with a sexy female. It's your duty to extricate him. It's for his own good!'

'*Hai rae,* Zia! Do you have to be so crude?' Meena muttered.

The next few days were spent by her friends planning impossible strategies for Amy to oust Anjali.

Zia lent Amy her turquoise-green shot-silk sari with dusky pink and gold threads woven into the border and the richly patterned *pullo*. The sari suited Amy perfectly. The blouse that matched the sari was very daring. It was high-necked and demure in front, with its own built-in brassiere, but the back was completely bare. The two sides of the blouse at the back were held together by silken cords. The cords had to be tied at the nape in a single knot, then crisscrossed through tiny loops in the two sides to the base of the blouse, where they were pulled together and tied in a bow. Amy was both worried and excited to wear such an audacious blouse.

'What happens if the knot comes loose, Zia?'

'It won't,' Zia answered matter-of-factly. 'Not unless Rayomand tugs at it.'

'You're awful,' Amy giggled. 'You're quite, quite sure I'll be okay?'

'Of course, you will. I've worn it several times and,' she added mischievously for Meena's benefit, 'Nothing like that has happened, more's the pity!'

Marina thought the blouse fitted Amy perfectly and saw nothing wrong with the ties holding the blouse together. It was Rosy whose sensibilities were offended. She held the blouse between two fingers, as if it were a dirty rag, saying, '*Chhee, chhee*, Amy*baby chhee*! You can't wears this. No, *Bai*, no,' she said to Marina. 'You can't let Amy*baby* go out in this. Shame on you Amy! No decent girl can be wearing such clothes. What is Zia's mother thinking? Allowing such shameless clothes? Just you wait no, an' see,' she opined darkly, 'That Zia, she will be coming to no good! A good girl, no, can be wearing anything once she's married. But,' she added primly, 'On'y if her husband allows, but oh my goodness me, not before that!' And pursing her lips in what Rustam called, 'Her sour prune face,' she walked out of Amy's room in a dudgeon, disgusted with Marina for not backing her and behaving as a proper mother ought.

Amy and Jamsheed had endured more strictures from Rosy than from either of their parents. When Rosy had complained to Marina and Rustam about their misdemeanors, telling the two of them to be more strict, Rustam had deliberately annoyed her by saying, 'We don't need to, Rosy. We have you to do our dirty work.'

Fond as Rosy had been of Rustam*seth*, there were times when he really annoyed her and she wished he could have been more like Hirjee*seth*, who always treated her with proper respect.

Amy skipped class on the day of the dinner. Rosy offered to wash Amy's thick straight hair with soapy *aretha* seeds and after drying it, rubbed it with a silk cloth till it shone. That evening after she was dressed, her mother clasped a coral pendant on a gold chain around her neck.

Marina too had dressed for the dinner with care, for her first evening out without Rustam's reassuring presence.

They reached Hirjee's house a few minutes after eight and after walking up a short flight of marble steps, they took the lift to the terrace. The September night was lit by floodlights and colourful lanterns strung at given intervals between slim poles. The coloured lights illumined the leaves of a large peepul tree in colours of dark green, indigo and purple, and a lone coconut palm in the garden glowed silvery against the inky sky.

A buffet table had been set discretely near some spiral stairs, to allow hired caterers access to the terrace from the kitchen below.

Philomena stood nearby, keeping a beady eye on the caterers, while Anwar Singh served the drinks.

Instrumental music floated from the speakers and potted plants cordoned off a corner of the terrace for dancing.

Stepping onto the terrace, Marina noticed the guests and had the ridiculous urge to flee. Her heart thumped wildly as she thought, I can't do this! I can't face these people without Rustam. What am I doing here? Why did I agree to come? Then her panicking eyes fell on Amy's face and seeing both excitement and trepidation in it, she willed herself to be calm. Then Hirjee was hurrying towards them with a big smile, his hands outstretched in welcome, and she found herself relaxing.

Hirjee had been on the lookout for Marina ever since his first guests arrived. His heart lurched ridiculously when he saw her, elegant as always, in a navy blue, silk Conjeevaram sari, with a triple row of pearls around her neck and pear-shaped pearl drops in her ears just visible below her perfectly groomed hair.

Taking Marina's icy hands in his, he saw panic reflected in her hazel eyes. He was fully aware of the effort she had made tonight. His own, silently conveyed how wonderful she looked and how grateful he was that she had made the effort. Turning his gaze from Marina to Amy, and taking her slim hand in his, said, 'Darling Amy, you look quite stunning. Take care you don't end the evening breaking too many hearts.'

Blushing at his fulsome compliment, Amy secretly wished Rayomand would think so too.

Rayomand was talking to friends when he saw his father rush to greet Marina and Amy. He saw Amy smile at something his father said and looking across the distance, thought he had never seen her look more lovely.

He was suddenly glad Anjali was not present. She had phoned earlier to say she was unwell and could not come. He hadn't believed her because they had been together last evening, and she had been fine. But secretly, he had dreaded seeing Anjali and Amy together. Anjali had sharp claws which she used with wounding effect if threatened by a good-looking woman and this evening, Amy looked incredible.

The evening took on a magical quality for Amy when Rayomand walked up to her and said that Anjali would not be at the dinner. Her heart leapt with joy, thinking, if only for tonight, she could pretend Rayomand was hers.

She was introduced by him to his friends and found herself warmly included in the group. When the music changed to catchy numbers by Michael Jackson, Bruce Springsteen, Aretha Franklin, and Tina Turner, some of the more energetic couples got up to dance.

Amy did several turns with Rayomand's friends, wondering all the while if he was ever going to ask her. When he finally did, it was after dinner, to Diana Ross' seductive voice crooning, 'Why do Fools Fall in Love?'

How apt, Amy thought wryly, to be dancing with him to that song.

'You look absolutely fantastic Amy, and you clearly are the most attractive person here tonight. Come to think of it,' he said with a mock frown, 'I'm not sure I approve of my men friends showering you with so much praise and attention. If you're not careful, your head will swell so much that Rosy will have to help support it.'

Amy giggled at this ridiculous scenario. 'If Rosy has anything to do with it, my poor head will shrink from sheer fright with all her scolding, to the size of a pea.' She told him how scandalised Rosy was, to see her leave home in a blouse that her mother thought was completely respectable.

'Rosy warned me to keep my pullo wrapped around my shoulders, at all times! Honestly Rayomand, having Rosy in the house is like having ten mothers-in-law!'

He laughed, but a part of him agreed with Rosy. Touching the smooth skin on Amy's back did disturbing things to his mind. He could not comprehend why he was attracted to her, or why he felt happy in her company. He was sure he had rid himself of the traitorous emotions experienced at the hospital, but here they were resurfacing again.

For Marina, the evening was one of mixed emotions. After her earlier attack of nerves, she relaxed and enjoyed herself. She was glad Hirjee had insisted she attend. His American guests were chatty and thrilled to be in Bombay, and excited by everything they had seen. Marina felt good to be with her friends, many of whom she had deliberately shunned, not wanting to see pity on their faces. But now, it was pleasant to know she had been missed. It was good to feel alive again and be admired. She found herself speaking easily of Rustam, to those who had known him well. The genuine affection they felt for him, was balm to her aching heart.

It was nearly midnight when the first guests began to leave, and she was surprised how quickly time had flown. The evening which had begun with her panicking had been a pleasurable one, and she thanked Hirjee for an enjoyable dinner, and for being such a kind and supportive friend.

On the way home, Amy was silent, but from the little smile playing on her lips, Marina knew she had enjoyed it as well.

Nineteen
Rayomand
September

Rayomand was relieved when the disturbing evening came to an end. He had spent far more time than he ought with Amy, but a part of him wanted to relive the hours spent with her at the hospital. She made him feel special and needed. Something Anjali never did. Latterly, he was beginning to feel he was just being tolerated by Anjali. She said she loved him and wanted to marry him and had apologised for her senseless outburst. And yet, when she was not around, doubts had begun to surface and were beginning to worry him.

Earlier in the evening, Ashok had taken him to one side, and asked, 'What's wrong, *yaar*? Stop staring at Amy. Aren't you forgetting something? That you're engaged to the beauteous Anjali. You can't have them both you know.' Then he added quietly, 'For God's sake, don't let Amy see you looking at her in this way. Don't play with her affections. If Anjali catches you looking at her like this, she'll scratch your eyes out and little Amy's. Just take care. Listen to my advice, which of course you won't, dump Anjali and marry Amy before someone steals her from under your nose.'

'You talk such rubbish, Ashok!' he had countered, annoyed by his friend's uncanny knack for reading his thoughts. 'I was just admiring her. Amy knows I'm fond of her and thinks of me as family. I'm only making sure she's enjoying herself.' Ashok had given him a disbelieving look and with an irritating smile, sauntered off to find Anu.

Once the last guest left, Rayomand agreed with Hirjee that the dinner had been a success, and everyone had appeared to enjoy themselves. The stylish spread organized by hired caterers was delicious and Hirjee considered the cost well spent. It was thanks to Anwar Singh and Philomena that everyone was well looked after. Before turning in, he gave substantial tips to each of his staff, in appreciation for their hard work. Philomena offered to make hot cocoa for him and Rayomand, but they both declined and asked her to get some sleep.

Rayomand entered his room and threw himself fully clothed on the bed. He mulled over the night's happenings and smiled at some remembered remark of Amy's. With her innate intelligence and ready sense of the absurd, she would make some man a delightful wife.

He lay on his bed unable to relax, then got up and prowled around his room, before deciding to phone Anjali. It was a quarter past one in the morning, but he knew she never went to bed till after two, unless there was an early morning film shoot. Her line was busy, which meant she was awake. On the spur of the moment, he suddenly decided to visit her and see how she was faring.

Arriving at her apartment, a sleepy sentry peered into the car, recognised him, and showed him to a parking space. Rayomand took the elevator to the fourth floor and stood undecided outside her apartment, staring at her nameplate, debating whether to disturb her or not. He was on the point of leaving when his fingers, of their own volition, rang the bell and a sleepy-eyed Savitri opened the door. She gazed owlishly at him and said in Marathi, that *Devibai* was resting and could not be disturbed. She disapproved of her mistress's shenanigans, but it was not her place to say so. Anjali was not an easy mistress, but a generous one.

Rayomand smiled and replied, that he did not think Anjali*devi* was asleep. He brushed aside her weak attempts to stop him and walked down the familiar, dimly lit corridor, past a row of oil paintings by famous Indian artists: two Husseins, a Shreshtha, one Gaitonde and four Hebbars. Anjali considered herself a modern Indian woman, having left her English roots many years ago.

Rayomand paused outside her bedroom. Indian music floated out and he recognised Allah Rakhah on the *tabla* and Ravi Shankar on the sitar. He could hear low voices and thought Anjali was watching television.

He turned the polished doorknob, entered her bedroom lit by scented candles, and went rigid with shock.

Anjali was in bed, but not alone. She was entertaining a man the way she knew best. She was riding him furiously, her great mane of hair swinging wildly from side to side. The man, in the throes of sexual excitement, was clutching her, his face contorted with the force of her gyrations. He was moaning her name over and over and Rayomand heard, as though from a vast distance, Anjali's high exuberant laughter, delighting in her supremacy.

Blood drained from his head. A film covered his eyes, and he felt nauseous. He tasted bile rising in his throat and his fingers curled into tight fists. He wanted to lash out at the man in her bed. He wanted to fling Anjali off the supine man with all the force that was in him, but the unnatural and sickening sight kept him rooted to the spot. He saw her turn her head and stare at him wide-eyed, as he spun on his heels to leave, forcibly slamming the door behind him.

He raced down four flights of stairs, taking them two at a time, desperately needing distance from what he had just seen. He came home with a haze of red in his eyes and sat in his parked car for a long time, gazing blankly at the garage wall. The earlier enjoyable part of the evening appeared to have occurred years ago.

He was not ready to go home, or to bed.

He had to walk.

He had to do something.

Leaving the parked car, he walked like a robot down Malabar Hill, past Hanging Gardens and down to Kemps Corner, sidestepping sleeping bodies wrapped in thin cotton counterpanes, on the uneven pavements. He walked all the way down Hughes Road, turned right at the Parsi Colony and then he was at Chowpatty beach, in front of Wilson College.

The beach, lit by neon streetlights was littered with dirty paper, the tideline edged with scum and dried garlands left behind by the waves. The stalls selling spicy snacks, drinks and ice cream were closed and shrouded in tarpaulins - a faint whiff of onions and spices lingering on the salt air. Kerosene lamps dangled from wooden posts were dark and silent. Stall owners slept on mats under their wheeled wooden carts, with light blanket coverings to keep out the chilly sea air.

Rayomand awoke as if from a bad dream due to the intense discomfort in his feet; his evening shoes, unfit for so much walking, were pinching him. He looked for a passing taxi but there was none and so he began his lonely trudge home, this time via Walkeshwar Road. He was almost at Teen-Batti, when he saw a cab at a taxi rank, the driver dosing at the wheel. He shook the man's arm through the open window, '*Bhaiya*, will you take me to Malabar Hill?'

The man agreed and within minutes, Rayomand was home. Opening the front door, he went into the darkened living room instead of his bedroom. Unlatching the veranda doors, he stepped out. The great city slept, its quiet only broken by the occasional yowling of stray cats and the plaintive barking of pie dogs.

Pulling up a cane chair and freeing his feet from their painful prison, he sat with his legs stretched out, in the first light of dawn. He listened to the rustle of waking birds and the rattle of Aarey milk bottles delivered by government vans, and the slap-slap sound made by a Parsi Dairy Farm, milkman's leather slippers, as he strode down the road carrying a metal milk can on his head.

Rayomand leaned his exhausted head on the back of the chair. He was unprepared for the shock, anger and disgust he felt. Why was she with that man? And more importantly, why was *he* not enough for *her*, when he worshipped her, and she swore she loved him. Only, she did not. She could not, if she could give that part of herself, which was precious to him, to another man. Were there others? He had always known she was not like most women. How could she be when she was so beautiful and adored by the public? He covered his eyes with his palms, to shut out the graphic images flashing before his lids. He had been warned, but he thought he knew best. He loved her. God, he loved her. But ... he wished ... what did he wish? That she was more like other women? No. She could never be that. A sane part of his mind asked if he still wanted to marry her ... could he trust her? He knew he could not trust himself to be near her. He was too physically attracted to her. She made other women pale in comparison. Amy flashed before him, but she was a child, just an innocent child; someone he was fond of. His head throbbed and his eyes burned, and with bitter thoughts whirling in his head, he finally fell asleep.

Hirjee was dressed and ready for work when he saw Rayomand sleeping on the veranda. It troubled him to see his son still in last evening's clothes and wondered how he could sleep through a cacophony of morning sounds: of Philomena's high-pitched voice scolding their *ganga*, the juddering and honking sounds of slow-moving traffic, crows cawing raucously and dogs barking, strays fed as an act of charity by their elderly tenants on the ground floor.

Sensing his father's presence, Rayomand blearily opened his eyes. The sun's rays pierced them like sharp knives and made them water. Raising his hand to shield them, he heard his father ask, 'Are you alright?'

Hirjee had heard Rayomand leave the night before and rightly assumed he was going to Anjali's. He had been woken at dawn, by the sound of veranda doors being opened and now it was worrying to see his son sleeping as though drugged. 'Are you alright?' he asked again.

'I'm fine Dad,' Rayomand replied, rubbing his painful neck and head. 'Sorry, I overslept. Philomena should have woken me! You carry on ahead, and I'll be at the office as soon as I can.'

Rayomand did not know how he got through that ghastly day, or how he coped with his busy schedule and dealt with the many problems awaiting him or kept his patience with Mrs. Pereira. His demons of pain were just under the surface and his head throbbed with the monotonous beat of drums.

Sometime during the day, Ashok called to thank him and Hirjee. 'We had a wonderful time. Thanks for inviting us. But what happened *yaar*, why didn't Anjali come?' and without waiting for a reply, asked, 'What do you think, of going to Goa for a weekend? Anu and I have been working hard and we need a break. What do you say? Will you come? I'll ask Asif and Fatima and you can bring Anjali. It will give us a chance to know her outside the party circuit. Satish Kulkarni has offered the use of his house and says we can go there any time we like. Well, how about it?'

'Sorry Ashok, I'm extremely busy. There's just too much work and I can't get away. But you carry on and I'll join you some other time.'

Later in the day, his secretary buzzed his desk to ask if he would take an urgent call from Anjali's agent, Pratap Khanna. He told Mrs. Pereira to say he could not because he was in a meeting and would be busy all day. He just wanted to forget anything to do with Anjali and try, if possible, to erase the terrible sight of the night before.

Twenty
Anjali
September

Hirok, in bed with Anjali, was unaware of Rayomand's presence until the door slammed behind him. He asked in surprise, 'Who was that? Your boyfriend?'

'Fiancé,' she replied ruefully.

Leaning against the headboard with his arm around her shoulder, he asked, 'So, what're you going to do and why are you still with him when you obviously don't love him?'

She mulled over his question once the shock of seeing Rayomand passed. Truly, if there was anyone she wanted to marry, it was Hirok; he was her friend and she felt alive in his company. But he would never marry her. They were too much alike. He liked his freedom and was unwilling to give it up, but that did not bother her. She was determined to keep his friendship even after her marriage. She would have to be careful, but she would do it. Men were strange creatures. Given half a chance, they would jump in and out of different women's beds; but if a woman did the same, she was pilloried.

'Why am I with him?' she repeated, with her head resting against Hirok's broad chest, 'It's because he's crazy about me and desperate to marry me. Our engagement, as you well know, was a result of a cover-up for those incriminating photographs. It is Pratap's advice to marry him. Not immediately, but certainly sometime in the future.' She then added, with uncharacteristic humility, 'But after tonight, who knows? He may not want me.'

Anjali was livid with Savitri for allowing Rayomand to enter when Hirok was with her and equally angry with Rayomand for coming unannounced, so late at night. She had gaped in shock on seeing him in her room, and only when the door had slammed behind him, had she finally exhaled.

Her mother was horrified to learn what had happened. She liked Rayomand and looked forward to him being her son-in-law. She could not understand her foolish daughter. How could she entertain another man while engaged to Rayomand, especially when he was desperate to marry her?

Pratap was just as upset. He liked Rayomand and was sorry he had found her with Hirok. When Anjali made it clear to him that she did not want her engagement to end, he rang Rayomand and tried to set up a meeting, but Rayomand refused his calls.

Pratap finally told Anjali, 'If you want him back, you'll have to phone him and use all your acting skills. But there's no guarantee he'll succumb to your guile after the shock he has received. No man likes to find the woman he plans to marry, cheating on him.' After pacing her room in silence, he counselled, 'Wait a few days for his anger to cool, and then call him.'

Rayomand was reading in bed when the phone rang; it was Anjali. Her low-pitched voice sent familiar electric currents down his spine and his first impulse was to slam down the receiver.

'Ray, sweety,' she breathed, 'I know you have every right never to speak to me. But, before you decide to do that, I need to talk to you. I want to make you understand a little of what my life is like before you sit in judgement. Please, darling? I just want to talk to you. Please? Please *jaan*, give me a chance to explain. And believe me when I say I love you.'

His mind rejected her honeyed words. He would not be swayed, and yet, knew it was only fair to hear what she had to say, and so agreed to meet her for tea at the United Services Club. They had, on occasion, visited the club with its sprawling grounds by the sea where members had respected their privacy.

The following day, Anjali arrived in her limousine and her chauffeur parked next to Rayomand's car. He opened the door for her, and she stepped out and walked up to Rayomand, who was waiting.

She smiled and his heart thudded as she leaned in to kiss his cheek, her eyes meltingly gentle. She looked ravishing in her cream *kurta* with tight-fitting trousers, a gold-edged *dupatta* covering her head, and her diamond engagement ring flashing in the evening sun.

They walked over scrubby grass to a shady spot overlooking the sea and sat on sun-bleached chairs. A waiter, recognising her, hurried to serve them. He took their order for tea and sandwiches, assuring them they would not be disturbed.

After chatting briefly about inconsequential things, Anjali skilfully led him through the story of her life. The tale she spun in her low passionate voice was so wretched, that she could have won an Oscar for the pathos. Sparkling tears slid down her flawless cheeks as she took the truth and removing from it her own single-minded determination to reach her goal, portrayed herself as an innocent girl arriving in India with her mother, in search of her father, the deposed raja of a minor state in Himachal Pradesh.

'Ray,' she confided with a break in her voice, 'You cannot imagine the shock and dismay my mother and I felt on arriving here, to find that my father had died, and we had no one to turn to. We were penniless in a foreign country, a country whose language we didn't speak. At first, my mother tried to find work, but she was unsuccessful. Then later, when an opportunity arose, she forced me into the life of modelling and into the sleazy cutthroat profession of acting.'

She added huskily, 'I was only fifteen and my mother made me lead a life that was anathema to me. She insisted we earn money, in whatever way possible, to buy return tickets to England. But once on this road, there was no going back for me, so, I decided to be the best model and the very best actress in India. Of course, there have been men in my life, but they were stepping stones to further my career. I have never loved anyone,' she uttered untruthfully, 'Until now.' She sent him a sideways glance through tear-laden lashes, pleased to see he was moved.

'And even though my mother forced me into this existence, I still love her dearly and have done everything I can, to care for her. But I'm tired of this existence and look forward to being with you and putting this nightmare behind me. But if it is your wish to end our engagement and never see me again, I'll understand, even though it will break my heart.'

She studied Rayomand from under her impossibly long-lashed drowning eyes and wondered if he had swallowed her tale. Seeing compassion on his face, she knew he had and was satisfied. Sitting beside him with her fingers clasped in his, she was delighted by her performance. She knew that once again she had woven her magic and he believed her. She had absolutely no intention of letting him leave her. Her mother was right. This man was not like the others. He would be faithful to her. Boring but faithful. If she played her cards right, he would wait for her until she was ready to give up her acting career, two or three years from now, sometime after she was thirty, thinking naughtily, he could be her 'Old Age Pension'.

After congratulating herself for being able to soften his shock, she thought ruefully of the wicked picture she had painted of her darling mother. Anna would rightly be annoyed if she knew. But knowing Rayomand, he would never divulge their conversation.

Though deeply moved by her tale of hardship and struggle, Rayomand was not fully satisfied. He could not fit the picture Anjali painted of her mother as mercenary and wicked, with the kind-hearted lady he knew.

But Anjali was still able to wake dangerous feelings in him. He needed time, to weigh it all in his head. To know if he could live with the knowledge of men who passed through her life and if she could truly live without their constant adulation.

Later that same evening, Anjali called her long-suffering agent, 'Pratap, I've done it. I told you I'd get him back and I have. It's incredible. Rayomand swallowed everything I put before him and more. I've decided that I want him for when I retire.'

Pratap listened to Anjali crow and thought what a strange and complex woman she was. How often she had said in the recent past that she was tired of Rayomand, that she found him boring; but now, with the possibility of him leaving, she wanted to hold on to him. He knew he was responsible for advising against letting him go, that she needed him for when she would no longer receive choice acting roles. Perhaps he was wrong to ask her to hold on to Rayomand when she could so easily close the chapter and move on.

Nevertheless, he knew of her stubborn, possessive streak. She did not let go of people or things until she wanted to. And here she was, delighting in her prowess as an accomplished actress, able to pull off an impossible feat.

Twenty-One
Amy
September

Amy was blissfully unaware of the turmoil in Rayomand's life. The day after the dinner party, she and her friends walked down the winding Sophia College Lane, to the busy shops at Breach Candy. Meena needed to buy satin material from Premson's, for a sari petticoat. They walked gingerly, side-stepping shallow potholes and rivulets of dirty water flowing out of a leaky pipe, from one of the high-rise apartments.

'Amy,' Pinku said, 'When are you going to tell us, what happened last night? Did Rayomand like your sari and did anyone comment on the blouse?'

'Girls,' Amy sighed dreamily, 'The evening was magical! Just magical!'

There was a joint chorus of, 'Oh, really?'

'Yes,' she repeated. 'The evening was wonderful!'

'You mean you liked Anjali?' Zia asked, perplexed.

'Anjali?' Amy repeated irritably, brought out of her reverie. 'Why ask if I liked her? She wasn't there. That's what made the evening so perfect!'

'Oh!' the three of them said, a second time, in unison.

Zia did a quick pirouette of pleasure on the lane and bumped into an elderly Maharashtrian lady trudging laboriously up the incline.

'*Kalji ghya*, take care!' she scolded Zia, annoyed at having her shopping jostled and not a bit mollified by Zia's embarrassed, 'I'm so sorry!'

They watched her shake her grey head and mutter about the bad behaviour of modern girls as she walked by, and appeared even more annoyed to hear them giggling uncontrollably, as they hurried away.

They made their way along the narrow Breach Candy footpath, to Premson's shop, past shoppers laden with parcels in plastic bags, and fruit sellers squatting on the curb, calling out to passers-by, '*ithe yaa bai*,' in Marathi, adding their calls to the roar of traffic and people conversing in a medley of different languages.

Once inside Premson's, and during the serious business of choosing the right coloured cloth for Meena's petticoat, their interesting conversation was put on hold. It was eagerly renewed once they were at Amy's. Marina was at work and as Jamsheed was involved with cricket practice, they had the place to themselves. They sat around the dining table and drank hot sweet tea, served by Rosy.

'Was there music and dancing?' Meena queried hopefully. 'And did Rayomand ask you to dance?'

'Yes, he did, and quite a few times. And he complimented me and stopped some of his more persistent friends from dancing too often with me. He also introduced me to his school friend Ashok and his wife Anu, who said she was related to you and that you'd spoken of me. What have you said?' Amy asked.

'Nothing very much,' Meena replied, guiltily.

And Pinku declared, with great conviction, 'Amy, I think he's fallen in love with you. If he danced with you as many times as you say, then he's definitely in love with you. Whee! It's bye, bye Anjali!'

After tea, they congregated in Amy's bedroom to continue the exciting conversation of Amy versus Anjali.

'Amy,' Zia said seriously, 'I think it's your duty as an old family friend, to save Rayomand from that witch's clutches.'

'What?' Amy exclaimed, 'How can I, save him? You do come up with weird ideas, Zia.'

'Amy, we all know that actresses have strange powers and somehow, she has bewitched him.'

Pinku and Meena joined Amy in laughing at Zia's pronouncement.

'Fine! Laugh all you like, but if I was as crazy about Rayomand, as you are, I tell you, a hundred such witches wouldn't stop me from saving the man I love.'

'Okay,' Amy said, trying hard to keep a straight face. 'How should I go about saving a grown man, from the woman he's chosen for his wife?'

'Well, for a start, you let him know that you love him. Then let him see how sexy you are.'

'Sexy? Are you mad, Zia? Have you got a touch of the sun? Can you see me acting sexy around Rayomand? He would die laughing and I would just die from embarrassment.'

'All right don't be sexy,' said the irrepressible Zia. 'I know you can't compete with the witch, so I'll show you what to do.' She simpered up to Pinku who was a head taller than her - Zia was barely five two. She looked at Pinku's face and batted her lashes a couple of times.

'I'd get a headache if I did that,' Pinku commented.

'Well, I'm not asking you to do it,' responded Zia. 'Then,' she carried on as if Pinku had not interrupted, 'perhaps a quick faint might help because he'll have to catch you to prevent you from falling. And as he is holding you close, he will suddenly realise how much he loves you, and then, you must look soulfully into his eyes and whisper, Rayomand I lo-ve you.'

By this time, it was too much for Pinku, who suddenly grabbed Zia and swung her around the room, singing in a high-pitched squeaky voice, 'Amy, Amy, I love you, I love you, I love you.'

At this point, the farcical nature of the situation got the better of them and they fell onto Amy's bed in peals of laughter so loud, that Rosy entered and told them to behave themselves.

After her friends left, Amy sat at her desk with her half-written essay before her. It was due the next day, but her mind was busy mulling over the recent conversations, and Zia's ridiculous and romantic turn of mind. She knew Rayomand found her attractive, but to think of him being in love with her? No. She was much too sensible to think that.

While Amy and her friends were discussing the previous night's dinner, Marina was busy with Gitu in her friend's flower shop. The two of them were working against the clock getting thirty exquisite arrangements ready to send by six in the evening, to a private dinner in Bandra. The morning delivery of the flowers chosen by their socialite client had arrived late and though they were close to completion, Gitu fretted they might not have them ready in time.

Whilst working, Gitu asked, 'How was the dinner? Did you have a good time? I'm so glad you went. It really is time you started going out. I was getting worried about you.'

'Oh Gitu, it's only been four months, but I did have a good time.'

'And did Amy enjoy herself?'

'Yes. Perhaps a bit too much! Rayomand has these good looks and easy charm and I think my poor daughter is definitely attracted to him. I may be totally wrong, but I sometimes think he likes Amy more than he knows; but he is engaged, as you know, and will be married soon.'

Gitu shook her head sadly. 'Thank God, in our Gujerati community, the parents choose the man for their daughters, and we don't have to undergo this sort of heartache. Look at me and Vineet, I met him only once, to see if he was acceptable and he did the same, to decide whether he wanted me for his wife. The next time we met was when we married. I know my Leena has chosen her fiancée Jeet, but fortunately, he belongs to our community and my mother-in-law is delighted.'

Marina tactfully refrained from reminding her that her older son had threatened to break away from the family if they prevented him from marrying a Marwari girl from a different Hindu community.

Gitu asked after Hirjee, intrigued by his affection for Marina and thought it all very romantic. Marina smiled and said, 'Hirjee looked well,' then changed the subject. She was uncomfortable discussing him with her garrulous friend. As she continued to work, she wished that Rayomand was free to marry Amy.

She remembered a day, many months ago, when she had said as much to Rustam and he had teased her, calling her, 'His dear romantic fool.' He had pointed out that Rayomand was much older and too sophisticated for Amy. He had agreed Rayomand was charming, witty, and extremely good at his work. But fond as he was of him, he disapproved of some of his friends; particularly his voluptuous girlfriend, whose physical charms were pasted on billboards all over the country. He had said, 'I can't understand how he can bear having men drool over her pictures. Poor Hirjee! I feel sorry for him. I know he doesn't approve of Rayomand's choice, and we must thank God, that Jamsheed is still too young to be thinking of the fairer sex.'

Marina smiled sadly, thinking of Rustam, missing him. She put the last finishing touch to her floral arrangement, while Gitu gave their van driver detailed instructions: the client's address, the speed with which to drive, how to lift the boxes containing the precious cargo, and what to say to the lady on arrival. The driver stood nodding patiently, having heard her strictures innumerable times before.

Marina dried her hands and thought longingly of a warm shower, Rosy's special tea, and her bed. It had been a long day and she felt unusually tired. She knew she was not fully recovered from her illness.

Twenty-Two
Rayomand
Late September 1985

Anjali was thrilled she had succeeded where another might have failed, but her delight in her thespian skill was tempered by the fact that Rayomand refused to visit her apartment.

Still, being supremely confident of her ultimate success, she agreed with Pratap that her fiancé needed time and was prepared to give it. Her careless attitude kept her from comprehending just how deeply troubled he was.

Rayomand struggled to block out what he had seen and be as loving as before. He made allowances for Anjali's childhood, admired her grit and single-minded dedication to her craft, and how hard she had fought to be at the height of her career. He acknowledged that he was bewitched by her looks and free spirit, unencumbered by mores of society. However, he was unsure if he was right for her. His liberal ideas had vanished seeing her in bed with another man. Though they still spoke most days, they met less often, because she was busy acting in a new film.

One evening, after a game of tennis, he asked Ashok, 'So, did you and Anu make it to Goa?'

'No *yaar*, you weren't available, and I've been busy with Dr. Hiranandani, so we shelved the idea. But Anu is still very keen. Are you saying you're free?'

'Yes. I need a change, if just for a weekend.'

'Great! Will Anjali come too?'

'No. She's busy.'

Ashok threw him a worried look; sensing all was not well. 'Okay, so which weekend suits you?'

'This one, or the next, I don't mind. But Marina's birthday is on Sunday, and I must be home in time for dinner. Dad has invited the Cooper family.'

'Fine, I'll ask Satish and get back to you.' He rang back the following day to say the bungalow was free that weekend, and that he had invited Asif and Fatima to join them.

Three days later, on a Friday afternoon, the five of them flew to Goa.

The bungalow at Baga was built close to the beach and though simple in design, was elegantly furnished. Just inside the entrance door, was a two-foot tall, antique stone carving of Lord Ganesha. In the living room, were glazed earthenware pots with palms and cut-away leaves, and a large bronze statue of the dancing god Nataraja stood in one corner. There were upholstered mattresses with bolsters and throw cushions in printed handloom cotton on the floor. Contemporary Indian paintings decorated the walls and faux antique lamps dangled from the ceiling. A wide veranda with stone steps leading down to the garden, encircled half the house, with the living room and all bedroom doors opening onto it. Each bedroom had low double beds, silk-shaded lamps, built-in cupboards, and brightly woven straw rugs on the floor. The bungalow's low roof was shaded by coconut palm fronds and pink and white flowering champa trees. The garden was ablaze with orange, yellow, and red bougainvillea, and scented white stargazer-lily bushes.

After a restless night, Rayomand awoke to the chorus of birds and a cockerel crowing loudly outside. He had slept fitfully, battling conflicting thoughts; the most worrying was Anjali's relationship with men. For all her convincing explanations, he felt she was not a victim. On that fateful night, she appeared to be enjoying herself. Her story did not ring true. And now, he was unsure if he still loved her. She, on the other hand, was much more loving, but for all her declarations, he did not believe her. Had she ever loved him, or had he just deluded himself into the fact?

Too awake to lie in bed, he changed into shorts and a loose cotton shirt and left the room. The cool dawn air carried the aroma of wood smoke, as villagers awoke and fired their *sigris*. There was just enough light to see the green of leaves and the white shimmer of *champa* flowers. He paused outside Asif's room to listen to his resonant recitation from the *Quransharif*, and bowing his head, added a prayer, to ease his mental turmoil.

Walking on the empty beach, with the heat of the rising sun on his back and yet to be warmed sand grains under his feet, he felt a sense of peace. The peace that had eluded him for many weeks.

Hearing a familiar 'chrrr', he shaded his eyes against the newly risen sun and followed the iridescent flash of blue, of a kingfisher flying from the top of a *toddy* palm, to swoop into the turquoise and white foamed sea. He waited and watched as it sped past him with a wriggling silver prize in its beak.

Studying Rayomand's solitary walk for a while, Ashok asked Anu as she poured his morning tea, 'Have you noticed *jaan*, that Rayomand isn't happy? He talks and laughs easily, but there's something wrong and I wish I knew why.'

'So, ask him, *naa*,' she replied, adding milk and two teaspoons of sugar to his cup, 'There may be something you can do.'

'No. I can't. I don't want him to think I'm prying.'

'Oh, you men! Prying-phrying! What nonsense you talk! If he were one of my oldest friends, I wouldn't be sitting here worrying and speculating. I would be with him, trying to help.'

'Help? Have you forgotten I tried giving advice and almost ended our friendship?'

'Advice? Not advice! I'm saying, be there for him. Get him to unburden himself. That's what friends are for. To share in each other's troubles.' She was about to say more, when Asif and Fatima emerged from their room and joined them, with a cheery 'Good morning.'

After a leisurely breakfast, Anu was keen to explore the village market and asked Fatima to accompany her. An auto-rickshaw was sent for, and they 'put-putted' away for some bangle and sari shopping.

Without wives or a fiancée to cramp their style, the men played in the sea, ducking each other's heads underwater, and calling out rude, long-forgotten names. and Rayomand had not laughed so much, nor been so relaxed, in a very long time.

Anu and Fatima returned at noon, delighted with purchases of fine silver jewellery, colourful bangles, leather slippers, and a nine-yard blue-checked sari for the caretaker's wife.

After tea, around four o'clock, they joined the men for a quick swim and a round of cricket on the beach, where they did all the batting and the men, with much good-natured grumbling, did the bowling and had the onerous task of chasing after the ball and retrieving it from the thorny undergrowth, above the tide line.

After dinner, the friends sat under a star-lit sky drinking hot coffee, listening to Rayomand recount an incident that had occurred when Asif, Ashok and he were schoolboys.

'We were holidaying in Tithall, when a *chowkidar* told us a scary story about a *mali* whose ghost wandered in the orchard on moonless nights, calling to his dead love. We were told that the lovers were prevented from marrying because they belonged to different Hindu communities. The *mali* was a lowly gardener, and she was the daughter of a rich Kohli fisherman. On being forced to marry another man, the young woman had rowed out to sea on her wedding night never to be seen again.'

'Aw, that's so sad,' Anu interrupted. Rayomand went on, 'The *chowkidar* said, that the unhappy man had sat on a raised mound staring at the sea and pined till he died.'

Asif grinned, 'Remember Rustam's take on it? He said the woman had not died but taken off with a handsome fisherman.'

Ashok interjected with, 'I remember him pointing to an elderly gardener sweeping leaves and asking us if we thought any woman would want to marry someone like him. When we protested that he was not the same man, Rustam insisted all gardeners looked like him! He also said that the man had sat and stared at the sea, not because he was pining, but because he was escaping a nagging wife.'

'We refused to believe him,' Rayomand continued, ignoring the interruptions. 'We decided to go and check it out ourselves. The next night, after everyone was asleep, we crept out of bed, and carrying torches in our hands, we went warily to the mound that seemed harmless in the daylight. We huddled close, tripping over ourselves, as everyday objects looked like monsters in the torchlight. As we neared the site, we heard a rustling in the shrubbery and suddenly, a white scary figure rose saying, 'Whooo, whooo, *maee ata houn*! I'm coming to get you!' We froze, then turning as one, ran screaming back to the house, the apparition flying behind us.

When we got to the house, we saw Marina and my parents huddled anxiously on the veranda, and as we pounded up the steps, puffing out of breath, we turned and saw the apparition throwing off a white sheet. It was Rustam, and seeing him convulsed in laughter, we scrambled down and leapt on top of him, and pummelled him as he lay laughing on the ground.'

Rayomand continued to sit in the dark, long after his friends had turned in, the quiet of the moonlight broken by the occasional baying of village dogs, scurrying sounds of nocturnal creatures, and the whooshing sound of the tide beyond the garden wall. The painful thoughts that he had pushed to the back of his mind during the full and happy day were back. He clearly saw his mistake in getting involved with Anjali. They were both just too different. Ashok had tried to warn him and he in his arrogance had thought he knew Anjali and been angered when told, 'Stay away from her.' How wrong he had been. He knew now, however hard he tried, he would never erase the sight of her in bed with another man. Slumping forward, he rested his head in his hands.

Unable to sleep, Ashok left his bed and went out onto the darkened veranda and saw Asif leaning against the railing looking out. Joining him, he noticed Rayomand sitting with his head in his hands. He glanced at Asif and without a word the two of them went down the veranda steps to join him, the sandy ground muffling their footsteps.

Rayomand was oblivious to their arrival until he felt a hand on his shoulder and Ashok's voice saying, 'Talk, *yaar*, we're here to listen.'

Covering Ashok's hand with his, Rayomand said, 'I've been thinking. I was an idiot to have been angry with you when you warned me about Anjali. Forgive me.'

'*Tchha!* No need for that,' Ashok replied, brushing aside the words, as he and Asif pulled a couple of chairs closer to Rayomand.

'I see now,' Rayomand continued, 'how wrong it was to be involved with her.'

'We wondered when you would figure out that outward beauty isn't enough in a marriage,' Asif added quietly.

'Anu can't stand her,' Ashok interjected. 'She has always felt you were being used. When she heard I asked you to bring Anjali, she almost didn't come.' Pausing, he said, 'You know *yaar*, who possesses genuine beauty?' and at Rayomand's questioning look, said, 'Amy.'

'Amy? Don't be so ridiculous, she's a child.'

'Child! She's a grown woman. Can't you see she's perfect for you?' and then, like any good matchmaker, began to enumerate her qualities. 'She's lovely, intelligent, and comes from an excellent family, one you've known all your life. She's Rustam's daughter and more importantly, if Anu is to be believed, her cousin Meena says Amy loves you. Come *yaar*, stop wasting time. Get married and join the married men's club. If you don't make a push to win her, someone else will.'

Ashok's late-night lecture amused Rayomand and when the three of them finally turned in, he slept peacefully for the first time in weeks. The next day passed quickly and soon after lunch they left for home.

Rayomand's plane was delayed by two hours, and it was nearing eight when he arrived home. Entering the apartment, he found the sitting room warm and inviting in the lamplight, ready to welcome guests. His father walked out of his room, buttoning his shirtsleeves, saying, 'You're back! Good. The Cooper family will be here soon. Daulat and Homi are here from the States and staying in the guest apartment. They arrived this morning and will be joining us.'

When Rustam died in May, his brother-in-law Homi had just undergone an operation. His wife Daulat, Rustam's older sister, had been distraught that she could not leave him to attend her beloved brother's funeral. But now, she and Homi were in Bombay at Hirjee's invitation and planned to stay till the end of November to attend Rustam's six-month prayer ceremony. She knew it had been Rustam's wish to send Amy to study in the States and knowing that Marina could not now afford to send her, she was determined to make it happen. She resolved to speak to Marina with the offer of paying for Amy's tuition and have her come and stay with them. She and Homi had not been blessed with children, and they looked on Amy and Jamsheed as their very own.

Rayomand entered the living room after a quick wash and change. He greeted his house guests and good-naturedly accepted their ribbing about the dark tan he had acquired at the beach. He shook hands with an unnaturally tidy Jamsheed, with his face scrubbed and hair slicked back.

He gave Marina a hug and wished her a happy birthday, then, turning to Amy, kissed her cheek, and was surprised by the quick flash of colour on her face.

As usual, there was general laughter around the dining table because Homi made the most mundane thing, sound funny, and later, a birthday toast was drunk to Marina and to the much-missed Rustam.

During the meal, Hirjee teased Rayomand by saying, 'There was a time Rayomand, especially when you first saw Amy, you thought her an ugly little thing.'

'What?' Amy grinned. 'Is that true? You actually thought that when you first saw me?'

'Not fair Dad,' Rayomand exclaimed. 'Come on, I was only nine, and didn't know better. But Amy, you've got to admit that newborn babies aren't pretty.'

Marina, watching the playful exchange, thought for the umpteenth time that Rayomand and Amy made a charming couple. Why can't he see my Amy cares for him and respond by falling for her? Life is so strange. Why did it never work the way one wanted? Why did it stubbornly follow a peculiar course, all its own?

After dinner, Rayomand sat on a comfortable armchair sipping his coffee and surveyed the living room. His father was chatting to an animated Jamsheed, Homi was conversing with

Marina, and Amy was listening avidly to her aunt. He suddenly became aware of Daulat's words, '... and we would love you to come and live with us.'

He walked over to join them and seeing him approach, Amy turned to him, saying, 'It's unbelievable. Aunty wants me to study in the States after my degree. She wants me to go live with her and Homi uncle because it was what Dad wanted.'

Rayomand felt a strange sinking feeling in his stomach. He did not want Amy to go away just when he wanted to know her better. It also struck him that had Anjali been with him, she would not have fit into their close family group. She would have been bored and found the group dull and ordinary. Sitting here with the people he loved, he suddenly knew for certain that he no longer loved Anjali and that their engagement had to end. The mist around his brain had cleared and he saw now what his friends and father had seen all those months ago, how ill-suited they were, and how stubbornly he had refused to believe them.

Twenty-Three
October 1985

Two days after his return from Goa, Rayomand received a call from Anjali, asking him to accompany her to Mount Abu. When he said he could not, she exclaimed, 'Why not? It's been ages since we've been on our own. It will be lovely. Please come.'

'Sorry, Anjali, I can't. Like you, I'm busy. But there is something we need to discuss. Can we meet sometime this week?'

'What about tomorrow? Come for dinner.'

'Can't, but I could visit around six if that's convenient.'

Savitri let him in and showed him to the veranda where a seated Anjali waited in a silk kaftan, her long legs crossed neatly at the ankles. He took her proffered hand and noted her surprise when he did not kiss her but walked to the balcony and leaned against it.

Studying her, Rayomand could not deny she made a ravishing picture with her dark flowing locks. The objective part of his brain continued to admire her astonishing beauty. Taking a deep breath, he plunged in, 'I've done a lot of soul-searching Anjali and I cannot put the thought of you with another man out of my mind. Neither can I forget and move on. The two of us are just too different in the ways we think and feel and would end up hating each other.' He paused, before saying, 'I'm sorry, but we cannot marry.'

Her eyes, warm and inviting an instant ago, hardened to bits of glittering green emeralds. How dare he stand before her and tell her he was breaking their engagement. Who did he think he was? She was not someone to be taken so lightly. He would pay for this!

She uncoiled herself from the cushioned seat and stood tall and regal before him; her strong perfume swirling around them. The fingers of her left hand curled painfully in his hair as she pulled his head down and kissed him deep and hard, her tongue darting into his mouth. Her right hand lightly stroked him, and his immediate response delighted her. She stepped away, saying huskily, 'You are wrong to think you can walk away from me. You are mine and no woman will ever satisfy you. If you leave me now, you will have to grovel before I ever take you back and even then, I may choose not to. Think about it, before you do anything you will regret.'

Then, turning, she walked away, her kaftan billowing after her, leaving him to see his way out.

For all Anjali's outward appearance of queenly pride, she was in shock. She had been so sure she had succeeded. How could he do this, after professing to be crazy about her? She rushed into her bedroom and after hearing the front door close, she called Pratap.

'Rayomand wants to break off our engagement.' Then, with anger replacing shock, she cried, 'Who does he think he is? If I find he's leaving me for another woman, I'll have her killed before I let her take what's mine!'

There was a silence at the other end of the line and then his voice said, 'I'll see you in fifteen minutes.'

When Pratap entered, he found Anjali pacing the floor like a dangerous tigress.

'So,' he said, grimly. 'You have finally done it. Managed to lose the one decent man who would have been true to you.'

'Don't lecture me,' she snapped. 'Tell me what to do. I don't want him to go.'

Pratap looked sadly at the beautiful but spoilt woman and thought of men who trailed through her life treating her like a goddess, only to be discarded like worn-out shoes. She was fortunate Hirok was still her friend. And that was only because he was strong enough to win her respect. However, having met Rayomand, Pratap knew that it was unlikely that Rayomand would change his mind. The sooner Anjali accepted it, the better. She was livid right now that he had ended their engagement but would soon realise it was a good thing.

'Calm down *beta*, we'll use this to your advantage. Tomorrow, we announce that you have ended your engagement and millions of men all over India will light *diyas*, because you are free again.'

Anjali smiled at the flattering scenario.

'All right, but Pratap, I will not allow anyone else to have Rayomand or to marry him. If need be, I shall have the woman done away with!'

She saw his eyes look coldly at her through his horn-rimmed glasses. 'Anju,' he said, 'You've been acting in make-believe films for too long. Do you truly imagine that such a thing can be done, and you escape its consequences? If you try to harm Rayomand, or anyone he chooses to be with, be prepared to find yourself a new agent. I've been with you these last ten years and watched over you as my daughter. If you stoop to the level of the Bombay mafia, be sure I will go to the police and inform them of the lakhs of illegal foreign exchange you have stashed in numbered accounts in Zurich.'

'Numbered accounts? What numbered accounts? There are no such accounts! I don't know what you are talking about or where you have heard such a ridiculous thing. Foreign accounts, you must be joking!' she lied, brazenly.

'Oh, they exist,' he replied. 'I know they do. I have the numbers and the name of the bank, Anjali. I have always tried to do my best by you. But now you must decide which way you want your life to go.'

His coldly delivered speech shocked her. He had never, in all these years, spoken so sternly. She knew what she implied could not be done as easily as in movies. In real life, the consequences would be most unpalatable. She studied him from under her lashes and with one of her mercurial changes of mood, smiled sweetly.

'*Arae* Pratap, my friend, there's no need to be so angry with your Anju. You are perfectly right! Thank you for pointing out my ridiculous behaviour. We both know I wanted to leave him. It's just that he got the words in first.'

Although she outwardly agreed with everything Pratap said, inwardly, she seethed. She was determined to make Rayomand sorry. Sorry in ways that were much less dramatic, but just as effective.

Twenty-Four

Rayomand

October 1985

With his engagement at an end, Rayomand wondered how he could have fallen for a woman to whom fidelity was unimportant. He had trusted her when she said she loved him and had forsaken other men. If he had not seen what he longed to forget, he would never have believed anyone telling him she was unfaithful.

Their break-up made headlines in all the newspapers and movie magazines. Friends and acquaintances rang, asking if it was true. He found it more and more irritating to be saying, 'Yes. Yes, it's true,' when all he wanted to say was, 'Stop, for goodness' sake. I don't want to talk about her at all!' If only he had listened to Ashok, he would have spared himself this heartache.

His thoughts turned more and more to Amy, and he deliberated if she was right for him. He wished he knew. He felt happy in her company, loved making her laugh, and enjoyed her offbeat sense of humour, so like his. When she was with him, he felt content and protective of her. He wondered if she would go out with him.

He would be more careful this time, especially after the terrible choice he had made in Anjali. He would use his head and not his heart. His friends thought she was perfect for him and his father would be overjoyed.

Could he marry her if she were agreeable? Yes, he could, and the more he thought about it, the better he liked the idea. More importantly, he wanted to settle down and start a family. He knew that his time in Bombay was short because their firm was opening a branch office in Madras, and he would have to be leaving soon.

He resolved to spend more time with Amy and see if what Ashok and Anu said was true. If it was, then he was willing to take a chance and propose. He knew Amy was sensible and if she disliked his proposition or felt she would rather go abroad for further studies she would tell him so.

Amy and her friends were delighted to read a write-up on Anjali, informing her fans of her breakup. They sat in the last row of their English class, eagerly studying a movie magazine, while Mrs. Advani, their English Professor, droned on about the merits and demerits of Indian writers, comparing them to their English and American counterparts Zia could barely contain her excitement and her low buzz drew baleful looks from the irate professor over her rimless spectacles.

One evening, Amy received a surprise call from Rayomand, inviting her to a piano recital at the Bhabha Auditorium. It was a recital she and her friends had longed to attend, but even the cheapest tickets were long sold out. Though his invitation delighted her, she was apprehensive about spending an evening alone with him. What would they talk about?

The recital was everything she hoped for. Their seats were close enough to the podium to watch the pianist's fingers glide over the keys. Amy could play, having studied the piano from the age of eight, but knew she did not have the dedication to achieve such magical sounds.

After the concert, they ate at the Shamiana and Rayomand was again surprised by how much he enjoyed Amy's company. It was so utterly different from those spent with Anjali, where there was always a strong undercurrent of sexual awareness. With Amy, he was relaxed and just himself. It was a relief not to be with someone continually in the limelight, never knowing when they would be photographed.

Up until this evening, he had not realised how tense that had made him.

The next afternoon, during their lunch break, Amy and her friends sat on the steps of the university building.

'Well, how was it?' asked Zia, her mouth full of potato puri.

'How was what?' Amy replied, obtuse on purpose.

'Your evening, with Rayomand.'

'Unh, that.'

'Yes, that.'

'And if you don't speak fast and tell all, I'm going to thump you,' Pinku threatened, as she and the others gazed at Amy with keen interest, intrigued by the new twist to the 'Amy Rayomand' saga.

'I loved every moment of it,' Amy affirmed and heard their general sigh of approval.

'Now don't go getting ideas,' she warned, 'Because he didn't get the tickets to take me out. They were given to him by a client, and he asked me I guess because he knows I like music and possibly ... Hirjee uncle couldn't go.'

'Yenh, yenh! Like he couldn't have invited anyone else! He has hundreds of friends, but no, he has to choose you!' Pinku chipped in.

'Did he say why he broke up with that witch?' Zia asked, and before Amy could reply, Meena interrupted, 'Honestly! As if he would. Men don't gossip.'

'But Amy, didn't you ask him?' Zia persisted, as though Meena hadn't spoken.

'No. Of course not!'

'Why not? Don't you want to know?'

'I do and I don't. I don't like thinking of her. And whatever happens, if you ever meet him, don't ask him.'

'So how will we find out if you don't and we don't either?'

'You just won't!'

And the four of them continued in this exciting vein, until it was time to attend afternoon lectures.

Amy felt she was living a dream. Being invited out by Rayomand was something she had fantasized about with her friends, but never believed could happen. She found that the two of them had lots in common and they laughed at the silliest things, and the difference in their ages didn't bother them. They were at ease with each other. Their lives had been entwined for so long that they understood what the other was saying without having to explain, especially when they spoke of their families. There was just one topic they both avoided and that was Anjali.

Spending time with Amy was a new experience for Rayomand. He was astonished at how easy it was to be with an undemanding companion. He also knew that after she completed her Bachelor of Arts degree, her aunt Daulat had invited her to live in the States to continue further studies. He suddenly woke up to the fact that he did not want Amy to go away.

Their evenings were mostly spent with friends at the Bombay Gymkhana Club because they both enjoyed the sport. Amy played tennis and swam, and Rayomand's friends made her very welcome. Fatima was friendly, but Anu with her zany sense of humour and her resemblance to Meena put Amy completely at ease.

Her friends were thrilled by her budding relationship with Rayomand and wanted to know every minute detail of her outings. Now, it was not, 'How to get rid of the witch', but 'How to make Rayomand fall desperately in love.' And because it was all so new and exciting, Amy enjoyed discussing him with them, but made sure they did not meet him often, and when they did, both Pinku and Zia were continually warned to curb their enthusiasm and their tongues.

She kept reminding them that he was just a friend. Someone she liked very much. He just saw her as a longtime family friend and nothing more.

Amy, in love for the first time, sensed that Rayomand was not completely healed. There were times when she saw sadness in his face, where before there was none. She was not to know that those were times Anjali had called him late at night and though he cut short their conversation, it sickened him that she still retained the power to make him want her.

In a few short weeks, he would be leaving Bombay to set up a new branch office for their firm in Madras. The knowledge that he would be living away for a while and that Amy was seriously thinking of continuing her studies abroad, distressed him. He did not want Amy to go. Not now, when he had woken to the fact of how special she was, and it seemed that she cared for him too. Looking back, he had been falling for Amy throughout the year. Being involved with Anjali had been a huge mistake. They were both too different. After debating back and forth with himself, he decided to take the plunge and ask Amy to marry him. There was a strong possibility that she might turn him down. They had, after all, been going out for only three months, but he knew he had to try.

Marina and Hirjee watched Rayomand's pursuit of Amy in amazement. There were times Marina worried that he was turning to Amy on the rebound. She felt it was all too soon since his very publicised break-up with Anjali. She prayed her daughter would be spared heartache. She had wished for this union since Amy's childhood, but now she was not sure she wanted it.

One evening, sitting with Hirjee on her veranda, she voiced her fears and he, taking her hand, told her not to worry. 'My prayers are coming true. I'm delighted he has come to his senses. Amy is the girl for him. I tell you, Marina, he's in love with her and it's only a matter of time before he wakes up to it.' Marina could only hope he was right.

Twenty-Five

Amy

Dec 1985

On New Year's Eve, Rayomand and Amy were invited by Asif and Fatima to a party at their home. Her friends were disappointed that Amy would not be spending the evening with them, but they accepted that Rayomand came first. They were impatient for him to propose; he could not take her out so often unless he was seriously thinking about it.

Amy was ready half an hour early and waited for Rayomand to arrive. Her eyes sparkled and her hair was brushed till it shone. Her well-fitting silk blouse, embroidered with crimson flowers, was tucked into a raw silk maxi skirt, and she wore gold-heeled sandals on her feet.

When Rayomand finally arrived at the appointed time, his eyes told her she looked beautiful, while she in turn thought he had never looked more handsome in his black tie and dress jacket.

Just as they were saying goodbye to Marina and Jamsheed, Rosy handed Amy a pashmina shawl and insisted she take it with her. Though unwilling, Amy obliged just to please her and told her not to wait up for her return.

Marina had refused all invitations and was staying home with Jamsheed, but Amy knew Hirjee uncle planned to visit them later that evening.

Fatima and Asif's apartment in Bandra was on the eleventh floor, with a spectacular view of the Arabian Sea. Asif greeted them at the door and led them into a room crowded with guests. There were flowers and scented candles everywhere, and in one corner of the living room a token Christmas tree still stood, decorated with baubles and twinkling lights.

On entering the apartment, a wave of nostalgia washed over Amy thinking of all the Christmases she had spent with her father. This was the first time Mum had not decorated their home or brought out the boxed, foldaway tree kept in one of the kitchen cupboards.

Rayomand introduced Amy to his friends and all the while kept a watchful eye on the men who tried to monopolise her. During the slow dances, she longed to tell him how much she loved him, but she could not, for though he was teasingly affectionate and funny, he never said anything romantic to her. She was not to know how she affected him or how much he wanted her. Or that while holding her, he was revelling in the clean fresh scent of her perfume and the silky touch of her hair, and her engaging laughter.

She was unaware that he had woken to the fact that he loved her. She was the one he had always loved but had not known it. She was his special Amy. Unconsciously, he had been looking for Amy's qualities in Anjali. With Anjali, he had been chasing a dream of his making and had learnt the hard way that the two of them were not remotely compatible.

By the time he brought Amy home, it was close to four in the morning and as the two of them sat chatting in the parked car, Rayomand took both Amy's hands in his, and said, 'Amy, you know I will be leaving soon to live in Madras. Dad has asked me to set up a new branch office there. I will be gone for at least a year…'

No, she wanted to scream. *No don't say any more. Don't say this is it and you don't want to see me anymore. You can't end our relationship. You can't!* Then, realising that he was still speaking, she forced her frantic mind to pay attention.

'.... there is something … I want to ask you,' and after a short pause, 'Do you think … you could? I mean, could you ..., er ..., I mean will you...,' then in a rush, 'Do you think you could marry me?' For a few moments, she wondered if she was hearing his halting words correctly. Her heart began to beat fast and she began to feel breathless. Had he just asked her to marry him? She could not believe it. And then, looking at him with eyes aglow with happiness, she cried, 'Yes! Oh yes! Yes!'

'You will?' he asked, startled by her immediate response, overjoyed by her answer; completely unaware that he was holding his breath or clutching her hands in a painful grip.

'You will?' he asked again, and then raising both her hands to his lips, he kissed them.

'Amy sweetheart, I promise I'll do everything I can to make you happy.' Then drawing her close, he gently kissed her lips. Curbing his instinct to rain passionate kisses on her lips, her face, her eyes, and to let his hands rove over her lithe form. But he curbed his impulse; unwilling to frighten her with the intensity of his desire.

Amy was mortified by his lukewarm response. To have her hands kissed and lips lightly brushed was not what she expected. She wanted more, so much more. It suddenly hit her that he had asked her to marry him, but not said he loved her. He was marrying her to please both their families, and even with this painful knowledge, she knew she was prepared to marry him. She had waited so long for him to propose, never once imagining it would be like this. She heard the steady beat of his heart as her head rested against his chest, tears smarting behind her lids.

Later, she wept in the privacy of her room, muffling her sobs under her pillow in order not to disturb Rosy, who was a light sleeper. I'm so stupid, she scolded herself, after the worst of her crying had passed. I've been given my dearest wish and I am wishing for more. Then, drying her tears, and before drifting off to sleep, she told herself she would work hard at their marriage and make Rayomand fall in love with her.

The next morning, she broke the news to Marina, Rosy and to Jamsheed, who whooped with delight. She told them that she and Rayomand wanted to marry before he left for Madras, because she wanted to go with him. Her mother said all the right things in front of Jamsheed but voiced her doubts when they were alone.

'Darling, you know how fond I am of Rayomand and overjoyed he's asked you, but shouldn't you give it some more thought? Are you sure you want to marry in such a hurry? What about your further studies? The two of you have only been seeing each other for, is it three months? Don't get me wrong, I know he's right for you, but you're so young and still to complete your degree. Why not ask him to wait a bit?'

'Why should I,' Amy replied, 'When I want to marry him now? I don't want to wait. You were married to Dad at the same age. Mum, don't you see, I love him!'

'But what about finishing your degree?'

'I'm sure my principal will help get me admitted to the Stella Maris College in Madras. I'll finish my degree there. Being forced to study during the day will keep me occupied when Rayomand is working.'

Marina instinctively felt all was not well with Amy, even though she appeared happy and Rayomand never happier. Her parents were delighted that Hirjee's son wanted to marry their Amy, and Hirjee couldn't contain his joy.

For Amy's friends, the 'Amy and Rayomand saga' was culminating in 'And they lived happily ever after.' But not even to them, would Amy share the shameful knowledge that she was marrying Rayomand knowing he did not love her.

The weeks flew by in a blur of excitement, with wedding preparations leaving her little time to be alone with Rayomand. Her trousseau was hurriedly organised, family jewellery was polished, caterers booked for the big day and the family priests notified. The wedding, due to her father's untimely death, was going to be a small affair with only immediate families and close friends in attendance.

Twenty-Six
Amy
Late January 1986

'Amy*baby* wake up! *Baby* wake up no, it's past seven o'clock!' Rosy's voice assaulted Amy's sleep-filled senses. Suddenly, the reality of what the fateful day held for her, made her bury her head under her pillow and pull her sheet over her head. She heard the curtains being drawn and the sheet yanked off her.

'Rosy!' she moaned, 'Don't do that, I can't stand the light.'

'Get up no and don't make fuss!' was the brisk reply. 'Tehmina*bai* is being busy from five-thirty in the morning and Marina*bai* is making that lazy good-for-nothing Raju hanging lovely garlands in the doorways. Get up no *baby*. Go see the luvely toran hanging outside the front door. It is so beeutiful, just like Tehmina*bai's* Swiss lace! And Anthony is cooking from early morning, *sev* for your breakfast and making food for lunchtime guests. Wake up no *baby*, Shavaksha*seth* and Tehmina*bai* and Mummy are waiting and waiting to have the 'wedding tea' with you. Come no,' she cajoled, and Amy reluctantly sat up in bed.

She looked balefully at Rosy who was already dressed, wearing a new gold chain and pendant in the shape of a cross, and gold earrings; both pieces of jewellery had been presented by Marina in celebration of the marriage.

'Go wash your face child, they are waiting for you.' She left the room, saying over her shoulder, 'Now I go wake that lazy Jamsheed and pull him out of bed.'

Amy pushed her feet into well-worn slippers and entered the bathroom. Seeing her sleep-swollen face in the mirror, she grimaced. Marrying Rayomand! How could she have agreed to this? And had it been just five weeks since she consented? And now the day was already here! Why am I marrying in such a hurry? I could have waited. Oh, why didn't I? Nobody forced me to do it so soon.

While brushing her teeth, she recalled saying foolishly and categorically to her mother that she was determined to marry before he left for Madras. Why had she said that? She had been fine during the engagement ceremony four days ago, so sure that she wanted to marry Rayomand. But now she was panicking. She was scared. Really, really scared and had no one to blame but herself. Within a few short hours she would be married to Rayomand who had still, not once said he loved her. She wished that she had asked him to wait.

In her numerous fantasies, he had begged her to love him, had said he could not live a day without her, and told her she was the most incredible woman in the whole universe. Declared undying love and said he would die if she did not agree to be his and only his, for the rest of their life.

And yet today, this was her reality.

He was fond of her, but he did not love her, nor pretended to. He was marrying her on the rebound to please his father, who loved them all so dearly.

Marina was up early, after a wakeful night. She busied herself arranging flowers with trailing silver ribbons in crystal vases, making sure that plates and serviette-wrapped cutlery were laid out on the dining table, and floors swabbed till they shone.

There was a carpet at the far end of the room with two chairs placed side by side and two side tables. Each table carried a crystal lamp and a filigree silver tray, with raw rice and fresh rose petals for the *mobeds* to use during the wedding ceremony. There was a small stool by one of the chairs with two silver containers. One with ghee and the other with chunks of brown jaggery, symbols of gentility, courtesy, sweetness, and good temper.

The living room furniture was lined along the walls to make room for rows of borrowed folding chairs. Tall floral arrangements stood in each corner of the room, and on a highly polished cabinet, the pride of place was given to a garlanded photograph of Rustam.

The day progressed with a strange and surreal quality for Amy. By mid-day, the apartment was buzzing with elderly aunts, uncles, and cousins; all curious to know the details of Amy's whirlwind romance, while tucking into Anthony's traditional lunch of rice with yellow dal sprinkled with fried onions, a spicy prawn patia, and ravo, a sweet made with milk and semolina.

By four-thirty in the afternoon her three friends were with her, dressed in their rich wedding finery; Meena, in a green and gold Kohlapuri silk sari, her hair tied back in a bun ringed with jasmine flowers, traditional Maharashtrian pearl rosettes in her ears, a gold chain around her neck and a red tikka on her forehead; Zia looking lovely in her red ankle-length silk skirt and short over-blouse heavily embroidered in silver and gold, long gold earrings and a heavy gold choker round her neck. Pinku's dusky tones were enhanced by a high-collared, cream brocade jacket worn over yards and yards of swirling, cream-and-gold brocade skirt. Her gold *nauratna* earrings were inlaid with nine precious and semi-precious stones, thought to bring good luck. Her curly hair was thoroughly brushed and for once, had a subdued glow.

They sat on Amy's bed, chattering like eager sparrows, thrilled she was marrying Rayomand. They made so much noise, that when Rosy heard Marina and her mother welcome the priests, she sternly banished them from Amy's room into the living room.

Tehmina introduced Amy to one of the two officiating priests who requested her to recite her *kusti* prayers, touch her lips to some liquid in a silver glass, and chew on a small piece of pomegranate leaf. Amy then showered and her grandmother, dressed in a crimson and gold embroidered chiffon sari, wearing a ruby and diamond necklace and diamond studs in her ears, helped Amy into the wedding sari.

Tehmina's face was wreathed in smiles, and she sang age-old traditional wedding songs accompanied by her older sister Shireen and Marina's neighbour, Piroja, while Marina, due to her widowed status, stayed away from Amy and kept busy, welcoming guests.

By six o'clock, the air was alive with excitement, and Amy, waiting in her room, knew it heralded Rayomand's arrival. She dug her fingernails into her palms to still her rising panic. Her heart thudded in her chest, and she felt faint. Sharp-eyed Rosy handed her a glass of ice-cold Coca-Cola, whispering, 'It's alright *baby*. Mary*mai* is watching. All will be well.' Smiling tremulously, Amy gratefully squeezed Rosy's fingers.

Rayomand arrived in his white wedding clothes, wearing a black *pheta* on his head and a shawl on his arm. He was flanked on either side by Hirjee and some of Hirjee's female cousins, and Philomena brought up the rear carrying Jeroo's precious jewellery to be presented to Amy, after the wedding.

Hirjee could barely contain himself, he was just so happy. Like Marina, he too had secretly wondered whether Rayomand was doing the right thing, asking Amy to marry him so soon after his much-publicised break with Anjali. But unlike Marina, he was ecstatic that Amy was to be his daughter-in-law.

Marina watched her mother take her place in welcoming Rayomand and his entourage.

Tehmina was at the front door with her sister Shireen and some elderly cousins, and she began the *aachhu michhu* ceremony by singing a traditional wedding song, with some of the ladies accompanying her in their off-key, high-pitched voices.

'Sukh sundariyo,
saja sau thaavo,
ne outaa jamai
ne vadhaavo rae, ae, ae, ae,
outaa jamai nae
vadhaavo rae!'

'Vaahalaa saasujee
tamae sopaaro laie aavo,
Nae outaa jamai,
Nae vadhaavo rae, ae, ae, ae,
Outaa jamai ne vadhaavo rae!'

(All you beautiful young women
come gather around and welcome the bridegroom,
and welcome the bridegroom!

Dearest mother-in-law
please bring the woven palm leaf tray
to welcome the bridegroom,
to welcome the bridegroom!)

As she sang, she dipped the tip of her thumb into a bowl of *kumkum* paste and applied it to Rayomand's forehead and then to each family member in turn.

After garlanding him, she took a raw egg from a silver tray carried by her sister and after circling it seven times round his head, broke it in a saucer. She did the same with a husked coconut, which she smashed with all her might on the tiled floor. She poured a small amount of water from a glass into the silver tray, and after circling it seven times around his head, emptied it into the saucer. At the end of the ceremony, she flung handfuls of raw rice over them and requested them to enter the apartment with their right foot.

Marina sat between Rustam's widowed aunt Gulan and her son Jaal, who bore a painful resemblance to Rustam. Jamsheed, dressed in traditional whites, was seated beside Jaal, while Daulat and Homi were directly behind her, watching the proceedings with great delight. They were back from the States, especially to attend Amy's wedding.

As befitting a widow, Marina dressed soberly in a silver grey shamu sari patterned with birds and flowers and edged in silver zari. Three rows of pearls circled her neck, and in her ears were matching eardrops given to her by Rustam on their tenth anniversary. Like all the other ladies, her sari too was worn the traditional way, with the *pullo* covering her head.

She smiled and conversed with everyone, but her mind was consumed with concern for Amy. She felt somehow, though Rayomand was fond of her daughter, he did not love her the way she had been loved by Rustam. It had been her dearest wish for Amy to marry Rayomand, but now when it was becoming a reality, she was wishing it were not so.

Rayomand was ceremoniously ushered in by Tehmina and invited to sit on one of the two waiting chairs. Amy emerged from her room and entered the frankincense and flower-scented room with her sari *pullo* draped over her head. She walked with downcast eyes, accompanied by her grandfather and her three friends, looking heartbreakingly lovely in her cream Chantilly lace sari, embroidered with seed pearls and transparent sequins. The sari had been specially made for her at the workshop of the well-known Miss Piroja Narielwalla.

Shavaksha smiled encouragingly into her pale and serious face and when she was seated beside Rayomand, gave her a reassuring hug, then stood to one side of her as witness in place of her father.

Tehmina performed the *aachhu michhu* ceremony by garlanding Amy, applying the auspicious red *teeli* to her forehead and handing her a bouquet, and a coconut, wound several times round with string.

Amy sat with her eyes trained on the tiled floor and when Rayomand whispered, ‘Hello,’ she was unable to look at him or speak, for her voice had deserted her.

Once the *aachhu michhu* was over, her grandmother and great-aunt sat on chairs behind her, and Rayomand’s two cousins, both married women, sat behind him.

Hirjee stood near him because custom required the marrying couple to have a male witness each: married men with children of their own.

Before the marriage ceremony could begin, Amy’s cousin Anahita presented a silver glass filled with milk to Rayomand and asked him to dip his fingers in it. He complied, and after wiping his fingers, dropped some gold coins into it as a gift.

Both officiating priests stood in front of Amy and Rayomand and the senior of the two, asked each in turn, repeating the prescribed words, ‘*passandae kadam*,’ ‘do you consent to the wedding?’ He asked it three times, to make quite sure they wished to be married and they both replied, ‘Yes.’ He then asked the witnesses for their formal consent and on receiving it, took Amy’s hand and placing it in Rayomand’s, prayed a benediction over them.

Amy stole a look at Rayomand’s serious face; one so familiar and yet on this day, so completely that of a stranger. She wished she knew what he was thinking. Her heart was beating fast and only the feel of Mitzi’s warm body lying near her feet, gave the proceedings a semblance of reality.

At first, the older priest objected to Mitzy’s presence and asked for her removal, but when Rosy tried dragging Mitzy away, she set up such a pathetic howl that the priest gave in and pretended not to notice her. Amy felt Rayomand's fingers lightly squeeze hers and she smiled nervously.

The priests began reciting Avestan prayers aloud and sprinkled rose petals and rice grains over Rayomand and Amy at given intervals. When the prayers ended, the senior priest invited them to exchange rings and gave advice on how to be good to each other to enjoy a long and happy life. Rayomand was asked to kiss Amy and smiling into her eyes he kissed her forehead.

Anahita came once more and kneeling beside Rayomand, sprinkled a little milk on his shoes to symbolically 'wash his feet,' and once again was gifted with gold coins. With the marriage ceremony over, Rayomand, Amy, and their two witnesses were invited to sign the Government Marriage Register.

The sun had set, and the apartment was aglow with lamps. Polished furniture and floor tiles gleamed in the warm light, along with the odd flash of diamonds worn by the ladies.

Misty-eyed, Marina hugged her newly married daughter, murmuring, 'May you always be happy' and to Rayomand, 'Bless you son and take good care of my Amy.'

Then, everyone present gathered around the newlyweds, to hug and wish them well and gift them with traditional money envelopes.

Zia unashamedly shed tears and told Rayomand how lucky he was to have their friend as his wife. Ashok and Anu warmly embraced Amy and Ashok whispered to Rayomand, 'Very well done, *yaar*.'

Hirjee kissed Amy's cheek and presented his beloved new daughter with a velvet box containing an elegant diamond parure, saying, 'If Jeroo aunty were here my darling, she would have wanted you to have this, because she loved you as much as I do.' Inside the box was a necklace consisting of a single string of one-carat diamonds, matching drop earrings and a bracelet. The one-and-a-half carat square diamond ring, belonging to the set, had already been presented to Amy four days ago by Rayomand during their formal engagement.

When everyone was holding a glass of champagne in their hand, Hirjee invited them all to join him in wishing the young couple a long and happy life. Amidst the shouts of cheers and laughter, another was drunk to the memory of two dear and much-missed family members, Rustam and Jeroo.

Once the general excitement calmed down, Rayomand drew Amy aside to say, 'You look stunning, sweetheart.' His unexpected words made her flush with pleasure. *He thinks I look good... he said I look stunning!* She wanted to whoop with joy, but instead, looking shyly at him, she whispered, 'You look pretty good too.' What she really wanted to say was, you look wonderful and so amazingly handsome. Suddenly, the alarming spectre of Anjali rose before her and she pushed it aside, thinking, *No I won't think of her, this incredible man is mine!*

Memories of her own wedding day flooded Marina's mind, as she watched Amy marry Rayomand. She had been so in love, but now, there was just an empty void and a constant ache. She missed Rustam. During the ceremony, she happened to catch a fleeting look of longing in Hirjee's eyes. Why, why did he continue to love her when she had never given him any reason to think that she cared for him more than as a dear friend. He had been Rustam's best friend and over the past years become hers as well. He was someone she could implicitly rely on to see to her best interest.

Earlier in the day he had informed her that as Amy's father-in-law, he had the right to look after Jamsheed's education and take care of any unforeseen bills that might arise. She had protested but seeing the pained look in his eyes had acquiesced. Her darling Jamsheed could stay on at his school.

It was a relief to know she did not have to worry about selling her apartment or move to Pune as she had planned. Her personal needs were few. She was not extravagant and from what remained of Rustam's estate after probate, she could manage to keep their home intact.

Her one constant regret since Rustam's death was the fact that she had not completed her university degree when she married him. It galled her that she had no formal qualification. Amy must complete her education and get her degree. She hoped that the Stella Maris College in Madras would accept her and allow her to do her B.A. exams in April.

Later, a traditional Parsi dinner consisting of lamb *pulao*, fish in spicy sauce, fried chicken, fried eggs on tomatoes and coriander, mango pickle, *chapattis*, wedding custard, and pistachio *kulfi* was served. It all looked delicious, but Amy was far too stressed to eat and barely managed to swallow a few mouthfuls.

The guests left soon after dinner and Amy and Rayomand changed out of their wedding finery into more informal clothes. Expensive jewellery was put away and they were able to unwind and laugh with the family over advice inflicted on them by elderly relatives.

But when it was time for her to leave home with Rayomand, Amy panicked at the thought of spending the night with him at the Oberoi. She almost said, *'Do we have to? It's still early?'* when it suddenly struck her that she was his wife now and would have to get over being terrified.

As usual, there were the typically long Parsi goodbyes, with Rosy holding on to Amy and shedding copious tears as if her baby was leaving for the far ends of the earth and not just five miles downtown to Nariman Point.

After being inundated with good wishes from all the family, the house-help, and neighbours, Amy finally got into Rayomand's flower-bedecked Maruti. Sitting beside him, she nervously sent up a quick prayer, to see her through the next few hours and all the days ahead. She had not spent much time alone with him these past weeks due to wedding preparations and now, she felt extremely shy. She fretted about his thoughts as he drove silently, concentrating on the road. *Was he sorry he was married to her and not Anjali? Would he grow tired of her and return to the actress? How would she ever hold his interest, a man nine years older?* Her agonising thoughts brought her perilously close to tears.

Sensing Amy's distress, Rayomand threw her a quick glance. Taking one hand off the steering wheel he covered her cold, tightly clasped hands lying on her lap with his warm one, his intuitive action succeeding in comforting her.

Twenty-Seven
Amy and Rayomand
January 1986

It was ten o'clock by the time they entered the hotel and were shown to their suite. Amy gazed at the room in awe, never having seen a bedroom so huge or so opulent, with thickly piled carpets, ornate furniture, and almost floor-to-ceiling windows. The drapes had been drawn back and tied with silken cords to give a clear view of the curving bay. She stood at one window and gazed down at the brightly lit city and at the streaks of red and white light created by vehicular traffic.

After tipping the bell-boy, Rayomand turned and, seeing Amy by one window, wondered at her thoughts. She had been unusually withdrawn all day; was she sorry she married him? He approached her and wrapping his arms around her waist turned her to face him. She stared wide-eyed as he raised her face to his and lowered his head to kiss her brows, her cheek, and her smooth neck. He heard her quick intake of breath as his hands stroked her hair, her arms, and down her slim back, pulling her closer. His mouth moved to find hers and to his sudden delight, found her kissing him with an intensity he did not expect. Her arms curled around his neck, and she was holding him as if she never wanted to let him go. A strange excitement surged in him. He wanted her, wanted to make love to her, but afraid he was rushing her, he looked into her dreamy eyes, and asked, 'Hungry?'

'Hmm yes,' she murmured, 'For this,' and smiling mischievously reached up again to kiss him.

He kissed her back, then pulled reluctantly away, saying, 'I meant for something to eat, sweetheart. I know you haven't eaten much, and I don't want you fainting in my arms.'

'I won't,' she said and suddenly began to giggle.

'What's so funny?' he asked.

'Just something Zia said a long time ago - that I should try fainting in your arms to make you aware of me.'

'Thank goodness you didn't,' he laughed. 'I might have run away in fright.'

Amy smiled, unable to say that the ruse was meant to make him hold her close and say, 'I love you, Amy.' He had not said those words and she wondered if he ever would. Perhaps if she was patient, he just might say them someday.

At Rayomand's suggestion, they dined at the hotel's rooftop restaurant, seated by a window with an amazing view. The night was cloudless, with a million stars, and the moon, late in rising, was clearly reflected in the Arabian Sea.

During their meal, Rayomand kept Amy laughing and only half believing the stories he spun for her. He held her close on the dance floor, reflecting how right it felt to be holding her and to have her as his wife.

Two hours later, they re-entered their suite and found it filled with an aroma of lilies and roses. Amy rushed to the beautiful arrangement, certain it was from Hirjee uncle, but her face lost its animation and she fell silent on reading the note tucked inside. Rayomand joined her, noting the change in her demeanor. At his approach, she handed him the card and turned blindly away.

It read, 'Remember I love you Ray darling and wait for your return. A'

Rayomand swore under his breath, hating Anjali for this; a deliberate act to make Amy and him unhappy. How had she known they would be staying here to order flowers sent this late at night? He picked up the unwelcome arrangement and put it outside the suite, saying, 'I'm so sorry Amy, so very sorry.'

She said nothing. The happy bubbling sprite was gone; she had retreated into her old, shy self. The wonderful mood of the evening was broken, and they got into bed as strangers. He whispered good night and turning unhappily on his side, tried to sleep.

Amy lay awake, staring at the ceiling, tears sliding into her hair, this was her wedding night, and her groom was asleep beside her. She mused over the happenings of the unreal day. Was it only this morning she had been afraid to wake up? And now, it already felt like a lifetime ago.

How could she compete with Anjali, who had just reminded Rayomand that she still loved him and waited for his return? Were they still together? If so, why had he married her? If Anjali meant nothing to him, why had he not held her and told her so. Why had he only whispered, 'I'm so sorry Amy, so sorry.' Sorry for what? That he had married her? She wept softly, unwilling to wake him, knowing regardless of what followed, she loved him. And holding on to the thought, she finally fell asleep.

Early morning light penetrated Amy's consciousness and she woke to unfamiliar surroundings. Her husband slept on his back beside her, with his right arm over his eyes. She marvelled that anybody could be so handsome. Turning over, she studied his strong aquiline nose, his mouth, his jaw line, and firm chin, and longed to touch him. The quilt they shared was pushed down to his waist and at some time in the night, he had removed his pajama top and slept in his muslin *sadra*. She noted that his forearms and chest were lightly furred.

She got out of bed and quietly walked to the window. She drew back the floor-length curtains just a little so that the pale morning light would not disturb Rayomand. Curling up on the window seat she gazed out, her very first morning as a married woman. The sea was a sheet of grey-green glass, speckled with white foam. Far out on the horizon were fishing boats and a white steamer, heading, who knew where?

She rested her head against the cool glass pane, thinking. Her life until her father's passing had been so predictable, boring but predictable. Her days had had a comfortable sameness to them, which at times had felt irritatingly tiresome. She remembered grumbling to Tehmina.

'I lead such a boring existence, Mamma. Nothing ever happens to me or to the Cooper family!'

'A boring existence? What are you saying?' her grandmother had snapped, 'What kind of excitement do you want? This is time for you to study, not time for excitement-bexcitement. You must wait until you're married. Then you can have all the excitement you want.'

How prophetic her words had turned out to be.

Twenty-Eight
Rayomand and Amy
January 1986

Rayomand opened his eyes and for a few seconds wondered where he was. His sleepy gaze soon grew accustomed to his surroundings, and all that had occurred the day before came flooding back. He was married. How extraordinary it sounded. He was married to Amy and not to Anjali. He turned to face Amy and saw that her bed was empty. The quilt they shared lay neatly to one side. He glanced at the clock on the side table; it was just after seven. The suite was dim, except for a bright sliver of light on the patterned maroon carpet. He looked across the room and saw Amy sitting cross-legged on the window ledge, hidden by the folds of the raw silk curtains.

Damn you Anjali, for wilfully causing trouble. Why had he not told Amy immediately that he had stopped loving Anjali, that he had seen a side to her which was anathema to him? He knew he had to make Amy understand and win back her trust. He now wished he had made love to her before going to dinner last night. He had been ecstatic when she kissed him with an ardour that had made him lightheaded. But fool that he was, unwilling to rush her, had waited till later.

He got out of bed and went to her, pulling open the curtains to allow morning light to flood the room.

'Morning sweetheart, slept well?'

Amy raised her head and nodded.

Rayomand reached down and drew her unresisting form from her sitting position into his arms.

Amy lay passively against his warm chest.

'You are just so incredibly lovely,' she heard him murmur and when he lowered his head to kiss her warm lips, her reaction to him was electric. She returned his kiss without inhibition. When his tongue teased her lips, she parted them to drink in his precious breath.

Amy wanted him so much it hurt. She yearned to have him make love to her and found she did not care if he still loved Anjali; she just wanted him. Her breath caught in her throat as his fingers lightly combed her silky hair, caressed the nape of her neck, and slowly moved lower. Wave upon wave of delight flowed through her.

Love me, love me my darling, she silently begged, giving in to the unfamiliar and breath-taking sensations he was awakening in her.

Rayomand felt a strange and unfamiliar need surfacing in him, for his lovely Amy. When his hands glided down her neck and over her firm breasts, he felt quivers go through her body and a deep intake of breath as he released her clothing and let it lie in a heap at her feet.

He stepped back to admire his beautiful bride standing unashamedly before him.

Amy reached for her husband and drew him to her, her hands moving inexpertly over him. Her exploring mouth moving over his bare chest, amazed by his immediate arousal at her wondering touch. She felt no shyness with her naked body pressed close to his, but instead, revelled in the feel of him.

This wonderful man was hers, and it was too incredible to be touching his bare skin with her hands, her lips, and the tip of her tongue.

Lifting Amy into his arms, Rayomand laid her on the bed; kissing and touching her with her newly aroused passion rising to match his. He let her exploring mouth, eyes and hands become familiar with him. He experienced this incredible feeling of rightness and tenderness, and an unexplained feeling of oneness.

He wanted their first time together to be perfect.

His loving touch brought Amy to a fever pitch; his own body reacting passionately to hers, aching for her; stunned by her eager response. Then, to his incredulous surprise, he found he could not wait. There was an urgency to take Amy, be one with her, and tenderly make her his wife.

For Amy, it was an experience, unlike anything she could ever have imagined. There had been times when she and her friends had tried unsuccessfully to picture what it would be like, to have a man make love to them. But this, this was unlike anything she had ever imagined; better than anything she had ever dreamt of. She adored Rayomand and gloriously gave herself to him. Her mind sang over and over, 'I love you, love you, love you.'

Later, snuggled contentedly against Rayomand, her cheek pressed against his chest, she blissfully breathed in the pure maleness of him. He held her close, his left arm encircling her naked waist and her shapely right leg entwined between both of his. To the newly initiated Amy, this was pure heaven.

She now knew that nothing she had ever imagined was as fantastic as this. All the books she and her girlfriends had read, could not match what she had just experienced. She was truly Rayomand's wife, and they would be together forever. Someday, she hoped he would say the three special words to her, and she could say them to him as well, but till then, she would be satisfied if he loved her in this way. She felt Rayomand raise himself on his elbow and say, 'Let's go for a swim. Do a couple of laps before breakfast?'

'A swim?' she said dreamily, 'Hmm, sounds wonderful.'

After showering, and a quick cup of hot chocolate, they went down to the pool on the first floor. By the time she walked to the edge of the pool in her swimming costume, Rayomand was already in the water, waiting for her. He looked at her in admiration and noticed that other men were doing the same.

After their swim, they sat under a large umbrella and ordered breakfast. Spicy scrambled eggs on toast, waffles with honey, and slices of sweet papaya. They were drinking their last cup of tea when a waiter informed Rayomand that he was wanted on the phone.

He excused himself and walking to the booth, lifted the receiver and said, ‘Hello.’

‘Morning, Ray darling,’ Anjali’s husky voice came silkily through the line. ‘I’m in the foyer with Pratap and so want to meet you and your wife.’

Rayomand’s mind froze at the sound of her voice. Why was she here after what she had done last night? He did not want to meet her now or ever again, nor did he want Amy to meet her. But knowing Anjali’s volatile nature, he was determined not to give her the opportunity to create a scene. Then again, he did not think she would in public, but he did not want her to meet Amy.

‘Hello? Ray, are you still there? Can you hear me?’

‘Yes, I can,’ he replied. ‘Wait for me in the lobby and I’ll be with you.’

He returned to Amy and unwilling to tell her the truth, he said, ‘Some friends of mine are in the foyer, and they want to join us. I don’t want to share this day with anyone but you, so I’m going down to send them away.’

Amy was surprised that he did not want her to meet his friends but was delighted that he wished to be alone with her. She poured herself another cup of tea and sat back thinking about their week’s honeymoon in Goa. Rayomand had said that they would be staying at a friend’s beach bungalow in Baga, where the colour of the sea water was a beautiful cerulean blue and not grey-green like the sea water washing Bombay’s shores.

Rayomand went reluctantly to the lobby knowing he must tread carefully. He suspected that Anjali would be at her most capricious. He saw her standing with Pratap Khanna, a long scarf partially covering her face to avoid attention. He approached and Pratap congratulated him, and Anjali, with a brilliant smile linked her arm through his and asked him to walk with her on the balcony, leading him away before he could refuse.

Looking out over the sea, she gazed at him, her emerald eyes bright with tears.

'Darling Ray, why did you do this? Why did you get married? You know I love you and miss you so much, and I know you must miss me too. How could you do this terrible thing? How could you punish yourself this way? Did you truly believe I wouldn't take you back? Oh darling, come back and I'll make it all up to you.'

Rayomand stared in a mixture of anger and shock, wondering why she was still pursuing him. He was sorry she could not accept a rejection, but he wanted nothing to do with her. His voice was cold when he spoke.

'It's over, Anjali. I'm married and believe me when I say I have absolutely no intention of being unfaithful to my wife. I wish you well, but please, you must leave me alone.'

His words made her seethe with anger.

While finishing the last of her tea, Amy wondered what time Rayomand wanted to leave for the airport. Then tired of waiting, she decided to change and go down to the foyer to join her husband.

Once in the foyer, she scanned the enormous hall and saw neither him nor his friends. There were some guests lounging on sofas and a well-dressed bespectacled man standing under the hotel's decorative mural. She noticed some glass doors leading onto a balcony and stepped out. To her far left, were a man and a woman. She saw the woman press herself against the man whose back was to her. There was something familiar about the woman's dark, free-flowing hair and the man's clothing.

Amy moved towards them in a hypnotic trance, as recognition hit her. It was Anjali. How could she not recognize her much-publicised face? She was kissing Rayomand and stroking him, where a shocked Amy would never think of doing, especially in public. She turned away from the devastating sight, heartbreakingly distressed that Rayomand, who had made the most glorious love to her, could turn so casually to his ex-lover. She was a fool to imagine that he could ever learn to love her. She turned and hurried blindly back to their suite, tears flowing unchecked down her cheeks.

The sound of the balcony door opening made Anjali aware they were not alone. She glanced briefly at the attractive young woman staring at them wide-eyed, and knew with certainty, that she was looking at Rayomand's new wife. She moved closer and pressed her voluptuous body to his.

Rayomand stepped back and found himself up against the hotel wall. Before he could react or push her away, she drew his head down and kissed him, and deliberately stroked him with one slim, beautifully manicured hand.

Her revenge, she thought gleefully, was complete. The 'new' wife was too far to hear a furious Rayomand tell Anjali to leave him alone. She knew his hands pushing her, would seem from that distance to be clutching at her.

She let Rayomand thrust her away once the door slammed shut and before he could say anything, she said in a falsely commiserating voice, 'Darling boy, I think your wife just caught you kissing me.'

Her words shocked him. Had Amy truly seen them, or was Anjali lying? He was livid with himself. He had not noticed Amy, but if what Anjali said was true, he felt sickened that Amy had witnessed a scene that he had not wanted to be a part of and would find impossible to explain.

Pratap Khanna, waiting for Anjali, idly noticed an attractive young woman walking past him to the balcony. A short while later, when he saw the same woman hurrying away in tears, he knew what Anjali had done. She had not come here to wish the newly married couple, but to create havoc. This was her way of punishing Rayomand for breaking their engagement. He felt a sense of remorse at being an accomplice to Anjali's diabolic machinations.

Rayomand raced to their suite, taking the stairs two at a time, not bothering with the elevator. Breathing hard, he pushed open the unlocked door and looked hurriedly around. It seemed empty. However, a keening sound made him turn and see Amy crouched in a corner, sobbing. Her arms were tightly locked about her knees, her head on her arms and her hands curled into tight fists.

His chest felt constricted, and it was hard to draw breath. How had this nightmare come about? He wanted to sit beside her and weep. What had he done? He knew he was inadvertently responsible for this shattering pain. How could Anjali have done this? How could she have been so cruel? This final act had destroyed the last vestige of attraction she would ever hold for him.

Sitting on the floor beside Amy, he tried taking her in his arms, but she threw off his touch with great distress. He waited until the force of her sobbing passed, before saying, 'Don't cry, Amy. Please don't cry! I'm sorry, so sorry! Please let me explain. It's not what you think! When I received Anjali's call, I went downstairs to tell her to leave me alone. She wanted to speak to me one last time and asked me to walk with her on the balcony, to have privacy from her fans. I went mainly to tell her not to contact me again. Sweetheart, it was a setup. It was only when she saw you on the veranda, that she forced herself on me.'

How ridiculous he sounded even to his own ears. Inexcusable and feeble explanations! How could he ever expect her to believe him? But he had to try.

'Please believe me, Amy. I stopped caring for her months ago. She has no idea how to be faithful and this terrible thing that she has done, this intentional hurt she has caused, is all due to her bruised ego.'

Amy heard Rayomand's anguished words, but her torn and bleeding spirit, rejected them. She just wanted to go home. Back to the room she had left so full of girlish hope, which now seemed a lifetime ago. She was so tired. She just wanted to go home.

Amy stared out at the sunny bustling streets, her head turned away from Rayomand, as he drove her home to an empty apartment. Jamsheed would be at school, her mother at work, and her grandparents would have left on the early morning train to Pune. Her head throbbed as she fought back tears. She longed to wake from this nightmare and find that they were in Goa on their honeymoon.

She waited at the door as Rayomand rang the bell. Rosy opened it and Mitzy rushed out, to cavort at their heels.

'You are home, Amy*baby*? What happened? Rayomand*baba* why is Amy looking ill?' and, scolding worriedly, she bundled Amy into bed, with Mitzy trailing behind, tail drooping, unhappy to be ignored.

Rosy rang Marina and asked her to come home then told Rayomand to phone Dr. Guzder. She kept wondering what had made Amy so ill and why Rayomand looked so intensely anguished. How had things gone so terribly wrong?

Twenty-Nine
Amy
February 1986

Amy was unwell for many days after her ill-fated stay at the hotel. She was feverish and shivery, but all her pathology tests were normal, confounding Dr. Guzdar.

Marina was beside herself with worry and Rayomand behaved like a man whose world had come to an end.

For the first few days, he sat silently in a corner of Amy's room, not daring to be too near her or to touch her, after the one time he tried holding her hand and she began crying piteously. Marina ached for them. How had this happened? She and Rosy nursed Amy, and Jamsheed wandered around the house like a ghost, never having known Amy to be ill.

Hirjee sent baskets of fruit each morning: sweet *mosambis, chikus*, large juicy grapes, and red *kashmiri a*pples, accompanied by bouquets of fresh flowers.

He spent most evenings after work with Marina, trying to comfort both her and Amy. He too, like Marina, wondered at the cause of this terrible distress between Amy and his son.

Amy's fever abated after a week and Rayomand finally went back to work. He called Marina several times during the day to ask after Amy's progress but stopped visiting their home.

Throughout the busy day, he concentrated solely on his work and was charming and professional with their clients. But when he came home, he went into his room and shut everyone out. He became totally unapproachable, answering in monosyllables when spoken to, and did not invite any confidences. For a while, he even ate his dinner on his own, much to Philomena's disgust. She most definitely did not approve of such behaviour and finally told him so in no uncertain terms,

'Shame on you, Rayomand*baba*! It is not right making poor Hirjee*seth* sit alone-alone at the dining table eating his food, and you sitting alone-alone and eating your food here.'

After her scolding, Rayomand made a special effort to dine with his father. He was grateful not to make small talk and appreciated his father being patient with him when he was both snappish and impossible. He shared the bare outlines of the sorry mess with Hirjee, saying he was entirely to blame for Amy's unhappiness.

The day Amy woke without painful drumbeats in her head, her eyes immediately travelled to the corner where she had sensed Rayomand's constant presence.

It was empty.

Had she dreamed of him sitting there, hour after hour?

She felt so tired.

She felt like a ninety-year-old woman.

It was an effort to raise her hand or lift her head.

Some days later, she horrified her mother and grandmother, who were both sitting beside her on her bed, by declaring, 'I want to divorce Rayomand.'

Both ladies stared at Amy in shock. Tehmina, who was leaning against the headboard, stopped stroking Amy's hair and Mitzy sitting on Marina's lap, nearly toppled out of it as her mistress suddenly sat up straighter.

A stunned silence filled the room, broken only by sounds from the street below and by the whirring of the overhead fan.

'A divorce!' Marina cried. 'Don't say that! We know something's wrong, but believe me, whatever it is, it will resolve itself. Don't think about it right now. You are still very unwell. Once you are up and about, everything will fall into place and begin to look better.'

'No Mum, you don't understand! Things won't get better. I know they won't. Our marriage is a tragic mistake, and I cannot live with him.'

Her grandmother's mouth dropped open. It was unimaginable that Amy should even consider such a thing. '*Dikra*, what are you saying? Leave Rayomand? You can't, not when your marriage has been sanctified with His blessings. No, no, no, there's no question of you leaving Rayomand. Can you imagine what everyone will say? That Marina Cooper's daughter is getting a divorce? You can't do that *dikra*. You'll ruin your name and ours.'

'Darling,' Marina asked, 'Are you saying there's something wrong with Rayomand?'

'No,' Amy cried in a choked voice, tears raining down her face. 'I know he still adores and wants Anjali, and that knowledge is tearing me apart. I cannot bear to be married to him! How can I possibly live with him, Mum? Tell me how? Tell me!'

Her distressed grandmother opened her mouth to say more, but Marina, getting off the bed, tactfully ushered her mother from the room, saying, 'Mumma, Amy is suffering from shock. Please don't say anything that will cause more distress. She needs time to heal and recover. Later, when she is more settled, we'll see what can be done. Her happiness must come first. She's very young and if there's been a misunderstanding, it'll work itself out. You know as well as I, that we must leave this in God's hands and be patient.' Marina returned to the room and held Amy until her bout of weeping stopped.

A week after her outburst, Amy sat in the living room with Mitzy on her lap, stroking her aging dachshund's golden-brown ears. She stared aimlessly at the sun shining on the feathery green leaves and dangling brown seedpods of a gulmohor tree. She watched a Rufus-backed shrike, the one she called a 'bandit bird,' perch on one branch and wait for an unwary insect to fly past. Her head ached and she felt unreasonably miserable that Rayomand did not visit anymore, even though he phoned daily to speak to Marina.

Sitting by herself it suddenly struck her that she needed to move out. To live away from home; get away from everything that reminded her of Rayomand and their disastrous marriage. Her mother had tried tactfully to get her to unburden herself, but the pain and humiliation were too raw, and she could not share it, not yet, with anyone. She saw enough pity in everyone's eyes without wanting to add to it.

She wasted no time in applying for accommodation at the Sophia College hostel and within a week, was fortunate to be allotted a vacant room.

Her mother was worried about her living away from home when she was not yet fully recovered, but helped Amy pack her books and clothes into two large suitcases, and drove her to the hostel, where she and Rosy helped settle her in. Rosy was emotional on parting, promising to visit often and though it was the last thing Amy wanted, she said nothing, unwilling to hurt her.

It was late April. Amy was sitting at her desk, gazing out of the Sophia College hostel window, doodling on a piece of lined paper. New buds and a smattering of flame-coloured flowers were visible on gulmohor trees. A spider, having spun its web in the corner of her ceiling, waited for its first meal of the day. Her eyes wandered around the room and rested on wooden shelves badly in need of fresh paint. A colourful rug lay on the floor and on her desk was a family photo taken in Mahableshwar two years earlier: Daddy laughing into the camera with his arms around Jamsheed, preventing him from wriggling away. Her own arm was around her mother's shoulder, and they were both smiling at Jamsheed's antics. Had there really been a time when they were so truly happy?

She glanced at her closet and thought of Rayomand's photograph hidden there. It came out at night to lie under her pillow when she slept. It had been drenched time and again by unchecked tears and become quite dog-eared, but his face yet was unmarked.

Why was she not sensible enough to hate him for the pain he caused with his lies? Or so impossible to stop loving him? Why did she cry, night after night, and yearn for him to hold her, and make love the way he had that one morning at the Oberoi?

The fan whirred loudly overhead, its only function, to blow study papers onto the floor. She stretched her arms above her tired head. Her final exams were imminent, and she wondered what the future had in store.

She knew that she could never have managed these past dreadful weeks without the support of her friends, although she had shared only a small part of her breakup with them. They had visited her soon after she moved into the hostel and when Pinku put her arms around her, her hard-won control had fallen away, and she had sobbed uncontrollably. They had wept with her until her paroxysms had abated and then, when Zia had pointed to their weeping faces reflected in the mirror, they had burst into fits of giggles.

Rayomand. She must not think of him. He had married her on the rebound. Rayomand, who had not loved her. She hated Anjali. Hated her for destroying her peace of mind and her marriage before it ever had a chance to succeed.

Two days ago, Zia had burst into her room, waving the previous evening's newspaper.

'Amy, Amy! The witch has jumped on her broom and whizzed off to Calcutta!'

'What?' she asked, unwilling to be reminded of Anjali, and Pinku, following behind Zia, added, 'She's trying to say in her best ridiculous fashion, that the witch has married some old man and gone to live in Calcutta.'

When the newspaper was spread open on her desk, Amy saw Anjali in bridal gear, standing beside a short grey-haired man.

'Yippee,' Zia crowed, and clutching both Amy's hands, swung her round and around the room until they both fell laughing dizzily on the bed.

Amy did not like living away from home, especially at night, when she missed her family and Mitzy. She found herself looking forward to Rosy's visits because she always came laden with food and caustic comments on the happenings in the Cooper household, and her ongoing battles with Raju and Jamsheed.

Rosy mentioned in passing that Hirjee uncle visited Mummy nearly every evening, which was surprising, because he had never done that before. Amy knew he had been a regular visitor when she was unwell, but to still visit so often? Was Mum growing fond of him?

No, she was imagining things; reading more into what Rosy said, than existed. Her books on John Donne and the metaphysical poets lay unopened in an untidy heap by her feet. She really ought to start revising, but her mind continued its own train of thought. Why did Rayomand call her so regularly, even when she often refused to speak with him? Was it guilt that he felt, and would she ever forget the gloating look on Anjali's face?

Rayomand kept pleading over and over for her to believe that he had not wanted to see Anjali, nor had he instigated the advance, but she refused to accept his explanation. She knew that she had been his second choice. He had proposed only after Anjali had publicly broken their engagement. Well, Rayomand would be free as soon as she could convince him and everyone else that she was in earnest about commencing divorce proceedings. But was she truly serious? A small nagging voice refused to be stilled. She continued to love Rayomand and that made her furious; furious for keeping his photograph and not being strong enough to tear it into pieces. To throw it away as he had thrown away their life together. She wanted to hate him, cut him out of her life; but he was with her in her dreams, night after night, holding her and telling her he loved her. Dreams, tiresome dreams, figments of her imagination and longings!

She lifted her study books off the floor and placing them on her desk, tried to refocus her thoughts. If she wanted to do well, she must put Rayomand out of her mind. With final examinations looming in a few weeks, she was unsure if she was ready.

Thirty
Marina
April 1986

The evening before Amy's exams, Marina stopped by to wish her luck and found her revising bits of poetry. She knew Amy was nervous, dreading the exams and studying hard, desperately wanting a First.

Marina entered and Amy flew into her arms saying, 'I can't do this. I am so unprepared. What if my mind goes blank? What if I flunk them?'

'Shh. You won't. You'll do brilliantly. You always do.'

Noticing how close she was to tears, Marina led her to sit on the bed, the only place other than the one chair by her desk, and drawing her close, spoke of nonconsequential things. She made Amy smile, recounting Rosy's ongoing battles with Jamsheed and his disgust at the mention of a bath and daily change of underclothes.

'Rosy insists that when Jamsa enters the bathroom, he lets the water run, but does not actually bathe. I tell her he will outgrow this aversion, but she disagrees, telling me I spoil him. You know her, she does not believe in being patient with him.'

Marina chatted lightly about things, but not of Hirjee's determined pursuit of her, unaware that sharp-eyed Rosy had already mentioned it.

Hirjee was forcing her to look inside herself and she did not want to become aware of feelings that might always have existed.

It was too soon.

What would people say?

When she said as much to Hirjee, he told her he could not care less what anyone thought or said. He reminded her that he loved her and had done so for years and wanted to marry her. He needed to know what she truly felt and if she cared just a little for him.

She was so confused.

She loved Rustam, so how could she even think of Hirjee? But think of him she did. He was her rock and she had leant on him even when Rustam was alive. Hirjee was not just Rustam's closest friend, but hers as well. She had invariably turned to him and trusted his judgement.

Life was so strange. What did her future hold?

After visiting Amy, Marina drove through the evening traffic to the member's shop at the Willingdon Club.

She was searching the shelves for a bottle of jam when someone tapped her shoulder. Leela*behn* Dalal, Gitu's mother-in-law, greeted her, saying in a carrying voice, 'Marina*behn*, how are you and the family? Gitu mentioned the other day that you have been unwell, but I can see you are much better now.' Then she added, 'I want to talk to you. If you have some time after your shop, come join me on the veranda.'

'I will,' Marina replied, 'but I can't stay long. I've had a long day and I am quite tired.'

After paying her grocery bill, she walked out to where Leela*behn* sat on a veranda sofa, with a waiter taking her order. Marina went up to her and sitting down, accepted an offer of a cold drink.

Leela*behn* commiserated on the passing of Rustam, then fell silent, leaving Marina to wonder what it was that she really wanted to say. After what seemed an interminable pause, Leela*behn* said, 'Child, you are like my own daughter and without a husband to look after you, I feel it is my duty to warn you.'

A worried tingle shimmied down Marina's spine.

'Gitu tells me that your husband's friend Hirjee is very interested in you, and now, with your husband gone, he has been openly pursuing you.'

'Leela*behn*,' Marina spoke, quietly, 'Hirjee is a dear friend, who has been of great help since Rustam's death. He is a wonderful friend and nothing more. Please do not concern yourself on my behalf.' Her polite reply hid the anger coursing through her. How dare Gitu discuss her with her mother-in-law?

'That is good. But there is something I feel you should know, something our family has known for a long time.'

Seriously disturbed, Marina wanted to get up and leave, but unwilling to be rude, she waited.

'Hirjee Dhanjibhoy has a ten-year old son. The boy's mother is Smita Dalal, a Gujerati woman living in Bandra. I'm telling you all this because her in-laws are distantly related to my husband. The boy stays with his mother, but Hirjee pays for his studies and his upkeep. The child has been brought up as a Hindu and thinks of Hirjee as an uncle, and not as his father. His mother once worked as a secretary, in Hirjee's firm, many years ago and he must have had the affair at the same time his wife was critically ill.'

'No! That's not true! That is the most slanderous thing I have ever heard, and I don't believe you. You don't know Mr. Dhanjibhoy! If you did, you would never believe or say such a thing about him.'

Marina stood up in great distress. 'It is getting late Leela*behn.* If I were you, I would not speak of it to anyone. Thank you for the drink.' She gathered her parcels with shaking fingers and though seething, politely *namasted,* before hurrying away.

Gossipy old so-and-so! How dare she spoil Hirjee's name. How dare she say Hirjee was involved with another woman and if that were not bad enough, to say he still visited her regularly. Oh! She could scream.

Later after dinner, with Jamsheed in bed, she sat on the darkened veranda mulling over Leela*behn*'s words.

At ten-thirty, Rosy looked in on her to say, 'Go to bed *Bai*, it is quite late. Again an' again you will be falling sick if you not taking care.'

'Don't worry Rosy, I'll turn in soon and remember to lock the veranda doors. Go to sleep. Good night.'

She sat on, rubbing her aching forehead, unable to imagine Hirjee being with another woman for all these years. To have a secret mistress and second son, ten years old? Was it possible to be so ignorant about people's inner lives?

She was suffused with sadness. Hirjee was her dear friend who always made her feel special.

Since Rustam's death, she had turned more and more to him, craving the sense of peace he imparted. And though she never openly acknowledged it, it was comforting to know he loved her and to have known for years, that two men loved her. Now to be told there was another woman in his life and someone who had been with him for many years was a terrible thing to accept.

He is a bachelor, she told herself, and a widower for goodness' sake. He has every right to his personal life. Why should he share this part with her or with anyone?

However, anger was building in her.

Yes, he was free to do whatever he wanted, but why make her believe that he cared for her? Go so far as to ask her to marry him. She felt violated by his hollow words. How could he live with the knowledge of his son being illegitimate, when he could have married the woman and given the boy the shelter of his name? It was not enough to just pay for his upkeep. How was it possible to be so mistaken about a person's character? Blinking back angry tears, she pummelled the chair arms with her fists.

Oh! The deception was unbearable!

She was angry with Leela*behn* for shattering her peace of mind. But what had been said, was said out of concern and not malice. It was good to be warned because she was relying increasingly on Hirjee. She was beginning to look forward to his daily calls and relax in his company. Since the night of his dinner, many months ago, there was an imperceptible shift in her feelings towards him. Though she would always love Rustam, an unexplained emotion was burgeoning in her, waiting to emerge.

However, she was now determined to help Amy file for divorce.

They both needed a break from the Dhanjibhoy men.

She would sell her apartment and move to Pune just as she had decided.

There was no question anymore, of accepting Hirjee's help towards Jamsheed's schooling.

No, she did not need him.

When Hirjee phoned the next morning, he was told by Rosy that Marina was busy. He rang a second time to ask if he could visit in the evening and was put off again.

After several failed attempts to reach her, he became seriously disturbed. This was so unlike Marina. What could he possibly have done to upset her?

He decided to stop by after work on the off-chance and find out.

Rosy welcomed him, saying, 'Marina*bai* is home and resting in her room.'

'Rosy, is Marina*bai* unwell?'

'No *seth*, she going to work today. She is just little bit resting.'

'Will you tell her I'm here?'

Rosy returned presently, saying, 'Sorry *seth*, but Marina*bai* has a headache.'

Unwilling to leave without knowing what troubled Marina, he walked to her closed door and said, 'Come out Marina. I need to speak with you. I only want a few minutes of your time.'

The door opened and her unsmiling face told him that something was very wrong.

Looking intently at her, he said in a low voice, 'We need to speak in private, where can we go?'

Noticing Rosy's inquisitive stare studying them, Marina said to her, 'I'll be on the terrace with Hirjee*seth*. If I'm needed, come, and call me.'

They went up in the lift in silence and stepped out onto the dusty, empty terrace. The evening sky above them was awash in shades of pink and mauve. The sea below was calm, its smooth surface sporadically broken by wavelets of rolling white foam, but the peaceful beauty of the evening was lost on them. Hirjee reached for Marina's hand, but she drew it away as though scorched by his touch. Shocked by her reaction, he asked, 'What's wrong, Marina? If I've inadvertently done or said something, I apologise. You've never shut me out of your life before and I can't bear it! Your friendship is everything to me. Please, my darling Marina, tell me, what have I done?' His anguished plea broke her outward control.

'Done? You ask me what you've done? I've never known a man so deceitful; so horribly deceitful, as you! Why pretend to care for me? Or ask me to marry you when you have a second family living in Bandra?'

Her words were daggers piercing his soul and his face drained of colour.

How had this reached her ears?

Who could have told her?

And then, anger began coursing through him because she judged him without giving him the benefit of doubt, or a chance to explain.

But the very next instant he knew he could not explain.

He was not free to explain. Looking into her stony face he stated, 'I'm sorry you choose to believe the worst of me. Yes, it's true. There is another family I care for, but I'm not at liberty to share the whole of it with you. Choose to think what you like, but don't ever call the love I bear, false or deceitful!'

They faced each other coldly, unable to believe the shocking situation they were in. Then without another word, Hirjee turned and walked down the stairs.

Hirjee drove aimlessly through the crowded streets, tears burning like red-hot pokers behind his eyes, as one refrain repeated itself over and over, he had lost Marina. He had lost her just when he thought there was hope she might begin to care for him. He parked in a quiet lane and rested his throbbing head on the steering wheel, gripping it in anguish, clearly recalling the day when he thought he hated Rustam.

He was working late, when Rustam burst into his room one evening, saying in a shaky voice, 'I'm in deep trouble and I don't know what to do, or where to turn.'

'What trouble?' Hirjee asked, perplexed to see Rustam pace the floor in agitation.

'Oh God, Hirjee! I don't know how to tell you this, but I'm in desperate need of help and advice.'

'Sure. Whatever it is, we'll solve it together. Sit down and cheer up. Nothing can be so bad. You're carrying on as if you've murdered someone.'

'Ah Hirjee, it's much worse! Much, much, worse!'

'Okay, so fill me in.'

'I don't know how to say this, but Smita is having my baby.'

'What? Did you just say Smita? Your young secretary is having your baby? No, that can't be true. And what makes you think it's yours?'

'I'm the father Hirjee, there is no one else. Oh God, I've been so reckless. When Smita said she loved me, I never thought our flirtatious behaviour would go as far as it has. I don't love Smita! I love Marina and would hate her to find out.

I don't want my marriage to end. If only I could put the clock back! But Hirjee, Smita is pregnant. With my baby! I told her not to, but she wants to go ahead with the pregnancy. What shall I do? Please help me!'

Hirjee stared at Rustam in horror, appalled by what he heard. He did not want to believe it. How could Rustam do such a thing? Have an affair, when the most wonderful woman was his wife? Hirjee gripped the arms of his chair to stop himself from physically striking Rustam.

'You idiot, Rustam. You absolute idiot! How could you? You don't deserve Marina!' he shouted.

'I know, I know. But please help me, Hirjee! I don't want my marriage to end! Tell me what to do! I will naturally pay for its support, but don't know how, without Marina knowing.'

Hirjee was silent for a while, then said, 'The only thing is for me to look after Smita. She is after all my employee, so I will take on the financial responsibility and look after the child.

'No! You cannot do that! I cannot allow you to pay for my mistake. All I want is for you to help me work this out. This is my responsibility.'

But Hirjee was adamant.

'There is no other way if you want to protect Marina. It's not fair to make her unhappy. She does not deserve this. It will have to be as I say.'

'Yes, I know it's not fair to make her unhappy. What can I say, Hirjee? I am truly blessed to have you as a friend. I promise I will make it up to her for the rest of my life. Thank you. Thank you!'

Rustam never strayed again and showered his family with love, and seeing this, Hirjee was satisfied. His beloved Marina was saved from unhappiness. But it had surprised him that not once in all these years had Rustam ever referred, even in passing, to his new child. It was as if he had blanked out the entire episode from his life.

Now that the secret was out, he knew he could never resolve the unpleasantness between him and Marina. He could not sully Rustam's memory, nor cause Smita grief by divulging her secret, or do anything to upset young Karan's safe world. Marina would continue to think unkindly of him and there was nothing he could do to rectify it. His act of unselfishness was a burden he would carry all his life.

He did not know how to come to terms with the knowledge that he had just lost the most precious thing to him, the one thing she had given him so freely - her treasured friendship.

Thirty-One

Amy and Rayomand

April 1986

The night before her final exams, Amy had a thought she could not stifle. She wished Rayomand had rung to wish her as his father had done.

Why do I miss him so much, when he cannot be bothered about something so important in my life?

Unable to sleep, she was up long before the birds were awake, to revise notes made the night before. With the first hint of dawn, she heard the koel's plaintive cry of 'coo coo' and the crimson-throated barbet begin its, 'pok, pok, pok', a repetitive call akin to an electric pulse.

At eight in the morning, there was a knock at her door and the hostel supervisor delivered a single, long-stemmed, scented white rose, with pink-tipped petals. Happiness flooded her on reading the card,

'Amy a white rose for luck. Love, Rayomand.'

He did know and had remembered to wish her.

Before entering the examination hall, she whispered to her friends that Rayomand had sent her a rose for luck and Zia smiled, glad that he had remembered.

On each subsequent morning of her five exams, a single, long-stemmed rose arrived; pale lemon, golden yellow, orange, bright red, and on the penultimate day, a perfectly shaped, crimson rose in full bloom. She collected her roses in a tall glass vase and her room was filled with its heady perfume.

Rayomand was determined to meet Amy on the last day of her exam, to learn if she seriously wanted a separation, or whether there was the smallest chance they could make their marriage work. When they last spoke, she had brought up the issue of a divorce and he had skirted around it. However, they had to resolve their dilemma, because now that he was living in Madras, he would soon be too busy to visit Bombay as often as he had.

He was parked in the shade of a piltoforum tree, the afternoon heat made bearable by a breeze blowing in through his open car windows. Small yellow flowers, with curved stamens, drifted down and settled on the hood and bonnet of his car. The gulmohor trees in the garden were ablaze with flame-red flowers, making a wonderful contrast to the yellow and white frangipani trees.

While waiting for Amy at this well-regarded lady's college, his hands sweating with nerves, he wondered if she would speak with him or turn and walk away. They had been apart for three months, with him living in Madras. He was working more than fourteen hours each day, desperately trying to erase the image of Amy weeping on the floor and later, though delirious in bed with a raging fever, aware of not wanting him to touch her. He was grateful that some weeks earlier, Zia had made it possible for him to sometimes see Amy around the college premises without her knowledge. He was like a lovesick hero in films, viewing his beloved from a distance. Nevertheless, he had neither burst into song nor run singing around trees, as in Hindi films, and that bizarre picture amused him.

His eyes continued their patient vigil till he saw Amy greet her friends at the entrance of the porch and then the four of them run down the College steps. He got out of the car and approached them. Meena saw him first and nudged Amy, to draw her attention. Happy laughter disappeared from her face, to be replaced by a look of apprehension. He thought she was about to turn and hurry away, but then, straightening her shoulders she spoke to her friends and walked up to him. She stood before him clutching her books for comfort and support.

'Hello Amy, how was your paper?'

'Good, thank you,' she replied noncommittally.

Rayomand nodded to her friends, who gave him uncertain smiles. He stood beside Amy with his hands tightly clenched in his trouser pockets, to keep from reaching for her.

'You and I,' he said, 'Have unfinished business to discuss. I'm leaving Bombay for good at the end of the week and will be gone for many months. If you're free this afternoon and it's not too inconvenient, let's spend it together? There is so much we need to discuss.'

Amy stared at the ground wondering what she should do. She and her friends had planned to watch a Clint Eastwood film this afternoon because Pinku adored him and later, Meena's mother had invited them for a Maharashtrian meal. She looked at Rayomand thinking sadly, *so this is the showdown. After today I'll be free from this dreadful mess. I should feel glad. Why then, do I want to run from him and be unwilling to hear his decision?*

She went back to the girls and excused herself from the film, promising to meet them later at Meena's. She then got into Rayomand's car like a prisoner facing execution. For weeks, she had intentionally avoided Rayomand, but now, as he rightly said, they had to decide. It would be good to finally resolve the situation and call it a day. The roses he had sent meant nothing. They were just a friendly gesture to wish her luck. How could she have imagined they meant more?

Rayomand drove out of the college compound and down the winding Sophia College Lane, concentrating on the heavy weekday traffic. He planned to drive her to the Sun 'n' Sand Hotel at Juhu.

Amy sat in silence until she noticed that they were heading north into the suburbs.

'Where are we going, Rayomand?'

'To the Sun 'n' Sand.'

'Why so far? I told the girls I'd meet them around six at Meena's house. Will we be back by then?'

And looking into Amy's wide apprehensive eyes, he replied, 'We'll try. Don't worry.'

They reached the beach hotel a little after two-thirty and went straight to the dining hall for a late lunch, but Amy was far too overwrought to eat.

'Shall we sit by the pool and order ice cream and snacks instead?' Rayomand inquired, to which she smiled uncertainly and nodded, ice cream would be infinitely easier to swallow.

The area by the pool had low almond trees and tall coconut palms with lights ringed halfway up the slender trunks. Some guests swam while some sunned themselves on loungers, mostly airline crew, turning their pale skin an unnatural orange.

Rayomand chose a table under a striped umbrella and beckoned a waiter, to give an order for a large peach melba for Amy, cold coffee with ice cream for himself and some spicy snacks and sandwiches. Amy protested that she couldn't eat so much, and Rayomand replied in a mock hurt voice, 'But I'm ravenous, even if you aren't.'

Amy always enjoyed Rayomand's company and today was no exception. It felt good to be with him and have him tell her about the new branch office in Madras, describe the house he had recently bought in Adyar, and having to learn useful Tamil words. He spoke easily of everything, except the one thing that lay heavy on her mind.

When their empty plates and glasses were cleared away, Rayomand stood up and drew Amy out of her chair, saying, 'Let's walk on the beach.'

A pleasant breeze blew, dispersing the day's heat, the sea was a shimmery pale green and the bright golden orb lay low on the horizon. It was just too glorious an evening to refuse. Amy had not visited Juhu for years and forgotten how much she loved it. Slipping off her sandals and rolling up her jeans, she followed Rayomand onto the beach.

As they walked, Amy sent her companion a quick sidelong glance, recollecting an incident from when she was little and their families had picnicked here. She remembered proudly showing her 'sand house' to the grownups; one she had built for the first time without anyone's help. And Rayomand, a gangling fourteen-year-old, getting his paper kite to fly, had backed into her 'sand house' and squashed it, making her wail. Jeroo aunty had comforted her and told Rayomand to remake her 'sand house,' which he had, helping her build a much bigger one. So many memories!

Maybe, just maybe, after they sorted out the difficulty of being married, they might possibly remain friends?

Rayomand took her hand as they walked along the water's edge, the silvery-white foam swirling around their feet, and after a surprised glance in his direction, she let it lie in his. They walked in silence, away from the hawkers and the public to where the beach curved and hit a bank of rocks with the ever-present gulls circling overhead.

They were truly alone.

Rayomand spread his kerchief on the sand for Amy to sit on, which she did, realising her feet needed rest.

'Amy,' he asked, sitting by her side, 'Do you hate me?'

Hate him? She recalled the innumerable times she had said she hated Anjali, but him? No. Not even when she was hurting and livid that he had lied to her, or even when she knew she was his second choice. It was true she did not want to see him, or ever feel his touch. A thought crept unbidden into her mind that she had never stopped loving him and staring silently at the frothing water by the tide line, shook her head.

Taking her chin in his hand, Rayomand turned her face to his, 'Amy, can you forgive me? Do I have the smallest chance of sharing your life? Are you certain you want this farcical marriage, as you called it, to end? Could you not learn to like me again? I'm not asking for your love, but please sweetheart, just like me enough to give our marriage a second chance? Perhaps someday, my love might kindle the same in you. Give me a chance, Amy. Please don't send me away. Believe me when I say I love you.'

He loved her? She stared at him in wide-eyed amazement. *How could he possibly love her?* He had never said it before; not when they first married, or even when they spoke on the phone. Never imagined, except in her make-believe world of dreams, that Rayomand would beg her to reconsider. She thought he would be happy to be freed from the shackles of a marriage on the rebound.

'How can you say you love me?' she cried. 'You have never loved me. It was always Anjali. I was only your second choice!'

'No. What I thought was love, was only a figment of my imagination. I imbued Anjali with qualities she does not possess. Instead, each time you and I met, it felt right. I was relaxed, we laughed at the same things, and I just felt happy being with you. I realised sometime during the year how much I loved you.'

'But you never said anything. You never said you loved me.'

'I know sweetheart, I know. I thought it was enough to show you how much you meant to me. I was wrong. I should have said I loved you. Forgive me Amy, forgive my foolish involvement, and please give me a second chance.'

He reached for Amy, and she moved unresistingly into his arms, her eyes bright with sparkling tears; her hands cupped his face and drew it down to meet her lips, yearning for his touch, the words she had longed to hear and only dreamt of, were being whispered over and over. He loved her! Unbelievable, but he loved her!

After what seemed like a blissful eternity, they sat and watched ribbons of orange pink, and mauve scatter in the sky and the reddish-gold disk sink into the sea. With Amy's handheld possessively in his, Rayomand asked, 'Where's your wedding ring? Have you lost it, or did you throw it away?'

'Neither' she replied and showed him her band dangling from a gold chain around her neck. 'I removed it but found I could not put it from me and decided to wear it round my neck instead.'

'Give it to me,' he whispered huskily.

Unclasping the chain Amy handed it to him. Taking her left hand, he kissed her empty finger and slipped the ring back in its rightful place.

It was turning dark when they began strolling back to the hotel, past hawker stalls bright with the white glare of kerosene lights and strident sounds of Hindi film music. Stray dogs scavenged among paper rubbish flung by customers greedily tucking into spicy *bhel puri, pani puri,* and potato patties.

The stars were out, by the time they entered the neon-lit hotel and Amy remembered her promise to be at Meena's by six, and now, it was after eight. She hurried to a phone box to call her and before she could say more than, 'Hello,' all three friends spoke at once.

'Where are you?' Pinku shouted.

'Why have you ditched us? What's happened? Are you alright?' Zia wanted to know, with Meena adding, '*Aayee* has kept food aside for you.'

Amy found it hard to respond, with Rayomand's arms wrapped around her waist and his head near the earpiece listening to their excited chatter.

'Meena, apologise to your mother and thank her for keeping dinner for me. But girls, I'm at the Sun 'n' Sand, and will be spending the evening with Rayomand.'

'Tell them,' he said, mischievously. 'You're not just spending the evening with me, but the night as well!'

Thirty-Two

Hirjee

Oct 1986

While driving to Bandra, because he had promised to take young Karan and his sister Monisha to the 'Great Russian Circus,' Hirjee's thoughts were filled by Marina. How had things gone so badly wrong? Why had he allowed his wretched pride and temper to get the better of him? He should have explained.

Explained what? He was not free to explain. Marina was hurt and there was nothing he could do. Her apartment was up for sale, and she would be moving soon. They had met only once, since then, at a celebratory dinner for Amy and Rayomand. Thank goodness the young couple had resolved their differences and seemed devoted to each other. In Amy's recent letter to him, she said she was delighted to be known as Mrs. Amy Dhanjibhoy, and with her new home in Adyar.

Arriving at a large building complex, consisting of eight uninspiring blocks of flats, he parked in front of one of them and took the lift to the third floor. He waited outside a door with white rangoli designs on the floor and rang the bell. The air all around was heavy with the aroma of ghee and asafoetida. Someone's radio or television blared Indian music, while two ladies on separate floors conversed loudly, craning their necks to talk to one another, and children raced up and down the narrow staircase, unceremoniously jostling unfortunates in their way.

Smita Dalal's fat but sprightly mother-in-law, Sitabehn, opened the door.

'*Aavo, aavo* Hirjee*bhai*, how are you?' and before he could reply, a small tornado flew into his arms.

'Hirjee uncle, Hirjee uncle, you've come!'

'Karan,' Sita*behn* admonished. 'Where are your manners? Is this how you greet your elders?'

Karan pulled away to touch Hirjee's feet in the traditional manner of greeting and Hirjee felt the usual tug at his heartstrings. He lifted the youngster and held him aloft, only to find Monisha pulling his trouser leg, wanting him to lift her as well.

Five hours later, after a tiring but exciting trip to the circus and a delicious meal cooked by Smita, the children were bundled out of the room by Sita*behn*, so their parents could chat to Hirjee.

During their conversation, Smita asked, 'What's wrong Hirjee*bhai*, Narendra and I have noticed a new sadness in your eyes, something that was not there before.'

Hirjee sighed, 'Marina knows about Karan. Someone told her a few months ago that I'm his father, and she's livid with me for what she calls, 'my deceitful behaviour.' She wants nothing to do with me and I can only hope and pray with time, she will relent and let me be her friend again.'

Smita covered her mouth with both hands, wide-eyed in shock, and turning to her husband, moaned, 'Oh Naren, what shall I do? Oh Hirjee*bhai*! I am so sorry, so very sorry!'

Hirjee reached over and patted her hand, 'Nothing has really changed Smita, so don't let it trouble you. I won't ever divulge the secret. Don't cry, Smita, please don't cry! Your life is not going to change. Your Karan is quite safe.'

Long after Hirjee left, Smita lay in Narendra's arms, unable to stop crying.

'Naren,' she whispered in Gujerati, unwilling to disturb the sleeping children, 'What possessed me to behave the way I did? Under what horrible stars was I born to inflict so much pain on everyone? Even though you say Karan is your son, anyone with eyes can see he looks nothing like you. Now poor Hirjee*bhai* is being punished and he has been so good to us!'

'Shh, Smita, it's alright. Karan is my son. I couldn't love him more if my own blood flowed through his veins. Hirjee*bhai* will sort things out. Don't distress yourself! Please don't!'

Long after Narendra fell asleep, Smita lay awake, thinking. She knew there was something she had to do. She needed to ask forgiveness from someone she had wronged. Afterwards, she would leave everything in compassionate Lord Krishna's hands, to do with her as He wished. She would pray for guidance and ask Him to give her courage.

Marina was surprised to receive a call from Smita Dalal, a name that was seared on her soul. Her first reaction was to replace the handset and not speak to her. But something in the low hesitant voice speaking Gujerati, made her listen to the request and agree, against her inner wishes, to meet with her on Saturday at three-thirty, in the gardens of the Prince of Wales' Museum.

Marina arrived before the appointed time and looked around her, noting the various changes since her last visit. People strolled in the garden, and she wondered what Smita looked like? If she was Hirjee's mistress, she must be very good-looking.

'Mrs. Cooper?' a soft voice asked, and Marina turned to see a plump, sweet-faced person in a sari. The woman put her palms together and *namasted,* and Marina returned the greeting.

'I am Smita Dalal.'

Marina stared unbelievingly. This very proper Gujerati housewife was Hirjee's mistress? There had to be a mistake!

She heard Smita introduce her to a short plump man with a receding forehead. '*Behn* this is my husband Narendra, and these are our two children, Karan and Monisha.'

As the three of them greeted her formally, Marina felt a strange sensation in her ears and felt faint.

She saw a ten-year-old boy with big brown eyes and a mischievous grin stare curiously at her, then turn to his father, saying, ‘Pappa, let’s go inside. You promised to show me the stuffed tigers and the giant Himalayan eagle. Please, Pappa please?’

‘Yes Pappa, please come! I want to go inside too!’ said his six-year-old sister. Narendra excused himself and clasping the children’s hands, walked off, leaving the two women alone.

Smita broke the silence by asking Marina to sit with her on a nearby bench.

‘Marina*behn*, I have come to beg your forgiveness for a wrong I did to you many years ago. You may not remember, but eleven years ago I worked as your husband’s secretary.’

Marina vaguely remembered a bouncy, vivacious young woman who was Rustam’s secretary for a short time. This married lady before her looked nothing like the young girl she remembered.

She heard Smita say, ‘I am deeply ashamed to tell you that I fell in love with your husband on the day I began working for him. I saw you occasionally at the office and was deeply jealous of you. You had the man I wanted, and I was determined to take him from you. At first, Rustam playfully fended off my advances. But there were occasions when I accompanied him to Delhi and Calcutta, and on one of those outings, we went to bed together.’

‘Stop!’ Marina cried. ‘Please. Don’t tell me anymore.’

‘Please *Behn*, hear me out. For I must try and put things right for someone very dear to us all.’

Staring at the dusty ground, she continued. ‘I was certain when I found I was pregnant, that Rustam would leave you and marry me. How could I have been so naïve? Married men may have a fling, but they will not leave their wives or family for some stupid girl ready to sleep with them!’ and dashing away tears, she bravely continued, ‘I told Rustam I was pregnant, and he was horrified. He told me to get rid of the baby at once. I was devastated. I could not believe he could say such a thing to me. That evening I handed in my resignation and left the office. I did not want to live. At night when my parents were asleep, I drank household cleaning fluid thinking to end my life. It did not happen. I just became violently sick and was rushed to the J.J. Hospital where my stomach was pumped. Naren and his family, who were my parent's neighbours, came to the hospital every day. I did not die nor lose the baby. A sympathetic Police officer, who visited me in hospital, did not file a criminal case, because a young man pleading on my behalf wanted to marry me. Marina*behn*, although I was entirely to blame for this horrendous episode, Lord Krishna took pity on me and sent my wonderful Narendra, into my life. He had wanted to marry me from the time I turned sixteen. But I, with my high ideals, looked down on him, because he was short and plump and just a lowly clerk in a government office. But now, I bless the day I married Narendra because he has been a true father to Karan. The other person, to come into our lives was Hirjee*bhai*. I do not know how he found out, but he came and said I would never have to worry about looking after Karan and promised to pay for his upkeep and all his education. Over the years we have grown to know and love Hirjee*bhai* as a member of our family. Karan adores him and so does Monisha.' Smita stood up and touched Marina's feet in abject humility.

'I beg your forgiveness, Marina*behn*. Be angry with me, I deserve it, but do not be angry at Hirjee*bhai* for he is the incarnation of a God! *Behn* do not throw him out of your life. Men like him are very rare!'

Marina listened to this tragic tale and her emotions swung from shock to anger, to pity, and then to utter dismay, for having treated Hirjee so badly.

She was amazed that Smita had intentionally bared her soul for Hirjee's sake. She could have kept silent, and Marina would never have known about Rustam's son. Her stepson!

She drove out of the museum in a daze, her mind in complete turmoil. She narrowly missed cyclists who swore colourfully and twice slammed on her brakes in the slow-moving traffic, to keep from bumping the car in front.

Frantic thoughts raced through her mind.

How could she have been so utterly unaware that Rustam had had an affair? Were there others? And if so, how many? Why had she not been enough for him? What was lacking in her that had made him look outside her love, for someone else?

She dashed away tears, blurring her vision.

'How could you, Rustam,' she raged. 'How could you do such a thing? Why was I not enough? Why? Why? Why?'

She felt sick. Bitter bile rising in her throat!

Hirjee knew. He must always have known!

Why did he never tell me? Stop being so stupid, she told herself angrily. He couldn't. He knew I would never believe him if he did.

No. If she had not seen the little boy, who looked like a miniature version of Rustam, she would never have believed anyone. Smita was incredibly brave to confess the way she did. Were all men unfaithful, or were they unfaithful because their wives were too trusting? Had she failed Rustam in some way? Her mind went back to the year Rustam was involved with Smita. Jamsheed was three at the time and she had just begun working with Gita. There had been evenings when she had come home tired, nights when she had not responded to Rustam's overtures, but he never let on that it troubled him. It had not mattered, because Smita had been ready to accommodate him.

She came home to a lonely apartment with only Mitzy to welcome her. Rosy was out visiting some friends of hers and Jamsheed was on a school trip. She lifted aging Mitzy and walked onto the veranda cuddling the little dachshund. She gently tickled Mitzy's ears, gaining comfort from the warm trusting body. The evening was humid, the sea a flat gunmetal grey reflecting her mood and the dark of the sky.

Marina did not recognise her life. Her placid, secure existence had been torn from its moorings since Rustam's sudden death and she was adrift.

So many changes had occurred.

She sat on a cane chair, a light breeze cooling her heated mind, mourning the death of her love for Rustam. Her intense anger lessened, leaving her drained.

She thought of the young boy she had met today, such excitement and innocence in his eyes, and marvelled at Narendra whose love was large enough to embrace another man's son. Smita was very fortunate.

Marina knew she must come to terms with what she had heard and the knowledge that a ten-year-old boy was her stepson, and her children's half-brother.

Her thoughts drifted to Hirjee, realising how much she missed him and how impossible it was to stop thinking of him and of his loving friendship. She longed to talk to him, but after her angry outburst, their relationship was limited to polite pleasantries. Soon after their heated conversation on the terrace, she had decided to sell up and move to Pune, wanting to get away from her apartment that held memories of twenty-three years with Rustam.

Rosy, noting that Hirjee had stopped visiting, asked Marina if she had quarrelled with him. Marina had fobbed her off with some lame excuse and Rosy, after giving her a disbelieving stare, had walked away with a hurt sniff. There was little one could keep from either Rosy or Philomena.

Those two sharp-eyed friends knew that Hirjee, who used to visit regularly, now came not at all.

When Jamsheed had been informed about the move, he had refused to go with her to Pune, threatening instead to move in with Hirjee. Hearing his rudeness, Rosy had scolded him, 'Say sorry to Mummy now! Spicking like this so rudely-rudely! What you mean by I go an' live with Hirjee uncle? Can you go and live with Hirjee*seth*? No! You cannot! Hirjee*seth* is Amy*baby*'s father-in-law, not yours.'

Marina knew that Amy and Rayomand were deeply concerned. They wondered what could possibly have caused such a rift between two friends and during a telephonic conversation with Marina, Amy had asked, 'Mum, Rayomand and I think something terrible has happened. Please tell me what's wrong? Let us help you two to be friends again. Help you clear this misunderstanding? Mum, Rayomand truly believes Hirjee uncle loves you!'

'Shh, Amy, don't say things like that. You are mistaken. There is no misunderstanding or problem. Darling, Hirjee was always Daddy's friend. With Daddy gone, it's only natural for him to be busy with his life. You know how busy I am, especially now, with the apartment up for sale and moving to Pune.'

'Don't move,' Amy had cried. 'Please Mum let us help with the bills so you can stay on in Bombay.'

'Thank you, darling, but there is no need for your concern. We'll be fine and it will be good to be near Mumma and Papa.'

When Rayomand questioned his father, he was told not to worry. There was no problem. Marina and he were good friends. But Amy and Rayomand knew something was terribly amiss because Marina had stopped Hirjee from paying for Jamsheed's schooling and was selling up and moving to Pune.

Marina felt calmer sitting with Mitzy, holding her and stroking her silky ears. She knew she would have to swallow her pride and beg Hirjee's forgiveness. He was her pillar of strength, and had been, even when Rustam was alive. He had made it possible for her to bear Rustam's death. His constant love had been a protective armour she had taken for granted.

She had insulted him so terribly and thrown away his love. How would she ever face him and beg his forgiveness?

Thirty-Three
Hirjee and Marina
Oct 1986

'You met Marina at the Prince of Wales' Museum and introduced her to Karan?' asked Hirjee. 'Why, Smita? What made you do that? How could you divulge Karan's parentage?'

'Forgive me Hirjee*bhai*, but when you said that Marina thought you were Karan's father, I knew I had to let her meet Karan. If I had gone alone and told her you were innocent, she would never have believed me. Naren and I have always known that you love Marina, and how painful it must be that she thinks ill of you. Hirjee*bhai*, I can never repay your many kindnesses, or the debt of gratitude I owe you. I disclosed my secret, to make her realize what a wonderful man you are. I would do anything to make things better for you!'

'*Arrae* Smita! You really shouldn't have. Marina doesn't love me. She has never loved me - only Rustam. Now her memory of him has been besmirched.'

'Hirjee*bhai* you are worth a hundred Rustams!' Smita said angrily. 'I know he was your best friend, but you were a better friend than he deserved! I don't say I was blameless. I know I was much at fault, but Rustam too was to blame. He was happy to be with me till I became pregnant, then wanted nothing more to do with me. If Naren and you had not come to my rescue, I don't know what would have become of Karan and me.'

'Well, what's done is done! Hirjee sighed. 'I do thank you most sincerely, Smita. It is a relief not to have this secret between Marina and myself.'

Hirjee paced his study after Smita's phone call, wanting desperately to go and meet Marina. But not sure he would be welcome. For years he had covered for Rustam, and she would naturally see it as terrible deception on his part. Whichever way he looked at it, he was in the wrong.

Since Jeroo's death, there had been women interested in him. But there was only one person for him. Just one person he loved, and that person did not want him. No, much as he longed to meet Marina, he knew he wouldn't. Not unless she called him.

Two days later, a handwritten letter arrived, addressed to him in Marina's neat script on the envelope.

What could she have written? He was afraid to open it.

Stop behaving like a child, he told himself, reaching purposefully for a letter opener. His eyes raced down the precisely penned missive.

Dear Hirjee,
Could we meet at your convenience so I can personally apologise for wrongly blaming you?
Marina.

He crushed the note in his fist, till his knuckles turned white. The letter showed she was still the same distant Marina, and nothing was changed.

She wanted to apologise for her outburst on her terrace. But he would rather have her anger than this polite aloofness. He paced the floor wondering whether to meet her or not, then decided to phone her. Just have a quick telephonic conversation and get it over with. He dialled her number and at the sound of her 'Hello,' said, taking a deep breath, 'Marina? Thank you for your note. There's no need for an apology. You were right to be angry, and ….'

'Please Hirjee,' she interrupted softly, 'Pease can we meet? I really need to talk to you.'

'Yes, of course.'

'Can we meet someplace where we might speak undisturbed?'

'Yes. Leave it to me. Shall I pick you up from the shop, tomorrow at six?'

'No. I'll meet you. Just tell me where.'

They finally agreed to meet in a lane opposite the National Sports Club of India.

Marina arrived five minutes after six, to find Hirjee parked and waiting for her. She felt a strange sensation as if she were seeing him for the very first time. She had forgotten how his eyes crinkled when he smiled and how they lit up when they rested on her. She felt shy, but taking a deep breath, she walked up to him. They met as strangers, politely greeting each other from a distance. Marina followed Hirjee through an ornate gate and onto the drive of his friend's garden. The house, built at the edge of the bay, was empty because his friend was away on holiday. An old retainer greeted them and invited them into a lush garden bright with cannas, cosmos, and marigolds. He showed them to some chairs on the patio before silently disappearing into the house.

Hirjee studied Marina's lovely profile and waited for her to speak.

Keeping her eyes trained on hands clasped nervously on her lap, she said huskily, 'I don't know where to begin Hirjee, but forgive me. Forgive my hasty words. I was so hurt and angry. But I should have known you could never behave in any way other than honourably.'

'Don't Marina, don't!' he interrupted. 'Don't ask for my forgiveness. You have every right to be angry and resentful. I was at fault. I did cover for Rustam and deserved everything you said.'

Marina asked, her eyes swimming in tears, 'Why Hirjee why? Tell me why was I not enough for him? Why was my love not enough? Why did he have to look for more outside our marriage? I feel so utterly worthless, so utterly, utterly worthless!' She dashed away tears with shaking fingers, trying desperately to prevent emotions from spiralling out of control. But it was like a tidal wave engulfing her and she suddenly gave in. Putting her face in her hands she started to cry. Unable to bear her distress, Hirjee stood up and drew her into his arms, clasping her unresisting form close.

'My darling, don't cry. Please don't cry!' he whispered over and over, holding her shuddering body, letting her weep unchecked on his shoulder, allowing the poison to flow out with her tears. He murmured words of love. Words he had longed to say, but until now, he had had no right to say them. Turning Marina's face to him, he wiped her tears with his kerchief and looking into her upturned face, lowered his mouth to taste her tear-drenched lips for the very first time. In the loving circle of his arms, her own crept around his neck and she willingly returned his kisses. To be held by Hirjee felt like the most natural thing in the world, as natural as being free to return his love.

Much later, they walked to the edge of the garden wall to gaze at the sea and watch lazy wavelets pour over black rocks. They saw the last of the gulls return to their nests and the first small fruit bats fly by in the darkening sky.

Standing in the circle of Hirjee's unswerving love, her love for Rustam seemed pale by comparison. For the very first time in months, she was utterly at peace.

Looking back over the years, she realized it had been Hirjee she had turned to in times of trouble, more than her fun-loving volatile husband. It was Hirjee's opinions and advice she had valued; Hirjee's quiet wit that always amused her and made her laugh, much more than Rustam's practical jokes and rough and ready humour.

She now recognised she had unconsciously returned Hirjee's constant love, something she must have been aware of in the inner recesses of her being, but never wanted to acknowledge.

Hirjee was her true-life partner.
He was her other missing half.

Epilogue
November 1986

Marina sat on a sofa repairing a tear in Jamsheed's school trousers with Mitzy beside her, floppy ears resting on her slippers. She heard Rosy's loud voice grumbling to cook Anthony, 'Where is that lazy Raju? He went hours ago to the Sahkari Bhandar, to fetch a kilo of sugar and some Amul butter and has not yet returned. It's five o'clock and Mitzy needs to be taken for her evening walk.' Anthony's long-suffering reply was muffled behind the closed kitchen door. Fond as Rosy was of Mitzy, she thought it beneath her dignity to walk a dog. She only walked Mitzy when Raju was away on leave.

The apartment was lonely without Amy and her friends, who now rarely visited. Jamsheed was still too young to afford her companionship. He was busy with his school, his friends, and his cricket. She spoke with Amy at least once every day, and this morning, she had been given some wonderful news; Amy and Rayomand were expecting their first child.

Marina thought back on the trauma they had been through, and the anguish Amy had suffered. Thank God it had all come right in the end. She recalled the early months when she and Hirjee had been worried sick, thinking Amy and Rayomand had made a big mistake in marrying.

Her Jamsheed seemed to have recovered from the painful loss of his father, transferring much of his affection and attention to Hirjee, who showered him with love.

Laying aside her sewing and with Mitzy trotting by her side, Marina went and stood on the balcony looking out at the sea. The old gulmohor tree in their compound was bare, with hardly a leaf on its low-hanging branches.

She mulled over last evening's conversation with Hirjee, when he had spoken of his involvement in the lives of Smita and Karan, the innocent little boy, who was the result of that association.

Hirjee's words churned inside her. She thought of the years Hirjee had guarded Rustam's secret to save her unhappiness. He had succeeded. Rustam had been exceptionally kind and loving these past ten years, and that had made his death so hard to bear. Hirjee told her that Rustam never saw his second son or ever asked after him. But Marina knew, had Rustam seen the scamp, he would have fallen in love with him. The fact that he looked so like Rustam clutched at her heartstrings and she knew she would never do anything to disturb young Karan's safe world.

She had dined with Hirjee at the Tanjore Restaurant last evening and when he brought her home and reached for her to wish her goodnight, she had gone willingly into his arms, their kiss an affirmation of their love.

She wondered what lay in store, in the years ahead.

She was at a turning point.

This past year and a half had changed her. She was different. She was not the same person who had been Rustam's wife for twenty-three years. The knowledge of his infidelity had changed her. Her love belonged to Hirjee who wanted her and had waited so patiently.

It was ironic they were in-laws to each other's children.

Would they ever marry?

She knew Jamsheed would be delighted because he adored Hirjee and Rayomand. Amy and Rayomand would most definitely approve and be happy for them. They were so relieved that all was well between the two of them.

Their friends, what would they say?

She could see her mother throwing her hands up in horror that Marina could even contemplate marrying Hirjee. Her loving father she knew would smile and wish her well.

But Marina also knew that in a metropolitan city like Bombay, most things were transient and usually less than a two-day wonder, with life carrying on just as before.

The phone rang and happy anticipation fluttered inside her.

Rosy answered and called out that Hirjee*seth* was on the line.

Marina stood up and turned to go inside. She suddenly realised that she did not care what anyone thought or said. She knew without a shadow of a doubt that she loved Hirjee and wanted to spend the rest of her life by his side.

A weight seemed to lift off her shoulders as she took the receiver from Rosy.

'Hirjee?'

Yes, my darling,' said his happy voice.

* * * * * * * *

Translated Words

A

Aachun-michun – a ceremony
Aferganyu - a metal urn covered by a flat metal plate, on which sandal wood is burned
Arrae - Oh
Aayee - mother in Marathi
Aavo - welcome

B

Baby - little girl
Baba - little boy
Bai - polite form of addressing a lady
Beti - daughter
Beta - child
Behn - sister
Bhai – brother
Bhaiya - brother
Bhajjias - a spicy fried snack
Bhel puri, pani puri - spicy Indian snacks
Behram Yazad - the angel who removes difficulty
Boomla - harpadon nehereus (family of sea lizard fish) commonly called Bombay Duck
Bungli - small bungalow

C

Chahram - Zoroastrian funeral prayers said in the early hours of the fourth day.
Champa - franjipani tree
Chappattis - flat wheat bread
Chhee chhee - sound of disgust
Chikoo - chickoo fruit - sapodilla
Chikan - embroidery in white thread

Chor Bazaar - thieves market - a market selling antiques
Chowkidar - sentry
Churidars - tight trousers
Cooli - porter

D
Daru - cheap liquor
Dastoor - Zorastrian priest
Dekho - look
Devi - term of respect,
Dikra - dear
Dil ki Dhadkan - The Beating Heart
Divali - Festival of Lights
Diya – oil lamp
Dupatta - long scarf

F
Filumwalla-types - film people

G
Ganga - a Maharashtrian housemaid
Gouss-goussing - slang for gossiping

H
Haan - yes
Hai – sigh

I
Ithe yaa bai - come here lady

J
Jamadar - sweeper
Jaan - term of endearment
Jaggery - molasses

K
Kalji ghya – watch out - take care
Kashmiri - from Kashmir
Kulfi - Ice-cream
Kurta - Indian dress
Kusti - a narrow flat sacred girdle worn over the sadra tied around the waist by Zoroastrians.

M
Mali - gardener
Memsahib - mistress
Mithai - indian sweets
Mobed - Zoroastrian priest

N
Naa - *no*
Nai - no
Namaste - Indian greeting
Nimbu-pani - lemonade
Navjote - initiation ceremony into the Zoroastrian faith
Nauratna – Indian jewelery with nine precious stones

O
Oonder - mouse

P
Paghri - turband shaped hat
Pheta – round cloth covered hat
Patia - spicy sweet and sour gravy
Pullo - a part of the sari taken over the shoulder.

Q
Quransharif - the Quran

R
Rangoli - chalk design on the floor
Ravo - semolina sweet

S
Seth - polite form of addressing a man.
Sadra - muslin vest worn by all Zoroastrians.
Safed jamun - water apple
Sahib - Sir
Sala - a friendly term used by men.
Salaam - greetings
Sev - sweet vermicelli
Sigri - stove
Sitaphal - custard apple
Sitar - a string instrument

T
Tabla - small Indian drum
Targola - a palm belonging to the coconut family.
Teeli - red dot
Tikka - red dot on the forehead
Tonga - a horse drawn carriage.
Toran - garland

U
Ukhra - a type of rice

Y
Yaa bai ithe yaa - come here lady.
Yaa seth ithe yaa - come here sir.
Yaar - friend

Z
Zari - silver or gold thread

List of Characters

Cooper Family:

Rustam Cooper, married to Marina Cooper
Their two children: Amy and Jamsheed
Rosy, their house maid
Anthony their cook
Raju, their house boy
Mitzi, their dachshund.
Amy's friends: Meena, Pinku, and Zia

Tehmina and Shavaksha: Marina's parents.

Dhanjibhoy Family:

Hirji Dhanjibhoy married to Jeroo Dhanjibhoy
Rayomand, their son.
Philomena, their housemaid

Anjali is an actress and Rayomand's fiancée.
Anna is Anjali's mother.

Smita and Naren Dalal, Hirji's friends.
Karan and Monisha, their son and daughter.

ACKNOWLEDGEMENTS

With thanks to my beloved Chotu for his constant love and reassurance. I am grateful to my editor daughter, Shaista, for her friendship, patience, support and guidance, and to my sons Rizwan and Irfan, and my brother Zubin, for their encouragement and for believing in me.

Printed in Great Britain
by Amazon

23302674R00148